Written by Paul Cunningham.

Thank you for buying this book. Releasing it
independently means I'm a tiny fish in an enormous ocean.
Your support is greatly appreciated. I hope you enjoy what
you read.

-Paul.

Follow me on Twitter:

@pcunninghamjnr

1. My First Time

It was late October 2009. I drove to a secluded, dark corner of a supermarket car park in Beaumont, North Dublin. The heavy rain kept most people indoors. For those that did venture out, they did so reluctantly. Shoppers made quick darts from their cars into the refuge of the overly lit main entrance. The deafening sound of the rain crashing down on the roof of my car did nothing to calm my nerves. My hands were trembling, I burrowed them firmly into the pockets of my coat. My left hand gripped the decoy phone, waiting for the signal.

The meeting was set for 7:00 PM. On the dashboard in my car, the clock seemed to sit at 6:47 for what felt like hours. It finally changed to 6:48, and a surge of anxiety started to kick in. The muscles in my legs jumped and twitched spontaneously. I tapped my feet on the floor of my car desperately trying to convince myself that the movements were voluntary. I closed my eyes tightly and tried to keep my breathing as slow and steady as possible. I counted to five while inhaling through my nostrils, held the air in my lungs for a few seconds before exhaling while counting to five again. This exercise failed to bring my heart rate down anywhere close to a 'normal' level. My stomach dropped when the decoy phone vibrated with a text message. It was Marty, and it simply read "I'm here!"

I turned the key in the ignition once. It wasn't enough to start the engine, but it gave me enough power to engage the windscreen wipers. Having cleared the stream of water from the glass, I had a clear view of the supermarket entrance. There were two employees, wearing high visibility jackets, smoking to the left of the main entrance. To the right stood a lone figure wearing a waist-length raincoat. The mysterious figure had the hood of his jacket pulled all the way up. He wore a dark baseball style hat with the peak pulled down as far as it would go over his

face. His effort to look inconspicuous had the complete opposite effect. He couldn't have stood out more if he tried.

I turned the ignition key all the way over to start the engine, but nothing happened. My once reliable and trustworthy Volkswagen decided to take that opportunity to show me it was feeling every mile of its fourteen-year existence. Turning the key again, repeated the scenario. On the third attempt, pressing the accelerator in frustration while turning the key, the engine revved into action. I drove slowly along the curb towards the main entrance. My crawling pace drew the attention of the two smokers. They glared at me under luminous hoods and light plumes of exhaled smoke. I flashed the headlights at Marty, brought the car to a stop and rolled the passenger window down about one-third of the way. All the doors remained locked as I repeatedly looked in the rearview mirror to ensure there were no sudden movements from the smokers that were now behind me. Marty approached, dropped a brown envelope into the crack in the window, and as instructed, turned on his heels and began to walk away. A mixture of €50 and €20 notes scattered onto the passenger seat and some fell onto the floor of my car. I leaned over and scooped the cash under the passenger seat, out of view. With the transaction complete I made no hesitation in getting the hell out of there. The adrenalin was pumping, the nerves subsided and a feeling of elation consumed me. It took me about a half an hour to drive home that night. Outside my house, I checked the footwell of my car to make sure there was no cash left behind. In my bedroom, I counted the cash. It was all there! Every cent. €10,000 in cold hard cash! I placed the cash in an old shoebox and tucked it under my bed.

When people think of the word 'Paedophile' they may think of a stereotypical dirty old man, a loner, an outcast. But paedophiles are everyday, ordinary people. They could be the guy in the local pub who's a great laugh and a really nice fella. They could be your lovely neighbour who always greets you with a smile and a wave. They could serve you coffee, drive your bus or pass you on the street without you ever suspecting a thing. But the secrets they keep are far from normal, far from ordinary. Some paedophiles can go through their whole life without ever being punished for their actions. Others just need an opportunity to show who they really are. That's where I came in. I set up my first fake profile on an Internet chat room in October 2009, her name was 'Erica-Iz-New'. The photograph for the profile was a stock photo from an American website. These images are non-sexual, completely legal and are used mostly for advertising purposes. On the profile I stated that Erica was eighteen, you had to be to sign up to the chatroom. But anybody who contacted Erica directly would immediately be told that she was in fact fourteen. To this day, I still don't know what drove me to ever set up a fake profile. Revenge? To make money? Did I see myself as a rogue vigilante? Maybe it was a mixture of all three. Either way, it happened, and little did I know it was that decision that would drastically change the course of my life.

The messages came almost instantly. People wanted to know all about Erica. Where she was from, did she work or go to college, did she have a boyfriend. But right after these people found out Erica was fourteen, the majority immediately backed away. Some even warned Erica about the dangers of being in a chat room intended for adults only. And then came the first contact from 'Marty_216'.

"Hi Erica, you look beautiful in your profile pic!"
"Thanks!" I answered. "But you should know that I'm only fourteen!"
"That's ok! Sure we're only chatting!"

I clicked into Marty's profile to try and gauge what kind of person he portrayed himself as. His profile picture was a close up of his face, his beaming smile was quite simply unmissable. He had medium length black/grey hair swept to the left side and wore thin framed silver glasses.

A bristly almost unkept moustache sat on his upper lip. It looked out of place compared to the rest of his clean shaved face. Marty had links on his profile to all of his other social media accounts. Between them all, Marty came across as a normal, respectful middle-aged man. The chat continued and appeared quite innocent, to begin with. Marty asked where Erica was from, what school she went to and what she did in her free time. I answered using my local knowledge, but more research was necessary if I continued to do this. I asked him the same questions and soon found out he was fifty-six, married with three kids and from Beaumont. We continued chatting for about an hour. It was getting late, so I made my excuses and ended the chat by saying...

"School in the morning, gotta go x".

"No problem hun. Will you be back on tomorrow?"

"Maybe ;-)" I replied.

Satisfied he was hooked, I logged out of the chat room. I lay awake that night not knowing how to feel. A fifty-six-year-old man was doing his best to befriend what he believed to be a fourteen-year-old girl. I had yet to learn his intentions, but my curiosity refused to be ignored. How did Marty feel when he got into bed beside his wife that night? The mother of his children lying beside him had absolutely no idea what Marty was doing.

Back in the chatroom the following night at about 7:30 PM. I was in there for all of two minutes when a private message came through reading "Hi hun how was school?" It was Marty. "Fine thanks, how was your day x?" I replied. The private conversation continued for nearly two hours. On three occasions Marty asked me if I was speaking privately to anybody else in the chat room. "No. Why?" I asked him.

"Just wondering, sometimes you take a little while to write back." As far as I could tell I was replying to all of his questions in good time. It seemed that Marty was a little jealous, possessive even.

"No. You're the only one I'm talking to in here." I replied.

"Good. I like hearing that!" He sent back.

At the end of my second day chatting with Marty, I told him Erica was logging off.

"Ok. Will you be here again tomorrow?" He immediately replied.

"I don't know, maybe."

"Well, you should give me your phone number, just in case your not on here tomorrow?" It was at that point I knew that I'd have to buy a decoy phone. The only number I could give Marty was my personal number. That was a bad idea, so I had to come up with some other excuse.

"Sure there's no point in swapping numbers," I replied.

"Why?"

"I don't have any credit to text you."

"I'll buy you credit so we can text!" The bastard had an answer for my excuse.

"You don't have to!"

"I don't mind at all. It means we don't have to meet in the chatroom anymore. Send me your number and I'll send you credit."

"I'm not sure." I told him. "My parents would kill me if they knew I swapped numbers with someone from a chatroom."

"They'd only kill you if they knew! Don't tell them. We're only chatting. Sure it's no harm."

"I'll think about it!"

"Ok. But it's much easier to text rather than arranging a time to meet on here! Will you be back here tomorrow?"

"Yea. Ok"

"Can't wait till then sweetheart!"

First thing the next morning I bought a decoy phone from my local supermarket, no contract, no sign-up, no bill. It was out of fashion, but it didn't matter, it could still receive texts, photos, and video messages. I made a point of not connecting the decoy phone to my home internet provider. The less data that was recorded the better. My plan was beginning to take shape. All I had to do was log into the chat room that night to see if Marty would really send credit to a minor so that he could have constant contact with her.

At the pre-arranged time of 7:30 PM I logged into the chatroom. There was no sign of Marty. Other people started to send private messages to Erica, but each one was ignored. There was only one person I wanted to hear from. A little before 8:00 PM, a private message came through reading...

"Hi gorgeous, sorry I'm late! how was your day?" It was Marty. After chatting with him for about an hour, I needed to see if he would ask Erica for her phone number again. "I'm logging off now. Shower then bed!"

"Ok. Will we chat tomorrow babe?" It was 'babe' now. I'd just been upgraded!

"I don't know, maybe...x"

"Have you thought about swapping numbers?"

"Yea. No harm I suppose. But I still have no credit!" I sent Marty the number of the decoy phone.

"Thanks. I'll send you some credit now! x" Was his reply.

About two minutes after logging out of the chat room, the decoy phone vibrated with a text.

"Hi hun, it's Marty216 from the chat room." Read the text. Attached to it was a photo message of a code for €20 credit. Marty followed through with his promise. He sent credit to who he believed to be a fourteen-year-old girl so he could text her.

"Thanks for the credit!!" I replied.

"No problem hun. Send me a cheeky shower pic! xx"

"No way! Off to bed soon anyway!"

"Night, night Princess," he immediately texted back. Fucking Princess.

The following morning at 08:04 I received another text from Marty.

"Morning sweetheart, have a great day at school." Erica had obviously been on his mind all night.

"Thanks, have a good day too xx," I replied.

Marty texted again later that night, asking Erica about her day in school. After filling him in with banal details, the conversation turned to Erica's dating life.

"Do you have a boyfriend?"

"No, never had one. :-/ "

"I don't believe you, I thought you would have been fighting them away!"

"No, Just never been asked out is all."

"But you have kissed boys before right?"

"Well, yea. But nothing serious"

"Are you a Virgin?"

"...Yea, I am"

"Have you ever touched a penis before?"

And there it was. Not that it was ok for Marty to be texting what he thought was a child, but that one question crossed a line. "Have you ever touched a penis before?" I knew right after that question, I was going to get the bastard if it killed me. The conversation continued and I answered questions like, "What bra size are you? What colour underwear do you have on? How often do you masturbate?" Marty was obviously getting himself hot under the collar. I could not have replied to his texts any longer that night if I tried. The anger in me was about to erupt. I had pins and needles running down both my arms while trying to type. My fists were clenched tightly waiting for him to fire the next question at me. I cut him off by saying Erica was going to bed.

"Send me a pic of you in bed!" He responded with.

"No! That's weird!"

"Weird how? Its only for fun!"

"No! I already turned the light off!"

"Goodnight so! Sleep tight sweetheart!"

I could have tracked Marty down that very night and beat him to within an inch of his life. But a strong whiskey had the desired effect in calming me down. My plan was working and soon I'd have Marty right where I wanted him.

Marty texted regularly over the next few days. Mostly at night time, presumably after he finished work. He consistently referred to Erica as 'honey, babe, and princess'. He sent two more codes for €20 credit which were never used. I wanted him to feel like he was doing Erica a favor by sending her credit. One night after texting back and forth for about an hour, Marty sent...

"I'm feeling horny!"

"Um, ok...." I replied.

"Don't you get horny too babe?"

"I guess, but not right now."

"What gets you in the mood?" In the mood? I had to stop and remind myself that this was a fifty-six-year-old man talking to what he thought was a child. From there, Marty started to ask about Erica's virginity.

"How do you picture it happening?" He asked.

"What do you mean?"

"Your first time. What would you like it to be like?"

"I don't know really. Haven't thought about it that much."

"A girls first time should be special, flowers, dinner, wine, somewhere nice!"

"That sounds amazing, but I'm not old enough to drink."

"Nobody else would know if it was just you and me."

"What do you mean?"

"I mean I could book a hotel room sometime and treat you the way you deserve to
be treated, like a Princess."

"Really? Wouldn't that be expensive?"

"No expense spared if you really wanted to do it."

"It sounds amazing, but what about my parents?"

"Can't you say you're staying with a friend?"

"hmm I suppose, but it's risky."

"I'll have you home bright and early the next morning, your parents would never
know."

"Ok then. But I've never done this before, I don't know what to expect. Does it hurt...the sex?"

"Don't worry about a thing darling. I'll make sure that I'm nice and gentle. Your first time will be an amazing experience."

And there I had it. Marty arranging to meet what he believed to be a minor, supply her with alcohol and take her virginity. We went through things in finer detail. Erica was to tell her parents she was staying with a friend. Marty's plan was that Erica would get the bus to town, then take the Luas to Heuston Street Station. Marty would pick her up, and begin their romantic evening. He never gave me the name of the hotel he booked but said it was close to the Pheonix Park. Everything was meticulously planned. The meeting was happening on Saturday, October 24th, 2009.

The Morning of the meeting, Marty texted Erica. "Cannot wait to meet you later." The text was accompanied by a picture of Marty's penis.
If I didn't already have him by the bollix, I well and truly did then. He continued to say all was set, room booked, condoms and flowers bought, the only thing he needed to know was, if Erica would prefer red or white wine. I told him red. Eating that day proved impossible. I was restless and constantly watching the clock. Every possible scenario played over and over in my mind while pacing from the living room into the kitchen. Printing out all the chat logs and every text message exchanged between Marty and Erica provided a welcome distraction. All in, there were seventy-two A4 pages of conversation. I highlighted the sexual content, where Marty talked about taking Erica's virginity, agreed to book a hotel room and asked what type of wine she wanted. All very incriminating evidence in itself. The front cover of this document was an A4 printout of Marty's penis. It was indisputable that Marty's expertise in grooming related to only one meaning of the word. I placed the printouts in my backpack and threw it on the pile of red envelopes that had been brushed behind my front door. Each envelope contained a bill, some dating back almost six months. The overdue bill would come in,

followed by the final notice and then the threatening letter. With no money to pay either one, there was no point in opening the red envelopes anymore. So they piled up and formed a mini red pyramid behind my front door.

We arranged to meet that night at 7:00 PM. With my backpack over my shoulder, I left my house with plenty of time to spare. Having told Marty that Erica lived in my area, I ended up taking the same route to Heuston Street as she would have. Sitting on the upper deck of the 27 bus into Dame Street, I wondered how Marty was preparing for the meeting. What did he tell his wife? How could she not know there was something suspicious going on? Had he done this before? Walking from the bus stop on Dame Street up through Temple Bar, music from the pubs and clubs spilled into the streets creating the 'buzz' that makes Temple Bar famous. Tourists flock there to soak up the atmosphere. In among the party guest are beggars, drunks, junkies and every type of degenerate imaginable. It's certainly no place for a fourteen-year-old girl to be wandering alone. I crossed the Ha'Penny Bridge, continued up through Liffey Street and onto Upper Abbey Street. It was a relief to escape into the relative warmth of a red line Luas carriage. If a fourteen-year-old girl sat on the Luas en route to meet a man she met on an internet chat room, what would be going through her head? Her parents would think she's going to stay in a friends house, she'd think she was going to be wined and dined like an adult. The truth is she would be on her way to be raped by a man over 40 years her senior. A man who would rape this child and most likely leave the hotel before the next morning, leaving a distraught young girl not knowing what had happened to her.

The Luas arrived at Heuston Station and there were at least twenty minutes to kill before the meeting. My stomach was churning as I crossed Sean Heuston Bridge. The sturdy October gust almost cut me in two as it hurtled its way down the Liffey. A strong drink was required before the confrontation. Part of me wanted to calm my nerves, the other part wanted to replenish the heat that had just been knocked out of me. I ducked into a small hotel bar and found a quiet corner to ready myself. Over a pint of Guinness and whiskey chaser, I thumbed through the printouts between Marty and Erica. My right leg was involuntarily shaking. I placed my right elbow firmly on my leg and rested my chin on my right fist to try and ease the convulsions. What the hell was I doing? Sitting, shaking in a bar about to confront a suspected paedophile. The thought crossed my mind to go straight home and forget the whole thing. But after re-reading some of the conversations, I convinced myself to see the confrontation through.

The decoy phone vibrated in my pocket and I immediately reached for it. A text from Marty read. "Hey babe, I'm parked on Infirmary Road. Let me know when you're off the luas! xx." The whiskey burned all the way down to the pit of my stomach as I gathered up the chat logs and left the bar. Leaving the hotel reception, I spotted a tourist map of Dublin and shoved it into the back pocket of my jeans. From Benburb Street I continued onto Conyngham Road purposely passing Infirmary Road. From the corner of the Criminal Courts of Justice, I had a perfect vantage point to try and spot Marty.

On the opposite side of the road, in a brand new blue Toyota Jeep facing me, a man in his fifties sat alone. His silver-framed glasses and thick black moustache looked overwhelmingly familiar. I stood back from the corner and called Marty from the decoy phone. I peered carefully towards the Jeep to make sure the driver was who I expected it to be. As the stranger answered his phone, that unmissable beaming smile, the same one from Marty's profile picture, was etched across his face.
"Hello? Hello, Erica?" The stranger excitedly answered.

I ended the call, turned the decoy phone off and placed it back in my pocket. There was no doubt in my mind it was Marty. It was time to ruin his life. Confident that Marty would be on the lookout for a young girl rounding the opposite corner, I began my approach. His car engine was still running, and there was enough space in front of him to escape in a hurry if he felt like doing so. So before crossing the road towards Marty's car, I removed the tourist map from my back pocket and began studying it while walking. My heart was pounding, almost as if it were propelling me towards the Jeep with every beat. Marty had his phone in his right hand and was holding it up to his right ear, no doubt frantically trying to ring Erica. He didn't see me closing in. I tapped on his driver window four times. It obviously startled him, he rolled down the window and asked...

"Can I help ya?"

"Yes, you can." I replied. There was an unwelcome quiver in my voice. So I tried to clear my dry throat, took a deep breath and continued.

"I'm looking to find the bus stop that the Tourist bus stops at. I'm trying to get back to town, I think it's around here somewhere."

I shoved the map uncomfortably close to Marty's nose. He grabbed it from me hesitantly and moved it away from his face as if trying to refocus. Before he had the sentence "Give us a look" out of his mouth, I had his car keys out of the ignition and in my back pocket. Marty immediately tried to open his car door. I slammed it shut against him.

"Who are you here to meet?" I fired at him. The colour seemed to drain from his face as soon as I asked that question.

"I..., I..., I'm meetin' a friend," He said.

"What's her name and how old is she?"

"Erica, she's eighteen." He lied.

"She is in me bollix." My voice unlocked a newfound confident tone. "There is no Erica, you were talkin' to me the whole time."

"She said she was eighteen."

"No she didn't, her first message was that she's fourteen!"

"But you have to be eighteen to sign up to the website."

"She clearly stated that she was fourteen in her response to your first message, I'll show you." I reached into my folder and took out the chat logs.

"By the way, IS THIS YOUR PENIS?" I showed him the picture of his genitals that was the front cover of my evidence.

"Yea, keep your voice down."

"Fuck off paedo, why should I protect scum like you?"

I stood by that statement, but I also didn't want to draw a crowd. I moved from his driver side door, around the bonnet and sat in the passenger seat. As I sat in, I heard the clinking of bottles underneath my feet. There were two bottles of red wine in a plastic shopping bag sitting in the footwell of the Jeep. A small bouquet of flowers peered out the top. They had a price tag of €7.99 still stuck to them. They were flowers fit for a Princess? But when you actually think about it... how would a child know what a decent bouquet of flowers is supposed to look like?

The interior of the car was uncomfortably warm and the 'new car' smell was overpowered by the stench of Marty's aftershave. I threw the printouts at Marty. The leather seat squeaked beneath him as he recoiled.

"Why do you think it's ok to ask a fourteen-year-old girl about her sexual experience?" I questioned.

"It's not but...I...I made a mistake...who are you anyway?" Marty stuttered.

"Don't worry about who I am. Answer my questions and we'll take it from there. What were your intentions in meeting a fourteen-year-old girl?"

"Nothing, I just wanted to talk."

"Oh, fuck off! You talked about taking her virginity! You told her you would buy her wine. The wine is right under my feet!! Why is there wine if you just wanted to talk?"

"I was going to tell her not to do this and be careful of who she talks to on the internet!"

"Then why send her a picture of your penis?"

"It was a mistake."

"A mistake? I've never once sent a picture of my cock to someone by accident!"

"Ok, I shouldn't have done it."

"Ok? No, it's not fucking ok! What would your wife have to say about this? She's a secretary, right? And your kids? Two of whom are married, one is a student. Your daughter is expecting her first child yea?"

"How do you know this? Who are you?"

"How do I know? You've got pictures of your whole family plastered all over social media! Did you think I wasn't going to look? Did you think you're hard to find? Life as you know it is over Marty, you fucked it up!"

"It was a mistake, I admit that! I shouldn't have been talking to her."

"Mistake? What will the Gardaí think of this mistake? How long will they give you to think about this mistake in prison? Have you been to prison before? Do you know what they do to perv's like you in prison? You're scum, the lowest of the low! You'll have to be sectioned off with the other perv's for your own protection!"

Marty's head collapsed onto the steering wheel. His thumb and index finger slid up underneath his glasses as he rubbed his eyes. I bet he wished this was all just a bad dream, and he would wake up at any minute beside his wife and go back to living his normal life.

"Have you ever been to prison before?" I asked him.

"No."

"Have you ever been arrested before?"

"No."

"It doesn't really matter. With everything I have on you, they're gonna throw the book at ya...unless..."

"Unless what? I fucking kill myself?"

"No... you can buy my silence... for €10,000 cash all this can go away! The only people that will ever know this happened is me and you. I won't go to your wife and kids, I won't go to the Gardaí. It won't leave this car."

"€10,000, where am I supposed to get that kind of money?"

"Maybe the same place you got the money for a new car? I really don't care. But that's my price. I'll give you until next Friday to pay me. If at noon on Friday I haven't heard from you, I will post everything online, post it all to your wife and send it to the Guards. Keep your phone on. I'll be in touch. And Marty, don't fuck around with me, because I can, and I will ruin your life!"

I opened the passenger door and was about to step out when Marty piped up.
"I'll give you €5,000."

I closed the door again.
"Who in the fuck do you think you are to negotiate with me? I'm giving you a way out here! I could go straight to the Guards right now and you'd be arrested tonight! Your house would be searched, computers and phones seized, and your family wouldn't know what hit them! How would you explain that? Fuckin' €5,000! You're staring down the barrel of years in prison and you try to bargain with me? It's €10,000 by Friday! If you don't have it I'll fuckin' hang you, and take great pleasure in it! I'll be in touch next week and tell you where to meet me, ya prick! I'm takin' the fuckin' wine as well!"

With that, I grabbed the shopping bag, threw the flowers into Marty's lap, and got out of the car. I threw his car keys on the passenger seat and headed back to Parkgate Street. Walking down the road, the two bottles of wine clinked together in the shopping bag. They sounded like the great bells of victory. After hailing a taxi and heading home I opened the wine and drank to a successful confrontation. I continued drinking while deleting Erica's profile from my computer. Before realising it, both bottles were polished off. With a whiskey, I collapsed on the sofa and reflected on the whole situation. It was a strange feeling, knowing I pretty much stopped a teenager from being raped. How it could have been if she was real. But instead of a lifetime of traumatic memories, therapy and guilt, all I created was a dilemma for Marty. Either come clean, ruin your life and face the consequences, or pay

€10,000 to make it all go away. At least that's what he thought.

Monday, October 26th, I texted Marty.

"What day is good for you?"

His reply was "I'll have it for you by Thursday."

"Great. I'll text you Thursday and arrange to meet."

This was the strangest point of the whole hunt. Did he really have the money? Did he come clean and go to the Guards, was he going to have me arrested at the meeting as part of a plea bargain? Was he going to spend a fraction of the money to pay some lads to rough me up? It was an odd feeling, but I had gone too far to turn around.

Thursday morning, October 29th, I texted Marty again. We arranged to meet in the car park of his local supermarket at 7:00 PM. He followed my instructions perfectly. "Stand at the main entrance, text me when you're there. When I approach I'll flash my headlights. Drop in what you owe me and walk away."

With my first transaction complete, I discarded the decoy phone. At that point, there was only one thing left to do. Hang the bastard. Donning a pair of rubber gloves, I reprinted all the chat logs and Marty's dick pic. I filled a self-adhesive envelope with all the evidence and addressed it to Santry Garda Station. It felt better sending the package from outside Dublin. I don't know why, but it made more sense to me to send it from somewhere else. Send the Gardaí on a wild goose chase if they tried to track me down. I took a drive to Wexford and sent the package from there. I didn't bother sending one to his wife. Let the Guards tell her what was going on. The trip to Wexford was a breath of fresh air, sometimes it's nice to get out of Dublin for a while.

I mulled over my first catch from start to finish. What could I do better next time? What needed to change? Using my own car was a big mistake. If Marty wanted to find out who I was, he could have done it very easily. Traveling to his area to pick up the cash was another mistake. In future, it was important to lure the paedos out of their comfort zone. There was no doubt in my mind that I was going to continue to hunt. Hook a paedo, blackmail him, and when he pays, screw him. It was beautiful. I knew I was on to something big and that there were many more paedo's like Marty to get caught in my web. But I'll never forget Marty. You never forget your first time.

2. Dr. Octave

I let the dust settle on my first snare. In the days and weeks after Marty paid me off, I used his money to pay my debts. The little red pyramid of unopened envelopes brushed behind my front door finally disappeared. It was strange not seeing it there anymore. For months it was one of the first things I saw at the end of the stairs as I tried to start my day. And whenever I ventured outside, it was the first thing to greet me on my return. A red blur sitting behind opaque glass. A constant reminder of the debt hanging over my head. But they were gone. The Banks, Credit Union, Electric and Gas Company all had what they were due, and that was the end of their letters.

Mid-November 2009, enough time had passed since my first snare so I set up the second decoy profile. Her screen name was 'Anna_Dub', she was thirteen and from Dublin. A new picture from the same stock photo website was downloaded and ready to go. This time I had everything planned out in advance. Her school, where she lived, where she went with her friends. A new decoy phone was ready and waiting to exchange numbers. It was time to go fishing for a paedo again.

The first time I logged into the chatroom as Anna_Dub wasn't very successful. Once Anna_Dub told people she was thirteen, they immediately backed off. But nothing is ever achieved by giving up at the first hurdle. I logged in again the next night and the night after until I hooked one. 'Dr. Octave' sent a private message simply saying...

"Hi Anna, a/s/l?". In chat room land a/s/l stands for Age/Sex/Location.

I replied "Thirteen/Female/Ballyfermot."

He responded with "Oh Ballyfermot? I live in Chapelizod. We're practically neighbours."

I found it strange that he picked up on the fact that Anna lived near him, and not the fact that she had just said she was only thirteen. I decided to remind him of Anna's age.

"Is it ok with you that I'm thirteen? I had to put eighteen on my profile or else I couldn't log in."

"Yea no problem. I'm twenty-eight but don't mind having younger friends," was his response.

The chat continued for a little while and he was getting to know Anna, making her feel at ease. I had to ask about his screen name, it was just so odd. Dr.Octave told Anna that he used to play in a band called 'The Dublin City Surgeons' and every member had to come up with a nickname for themselves with 'Dr.' in front of it. Octave is a musical term, he started to explain, but I got bored and changed the subject.

Dr.Octave's profile picture was a picture of a small black dog.

"Is that your dog in your pic?" I asked.

"Yea, his name is Leroy." Dr.Octave responded.

"He's so cute!"

"Thanks. Do you have any pets?"

"No. My parents won't let me have any!"

"Oh, that's terrible. Everyone should have pets. They're great company!"

We chatted for a little bit about the dog, he was a miniature schipperke. I feigned interest in the conversation while clicking into Dr.Octaves profile. It was vague, to say the least. Three pictures of the dog were on his profile and it said he lived in Dublin. That was it. No pictures of himself, no clue as to what he did for a living, if he was married, nothing. It seemed I had my work cut out if I wanted to know who was behind the profile.

We chatted for about three hours on the first night Dr.Octave contacted Anna, but I wasn't sure where the chat was leading. He wasn't bordering on a sexual conversation, not even close. I decided to see where I stood with him, see if he gave me any indication that he was interested in talking again.

"It's getting late, I have school tomorrow. I better get to bed!"

"Ok. It was nice chatting to you Anna. Will you be on here again?" Was his response.

"Yea. If I log back on the same time tomorrow I might see you here?"

"Sure. That sounds like a plan. Nite nite. x"

I still couldn't make out where I stood. Dr.Octave was a twenty-eight-year-old man chatting to who he believed to be a thirteen-year-old girl. It was wrong, but not wrong enough to hit him for €10,000. The only chance to catch Dr.Octave was to play it by ear and see what happened. I'd give him at least a few days, if the conversation wasn't going where I wanted it to, I would have deleted the profile and started again. The following night after our first encounter, I logged onto the chatroom again.

"Hi Anna. How was your day?" Was the private message I received shortly after logging on. It was Dr.Octave.

"Hi! Yea, my day was fine. Too much homework lol. Yours?"

We chatted for a little while, again the conversation was banal and generic to the point of being boring. Dr.Octave then complimented Anna on her profile picture. "You have beautiful eyes."

"Thank you. Nobody ever told me that before." I replied.

"That's surprising. It's the first thing I noticed about you."

"Thanks! Do you have a picture?"

"I have pictures. But not on my profile."

"Why not?"

"I'm just more private than others I suppose."

"Ok. But I'd like to know who I'm talking to."

"I have pictures on my phone. I don't know how to upload them on here though." A rich comment coming from a man who had already uploaded three pictures of his dog.

"Oh, ok. I'll just have to imagine what you look like! lol"

"I could text you one?" It was about time the conversation moved in that direction.

"Ok. No harm in it I suppose." We exchanged numbers and soon afterwards I received a text.

"Hi. It's Dr.Octave from the chatroom."

"Hello! Wheres my pic? lol" Dr.Octaves reply to that message was a black and white picture of a man playing guitar on stage. It must have been taken at one of his gigs because it looked like he was in motion when the photo was taken. The photograph was blurred and unclear. The man in the picture was dressed in a white jacket with a stethoscope around his neck. He had long dark hair tucked behind his ears and wore black framed glasses.

"Oh. Now I see you!" I sent back to him.

"Yup. That's me. Like what you see?"

"Of course. I like your hair!"

From that point on we texted back and forward, the chatroom became obsolete.

"Can you send me some more pic's of you?" Dr.Octave asked.

"No! You saw my pic on the chatroom and I only saw one of you, so we're even!"

"If you send me more pictures, I'll send you some."

"No. My mam would kill me if she knew I was sending pictures." It would have been beneficial to get more photos of Dr.Octave, but I couldn't send him any more of the decoy. Using the excuse that Anna's mother might find out she's exchanging pictures with someone would have to work for the time being.

We continued to text each other over the next few days and I could feel Dr.Octave beginning to trust Anna. He let his guard down a number of times and revealed a little more about himself. He told Anna that he was a taxi driver. He also mentioned he had a daughter, but his ex-partner wouldn't allow him to see her. After they broke up she took the girl and moved out of their shared home. Dr.Octave said he has barely seen his daughter since. He said this was the reason why he got Leroy, for company as he was so lonely. I felt the conversation beginning to turn the way I wanted it to.

November 10th was the first time Dr.Octave rang Anna. I couldn't answer the call so let it ring out. He left a voice message...

"Hi Anna. I thought I'd ring you so I could finally get to hear your voice. But you must be busy. I'll try again later." This was going to be a big problem if he continued to ring Anna.

The following morning I woke up to another voice message left by Dr.Octave. I must have been sleeping off a hangover as I didn't hear the phone ringing at all...

"Anna, it's me again. How come you never answer your phone? You don't want to leave me lonely and on my own do you? I'll try again later."

It was a clear change of tactics by Dr.Octave. He was playing the sympathy card and trying to coerce Anna into talking to him. I had to set up a meeting soon. The longer I tried to string him along, the risk of losing him grew. I texted him after hearing his voice message.

"Sorry I couldn't answer earlier. I was on the bus to school."

"No problem." He started. "Good idea not to answer when people are around. They don't need to know about us."

"I'll text you when I'm home from school."

"Talk later x"

That afternoon I texted Dr.Octave. I wanted to keep his mind away from calling Anna. Keep him occupied on something else and try to steer the conversation into a meeting. The dog was my best bet.

"How's Leroy?" I asked.

"He's good." Was his reply, accompanied by another picture of the dog.

"Aww he's so cute! I wish I had a dog like him."

"You can meet him sometime and take him for a walk if you like?"

"Really? I'd love that!"

"Of course! Come over and meet him anytime you want." After he sent that text he gave me a clear description of where he lived. I vaguely knew the area but wasn't quite sure where his house was. A meeting in a public place worked better for me. I still didn't know exactly who I was dealing with.

"Thanks. Maybe we could meet in the park instead? It would be better for Leroy!"

"Yea, that sounds like a plan! I can meet you in the park at the top of Chapelizod Hill Road. When suits you?"

"Great. Tomorrow? After I finish school, does that work?"

"Yea perfect! And what do you wanna do after?"

"What do you mean?"

"After you meet Leroy. What will we do?"

"I dunno..."

"You can come to mine and we can watch a film or something?"

"Yea, ok. But I have to be home by 9:00 if it's a school night."

"No problem. As long as your boyfriend doesn't mind, lol"

"I don't have a boyfriend."

"Oh, so we're both single!"

"I guess so."

And then it started. I finally lured Dr.Octave into the conversation I needed in order to hit him for €10,000.

"Have you been with a boy before?"

"I've kissed a few boys, but never gone out with one properly."

"How far have you gone with a boy?"

"How far? I've only kissed boys before!"

"So you're a virgin?"

"Yea." It was as if the word 'virgin' flipped a switch in Dr.Octaves brain. From that point on he asked a barrage of questions relating to Anna's sexual experience. I answered questions like "Have you seen a boy naked before?" "Have you seen a penis?" "Have you ever touched one before?" "Have you masturbated a boy before?" By telling Dr.Octave that Anna had no experience with boys seemed to keep him hooked.

"Do your friends all have boyfriends?" He asked.

"Some of them do yea."

"And how come you don't?"

"I dunno..."

"Did you ever think its because you don't know what to do with a boy?"

"No. Not really,"

"I bet all your friends are having sex by now. You don't want to be left behind do you?"

"No."

"Well after you meet Leroy you can come back to mine and I'll show you how to treat a boy. That way you'll know what to do and you won't be left out."

"Show me what exactly?" I needed him to answer. Then I had him.

"I'll show you what boys like. How to masturbate them, how to perform oral sex."

"I might be a bit nervous." "That's ok. I'll get some condoms in case we want to go all the way. Then you won't be a virgin anymore, and your first boyfriend will know your experienced."

"Tomorrow yea?"

"Yea. Me and Leroy will meet you in the park at about 6:00. Then we'll walk to mine. And don't worry, I'll make sure your home by 9:00."

"Ok."

"Tell your mam you're going to your friend's house yea? Don't tell her your meeting a dog. You know how much she hates pets!"

My jaw and fists were clenched and every muscle in my body was tense with rage. I poured myself a whiskey to try to calm down. A twenty-eight-year-old man used his dog as bait to lure a child into a meeting. Then he made the child feel like she was being left out by not having sex. Isolating her and making her feel like the odd one out, he had her right where he wanted her. The meeting was set for Thursday, November 12th.

Another agonizing day was spent pacing the house and watching the clock. After printing out all the chat logs and photos of Leroy that Dr.Octave sent, I devised a plan on how to confront him. It was best to try and blend into my surroundings as a jogger. A pair of tracksuit bottoms, an old dark hoodie, and a black wool hat made me look the part. At 5:15 it was finally time to leave my house. That gave me plenty of time to get to the park at the top of Chapelizod Hill Road, just along the Kylemore Road. I took my own car again but parked on Colepark Drive. It was just a short walk to the park and if necessary, I could have left the car there overnight if the meeting turned sour. The radio was a welcome mental distraction while preparing myself for the confrontation. I closed my eyes, took deep breaths and began to relax a little. My new found peace was rudely interrupted by the vibration of the decoy phone.

"Leaving now hun x." Was the text from Octave.

"Me too, see you soon x." I replied.

The chat logs were rolled up and tucked safely into the sleeve of my hoodie. Earphones were placed in my ears, although they weren't attached to anything. I wanted to create the illusion that I was in my own world listening to music while being fully aware of my surroundings at all times. Stepping out of the car, making my way to the park, the nip of a sharp November night greeted me immediately. Every breath exhaled seemed to blend in with the light fog that had descended over Dublin that night. The park was eerily empty and only illuminated by the dim, hazy street lamps that dotted the perimeter of the interior footpath. I started to lightly jog around the park. It was a good way to keep warm, plus my panting would disguise any nervous quiver in my voice when talking to Dr.Octave. Two laps of the Park, still no sign of him or the dog. I slowed my pace to a walk as I turned back towards the Chapelizod Hill road end of the park. The only other person around was a heavy-set man in a grey jacket walking a small black dog just at the crossroads of Kylemore and Le Fanu Road. The dog fit the profile, but the person walking him looked nothing like the photo Dr.Octave sent to Anna. It couldn't be him. The dog walker had a very peculiar gait. Rather than walking one foot in front of the other, he seemed to waddle from side to side as if his right leg was an inch or two shorter than the left. Every step seemed like a chore as he made his way to the park entrance. All his concentration was entirely focused on his phone as he entered the park. We continued to approach each other. The decoy phone vibrated in my pocket. As we passed, I looked closely at the dog. There was no doubt it was Leroy.

The walker paid no attention to me. His breathing sounded deep and heavy. He wore silver framed circular glasses, his hair was shaved tight to the bone and his double chin sat on the collar of his jacket. When I was a safe distance away from the man and his dog, I checked the decoy phone.

"Just in the park now. Where are you?" Was the text from Dr.Octave. It had to be him. But it made no sense. Who was the heavy set dog owner? Who's picture did Dr.Octave send to Anna? There was only one way to find out.

At the entrance to the park, I turned and walked slowly in the footsteps of the dog walker, maintaining a safe distance. He followed the footpath along the Kylemore Road, passing the small playground along his way. Luckily it was dark and too cold for any children to be around. He then took a left and was heading towards Rossmore Road. It was time to nab him. It didn't take long to catch up to him. His odd walk meant he didn't get anywhere with speed. When I was within earshot I let out a whistle and said...

"Leroy, Leroy." The dog turned around, his tail wagging excitedly. I bent down and started to pet him.

"Hi, do we know you?" Asked the dog owner, his heavy breathing almost sounded like a snore.

"Oh yea," I said, "We've met before."

"Sorry I don't remember you, what's your name again?"

"Oh, no worries, my name is 'Anna', we met a few nights ago on the chatroom Dr.Octave." I answered while rising to my feet.

"You have the wrong person, it wasn't me." He said.

"So your screen name isn't Dr.Octave and your dog's name isn't Leroy? Your dog certainly thinks it is!"

"No, it's not me."

I took out the decoy phone and said to Dr.Octave...

"So if I call the number you gave to 'Anna' right now, your phone won't ring?"

"No," he said, "I don't know what you're talking about."

With that, his phone started to ring...

"So, you're trying to tell me that you didn't give your phone number to who you believed to be a thirteen-year-old girl in a chat room?"

"She said she was eighteen!" He fired back.

"So it is you?" I asked. "And who the fuck is the person in the picture you sent to Anna? If you're twenty-eight, I'm the fuckin' tooth fairy!"

"You have it all wrong, I knew it was a setup. I wanted to satisfy my own curiosity by proving that it was!"

"So, you arrange to meet a thirteen-year-old girl to let her walk your dog. You invite her back to your house to teach her about sex so she won't feel left out around her peers. Do you realise how this makes you look?"

If he could, I'm sure Dr.Octave would have started to run at that point. But instead, he turned and began a more strained version of his original waddle. I could only guess he thought he was getting somewhere faster than before, but all he seemed to do was to sway to the left and right more strenuously. I removed the chat logs of our conversations from my sleeve and told him...

"I have everything here, every word you sent to 'Anna', you can't deny it's you. What would the Guards have to say about all this?" He stopped momentarily and looked me dead in the eye.

"No, please. I can't go through all that again." It was obvious that wasn't his first time dealing with an issue like this. "I wasn't going to do anything". He said.

"Then why are you here?" I asked. "And how the fuck were you going to explain that you were the man in the photo you sent to Anna?"

"The photo is me!" He shot back.

"Fuck off! How many decades ago was that? How old are you?"

"None of your business."

"Play it like that if you want, but I have everything I need to hang you!"

"You have it all wrong. I wasn't going to do anything."

"Then why are you here?" I asked.

"I just wanted to prove to myself that it was fake...it's all fantasy, just fantasy."

"But you're here Doctor! That's very real! I have it all documented, your every word. You typed it! Nobody forced you!" With a grunt, Octave began to waddle towards where he first entered the park.

"You know the Guards will search your house, seize all computers and smartphones. You're looking at serious time here! We both know this isn't your first Rodeo, Doc!"

"Oh, Fuck off," he said, between jaded breaths, "I didn't do anything wrong."

"You didn't do anything wrong? The information I have on you will ruin you, and you know it! Your job, your house, whatever friendships or relationships you have left, everything will go up in smoke!" He didn't respond, the good old silent treatment.

We exited the park and crossed the road back towards Chapelizod Hill Road. I remained silent until we began our descent down the hill. The further we got from my car the better. Even if he wanted to, Dr.Octave wouldn't have been able to give chase after I told him why I was really there. I stood in front of him and he stopped dead in his tracks. His breathing became an exhausted wheeze. There was sweat rolling from his forehead all the way down his chubby face, dripping from his chin onto his jacket. "Look," I started, "You can try and ignore me all you want, but you can't ignore what you've done. But you can make it go away... €10,000 in cash is the cost of my silence. I'll give you one week to get it. Ignore me, I go to the Guards, try to fuck around, I go to the Guards. I'm your only way out of this, so the choice is yours! Keep your phone on, I'll be in touch." ...Still nothing.

He stood there with his mouth wide open, desperately trying to catch his breath. I walked around him and back up towards the crossroads. I couldn't stop myself from saying "See ya later Leroy!" as I left. At the top of the hill, I turned back and looked for Dr.Octave. I watched his overcautious pathetic limp make its way down the hill until he disappeared from view. After returning to my car, I went straight home and deleted any trace of Anna from the internet.

Giving these perverts a few days to get my money together gave them time to destroy evidence too. But there was no other option. If I leaned on them too much they might have cracked and handed themselves into the Guards. That was no good to me, okay there'd be one less perv online trying to contact kids, but all my efforts would have been wasted.

Monday night, November 16th, I texted Octave... "Do you have what you owe me?"
"Most of it, yea." Was his response.
"We're meeting on Thursday. I'll text details then." I sent back.

Thursday, November 19th. Another day going over and over all the 'what if's' that could go wrong. But my confidence in my plan was strong. It had to work. At about 3:30 that afternoon, equipped with a small roll of black masking tape, I drove to a car rental company in Ballymount Industrial Estate. I purposely parked about a two-minute walk from the rental company. It was just around the corner and out of view of the main reception area. During the procedure of renting a car, they asked me what make or model I wanted. That made no significant difference to me, all that was required was the registration to have a '0' in the latter part of it. That way, with a small piece of the black masking tape, I could make the '0' look like an '8'. Even if Dr.Octave or any bystanders got the registration of the rented car, it would never be traced back to me. A new Ford Mondeo was recommended to me and it was acceptable once the registration plate had what I was looking for. Just after 4:00 PM I drove out of the rental company and got a feel for the car. It was my first time driving a new car, it felt slick as if the steering wheel anticipated every move I was about to make. It got me thinking, if I made some real money from snaring paedophiles, maybe a new car would be top of my shopping list. But then again, after months of being out of work, how was I supposed to explain the sudden appearance of a new car?

With time to kill before the meeting, I made my way to the Square Shopping Centre. In a fast food restaurant, I toyed with the burger and chips I ordered, barely able to take a bite.

"7:00 PM, Acres Road, Phoenix Park, by the football pitches. Text me when you're there!" I texted to Dr.Octave.

"OK." Was his only response.

The Phoenix Park was a logical place for the exchange. It was close to Chapelizod, so Octave would have no problem getting there. Acres Road was ideal because it's more secluded than the main road, Chesterfield Avenue. I could get the money and get out of there quickly. At around 5:45 PM I left The Square and headed for the Phoenix Park. The most probable entrance that Dr.Octave would use to access the park was via Chapelizod Road. By parking on the North Road, on the opposite side of the park, it was highly unlikely that we would encounter each other before the agreed time.6:40 PM, sitting alone in the rented car, the anxiety took over again. Was Octave going to pay? What if the Guards were there? Do I have it in me to drive off with the Guards in pursuit? What if the car got wrecked? What if Octave attacks me? I turned up the radio to try and distract my mind from the agonizing self-doubt. 6:55 PM my decoy phone vibrated with a text from Dr.Octave...

"At the pitches."

My stomach was doing somersaults and providing a chorus of unwanted noises. I fumbled to start the car. Once the key turned in the ignition the car immediately jolted forwards and cut out. The car was still in first gear, a detail that escaped me when I parked. Deep breaths, steady, start again. From the North Road, I approached the roundabout on Chesterfield Avenue, taking the exit adjacent to the American Ambassador's Residence which leads to Acres Road.

While slowly driving past the Papal Cross I rang Octave from the decoy phone. After two rings he answered.

"Turn your hazard lights on."

As I rounded the slight right-hand turn to continue on Acres Road, a silver Toyota with a taxi plate on its roof grabbed my attention. The blinking hazard lights intermittently threw an orange glow onto the overweight driver who sat facing me. On closer inspection, there was no doubt that the swollen red face was the now familiar figure of Dr.Octave. With barely any traffic on the road, I was able to pull the rented car right up to his so that our driver windows were right next to one another. Our windows rolled down almost simultaneously. His breathing was hard and heavy, almost panting, giving me the impression he was as nervous as I was.

"Throw it in." I told him. Octave reached down to the footwell underneath him, pulled up a blue plastic bag and threw it in my driver's window. The blue package landed on my lap, and without having to think about my next movement, I was already driving away. The flashing hazard lights of the silver taxi faded into my rear view mirror.

Driving down Acres Road I opened the package. The light blue tint of the €20 notes and the orange shade of the €50's were neatly lined up and bound with elastic bands. It was a pure adrenaline rush and the nerves finally subsided. With the cash tucked safely into my jacket pocket I headed back to Ballymount. Parking the rented car behind my own I removed the tape from the registration plates, turning the '8's back to '0's again. It was time to go home and celebrate another successful snare. With whiskey in hand, I double and treble checked the amount. €6,240, the bastard tried to shortchange me! Did he think I wouldn't notice? The thought of ringing or texting Dr.Octave to get the rest of the money did spring to mind, but it was too risky. Another meeting with the same pervert didn't appeal to me. I'd follow the procedure and send everything on Dr.Octave to his local Garda Station.

Friday, November 20th, with the conversations between Dr.Octave and Anna printed and sealed in an envelope, addressed to Ballyfermot Garda Station, I took the 27 bus up to the Walkinstown Roundabout. The decoy phone was in my pocket ready to be dumped somewhere along the way. Walking to Ballymount where the rented car was parked, I made sure to search the interior to see if any of Dr.Octaves money may have fallen from the bag and scattered in the car. But there was nothing, the fat bastard tried to pull a fast one. The decoy phone vibrated with a phone call. It was Dr.Octave calling, but any further correspondence with him wasn't going to lead anywhere. I ignored the call and followed through with my plan.

Having dropped the car back to the rental company, I boarded a bus bound for the City Centre. My plan was to send the envelope from somewhere outside Dublin again. Get off at Dame Street, walk to Pearse Street Train Station, get a train to another county. Post the package from there, dump the decoy, spend a few hours exploring and then return home. Walking up College Street, right outside Trinity College, that plan changed. A junkie, swaying his way through pedestrians looked at me and asked in a sluggish nasally voice...

"Here buddie got any spare change man?"

"No." I snapped back at him.

But then it hit me. If I could pay this fella to drop the package into Pearse Street Garda Station, it would save me a train journey. Ok, it was the wrong Garda station, but the information would fall into the right hands either way. I called the junkie back...

"Here mate, come here a sec!"

The junkie staggered back towards me. His once white runners were filthy and in tatters. The ends of his grey tracksuit bottoms were torn and damp. There were a number of questionable stains dotting the front of his tracksuit bottoms. He wore a heavy blue puffy jacket that was fully zipped up. His bony gaunt face poked out the top of the jacket. His jawbone was razor sharp, no doubt a result of his body being ravaged by heroin. His bulging eyes were half open. His hands were clasped in front of him thinking he was getting some change. He looked like he was trying to receive communion.

"I have a little job for ye," I told him.

"Yea?" He asked.

He looked up at me trying to focus on my face, his mouth was gaping open.

"I'll give you €20 to drop this envelope into Pearse Street Garda Station."

"No way bud." Was his answer, "If I go back in there, them fuckers won't let me out." He laughed as he finished that sentence. At least that's what I thought it was. But all he seemed to do was raise his upper lip high enough to reveal his yellow, rotting teeth.

"€50 then," I said, "All you have to do is say you found this on the street and you want to hand it in."

"Fifty notes? Alright then!" He replied.

"Fine, but I'll be watching you. Go into the Station, if you don't go in I'll follow ya and get my money back."

"Sound man, sound I'll do it, no bother." I handed him the envelope, which he tucked under his arm. I paid him the €50 as promised. He immediately unzipped his puffy blue jacket to reveal a red bum-bag clasped around him. He wore it hanging over his left shoulder and fastened behind him so that the main storage part of the bum-bag hung over his heart. He unzipped a small pocket on it and tucked the €50 inside. God only knows what secrets the other pockets were hiding. I wouldn't dare to find out.

We walked up along College Street and junkie started asking me about the envelope.

"What's in it man."

"Haven't a clue, I found it up the road, I don't have the time to drop it in myself."

"Ah, right yea." He was probably too high to pay attention to the obvious lie.

"I'm gettin' the bus here," I said to him. "But you go in and drop the envelope off. And don't forget, I'm watchin' you!"

"Sound buddie, see ya later," he said while veering onto Pearse Street to make his way towards the Garda Station. Paying no attention to his surroundings he stepped into the road while the traffic was still moving. Cars slammed on their brakes and beeped their horns as junkie carelessly crossed the road. He gave the agitated drivers the thumbs up and waved to them like he was the Lord Mayor. He miraculously made it across the road in one piece. I kept a close eye on him and watched him go into the Station. He was taking longer than he should. Standing, watching for any sign of junkie leaving the Station, the decoy phone rang again. It was Dr.Octave. I ignored the call. Junkie was escorted out of the Garda Station by two Gardaí. There was no envelope in sight, so mission accomplished. I walked away quickly before junkie could point me out or get me involved in any way. Walking up through Temple Bar the urge to stop off for a drink was far too tempting to ignore. Two paedo's down, and over €16,000 made. I was on a roll.

Getting home that night was hazy. The last thing I remember was tossing the decoy phone into the Liffey. The following morning the sound of a vibrating phone eventually woke me from a drunken slumber. With the taste of whiskey at the back of my throat and my head pounding, I frantically searched for the vibrating phone to shut it off. I found it and the person calling was Dr.Octave. Bollix! I must have thrown my own phone into the Liffey and kept the decoy one. Smart move. The phone rang out and notified me that I had a new voice message...
"Look. I know I left you short. But if you just give me more time I'll get the rest of the money for ye! Please, just give me a chance. I can't go back to prison. You don't know what it's like in there for someone like-"

Ignoring Dr.Octaves pleas, I ripped the battery from the phone. As soon as my hangover subsided I ventured out and dumped the decoy. Confident that I was going to hunt again I bought two new phones. One for my personal use, and another decoy. But it was important to allow a few weeks to pass before setting up the third profile.

3. JJ

Early December 2009 my third profile was set up. On that hunt, I changed tactics. I thought it was better to stay away from the chat room where I already caught two paedophiles in the space of two months. This time I went for a gay chat room. Decoy phone purchased. Photo downloaded. Profile set up. Background story ready. Screen name 'Darren_Dot_ie'. I was all set. As with my first two hunts, the decent people warn you off a chat room like that one. When I revealed Darren's age, most of the men chatting to him made their excuses and stopped. But one stuck around even after he warned Darren he was too young to be there. 'JJ_38'. From his profile picture, JJ looked like one of those guys that never had a hair out of place. His jet black hair was slicked back, looked soaking wet, and you could see the comb marks stretching from his forehead all the way back through his scalp. He seemed to take great pride in his appearance. I learned that 'JJ' was thirty-eight from Dun Laoghaire and ran his own restaurant in the City Centre. From the restaurant's website, I learned they were in business for six years and that JJ employed twenty-two people. Pictures of Irish celebrities and well know public figures dining in JJ's restaurant were proudly displayed on the website. It looked like JJ was doing very well for himself. It was time for me to take a piece of that.

JJ and 'Darren' spoke online for two consecutive nights. But I could tell JJ was a little cautious.
"I really shouldn't be talking to you!" he said.
"Why not?" I replied.
"I could get into a lot of trouble."
"For talking? lol."
"You're thirteen. You don't understand!"
"We're only chatting!"

JJ appeared to relax and started to reveal a little more about himself. He began to tell Darren about his 'coming out' story.

"I left it late by today's standards! I was twenty-four before I told anyone." JJ said.

"Oh. Why is that late?"

"Well, when I came out it wasn't as widely accepted as it is now."

"How come?"

"I don't know, it was just a different time. My Dad still barely talks to me."

"OMG. Why?"

"He's a man's man. A rugby loving, beer drinking fisherman. He said he couldn't stand the thought of his only son prancing around town with another man!"

"That's terrible."

"Yea. But I can't change who I am! Mam was great though. She acted like nothing happened!"

"Thank God!"

"So how about you? Are you out yet?"

"No way!"

"I know the feeling. It's difficult to tell anyone."

"When did you know you were gay?" I asked.

"I knew since I was a kid. I wasn't like the other boys!"

"Same here!"

"So what are you on the chat room for? Trying to meet your first boyfriend?"

"I don't know. I have no experience with guys."

"Not even a kiss?" JJ asked.

"No. :-("

"Awww!! Do you have a cover-up girlfriend?"

"No. I did have, but she just got annoying."

Our chat was cut short when my computer unexpectedly froze and closed down the website. I shut the computer down and restarted it after a few minutes. After logging back into the chat room I was relieved to see JJ was still there.

"I thought I lost you! lol" He sent to me as soon as I was logged back on.

"Sorry. My bloody computer crashed. It never does that!"

"It happens a lot with this website, it's glitchy as fuck!"

"Oh." I replied. "So I'll just have to get used to it!"

"Well not really. We could text instead."

I wasn't sure if JJ was being honest when he said the website we were using was actually faulty or if he used this as an excuse to get Darren's number. Either way, I didn't care. The conversation was moving exactly along the path I wanted it to.

"Sure. No harm in swapping numbers I suppose." I replied.

We exchanged numbers and continued the conversation by text.

"Hey!" Was the first text message JJ sent.

"Hi. Oh, your picture on here is a different one from the chat room." I replied. The profile picture on the app JJ texted Darren from was obviously the same person, but his hair was shorter than it was in the picture on his chat room profile.

"Yea. Same queer different hair."

"I like it shorter!"

"Thanks. How about this one? I used to have it shaved." With that, JJ sent two other pictures where his head is shaved to the bone.

"OMG, you look so different."

"lol, thanks. Ok, your turn now."

"What do you mean?" I tried to play the fool.

"Send me some more pic's. I want to see some more of you."

The bastard had me. I only had one photo for the decoy profile. If I downloaded more than one photo of the same model from the stock photo website, it would have been obvious the profile was fake. The pictures were all professional, portrait style. I had to try bluff him somehow.

"I can't. If my parents found out they'd kill me."

"Do they know you were on a gay chat room?"

"Of course not!"

"You weren't afraid of them catching you on there!"

"I was. They don't even know I'm gay! My life would be over."

"Oh stop. Such a drama queen. Send one pic. Just one of what you look like now!"

"I can't. Seriously they'd disown me."

"Oh, what's the point then? I knew I shouldn't have bothered talking to you!"

"Wait. Hang on!" I replied. A notification reading 'unable to deliver message' appeared on the screen of the decoy phone. JJ had blocked Darren's number.

It was infuriating knowing that I had wasted time talking to JJ. I'd have to start all over again and try to hook somebody else. I kept Darren's profile online and logged back into the gay chat room. It was tedious and the conversations with people in there were not heading where I wanted them to. Sometimes I'd log in to the chat room and contribute to the open conversation, in the hope that somebody would click on Darren's profile picture and send him a private message. I wasted three days doing that without a single message.

I was contemplating deleting that particular profile and trying with another, but as I was searching for a female model to become my next decoy profile, I received a notification from the gay chat room to inform me that Darren had been contacted via private message.

"Any luck finding your first boyfriend yet?" It was JJ.

"Hey! No! I'm so glad it's you." I replied.

"Still here looking I see!"

"Yea. Since you blocked my number! :-("

"Sorry! Hang on..." With that, the decoy phone vibrated with a text message.

"Sorry I blocked you!"

"It's ok. How have you been?"

"Fine. I'm a little tipsy. I arranged a team building thingy for my staff today and we ended up in the pub!"

"That sounds fun!"

JJ was back and I knew he was vulnerable because he had been drinking. It was time to see if I could finally reel him in. We talked about the team building day, the time he spent with his employees and how it will improve his business. Then I started to get personal.

"Did you meet anyone tonight?"

"No. Wish I did though!" He replied.

"lol. What was your first time with a guy like?"

"Ha. I was fifteen. He was about thirty. He was gorgeous, married but I didn't care."

"Wow. A married guy?"

"Yea. I was his little secret!"

"Fifteen! So I have to wait at least another two years!"

"Not necessarily."

"What do you mean?"

"We could meet up. I'll book a hotel room. An older man did it for me, now it's my turn to help someone else!"

"Yea right. You're full of shit!"

"Really??" Straight after JJ sent that reply, I received two pictures of JJ naked. They were taken in what I guessed was his bedroom. He stood and took the photos in the reflection of the wardrobe mirrors. I knew I had him. There was no way out for JJ.

I found it hard to believe that a gay man who only came out at twenty-four would have his first sexual experience with another man at the age of fifteen. I guessed this was JJ's way of making Darren feel at ease. Make him believe that it happens all the time and that it's nothing out of the ordinary. We chatted for a little after he sent the pictures. To my relief, he never asked for any in return.

"Ok. I believe you! So where and when?" I replied to his naked pictures.

"What are you doing this weekend? I'll book a hotel out this way."

"OMG. I can't believe I'll actually meet you! You know I can't stay the night right? My parents would know something was up."

"Jesus your parents are so controlling. I'll book a room for the day and you can go home that night."

"It sounds great. Thanks. xx"

We went through the finer details of how we'd meet. Darren would tell his parents that he was going out with his friends, instead, he would spend the day with JJ in a hotel room. The meeting was set for Saturday afternoon December 12th at 2:00 PM. Darren would travel to the City Centre and get the DART (Dublin Area Rapid Transit) to Dun Laoghaire. JJ would meet him on the East Pier and from there they would take a short walk to the hotel.

In the days leading up to the meeting, JJ texted Darren constantly. I could tell when JJ was home from work because the texts turned more sexual. He'd talk about the things that he and Darren would do once they met and on one occasion he sent me a picture of his bed with the caption 'Wish you were here!' Two pictures of JJ's erect penis soon followed, and just when I thought it couldn't get any worse. JJ proved me wrong.

On Saturday morning, the day of the meeting. JJ sent a video to Darren. It was a 15-second clip of JJ masturbating. He climaxed before the video ended. Right after JJ sent the video he texted Darren...

"What do you think of that? lol"

"OMG. You're mad!"

"You could say I'm a little excited about meeting you!"

"Looking forward to seeing you too!"

It sickened me. A thirty-eight-year-old man sending a video like that to who he believed to be a child. I printed out all the chat logs and the pictures that JJ sent, and put them in my backpack. The earlier meeting suited me. It gave me less time to hang around the house overthinking every possible outcome. I left at about 12:30 PM, plenty of time to get the bus into town and get the DART to Dun

Laoghaire. Again, all that ran through my head for the entire journey was what would be going through Darren's mind if he were real and if he was actually on his way to meet JJ. A thirteen-year-old kid who thinks a man over twenty years older than him is doing him a favour by booking a hotel room and 'introducing' him to homosexuality. I made it to Dun Laoghaire Train Station a little after 1:40 PM. With time to kill before meeting JJ, I contemplated going for a drink, but in the end, there wasn't enough time. I strolled aimlessly around until it was time for the meeting. There's something about the sound of waves crashing against the coast that I love. It's soothing, and it certainly played its part in keeping my nerves at bay. Deep breaths of the crisp sea air had an almost medicinal effect. Although it was cold there were still some people, well wrapped up in coats, hats and scarf's walking along the pier and the shoreline. I wasn't the only one basking in the glory of the chilly December sea breeze.

I stood on the Queens Road, a stone's throw away from the entrance of the East Pier. At 1:55 PM I texted JJ. "I'm just at the entrance to the East Pier."
"On my way." He replied.

I maintained a watchful eye on everyone walking close to the East Pier. Nobody loitered around, everyone either walked to or from the pier or continued walking along the Queen's Road. I spotted a sole male crossing the traffic lights, and approach the entrance of the small park just opposite the East Pier. He was quite tall and well dressed, he wore a black winter jacket and a flat old style tweed farmer's cap. He walked with his head bowed against the wind, so it was difficult to get a clear view of his face. He sat on the first bench in the park, the bench faced the sea, he then reached into his pocket and pulled his phone out. Soon after, the decoy vibrated in my pocket. The man was looking all around him as if looking for someone in particular. I figured it was JJ. I discreetly checked the decoy phone...

"I'm in the park just beside East Pier, Where are you? :-)"
The text from JJ read. It was him. Everything was in place.

I fought the urge to let my feet keep rhythm with my heart and consciously walked slowly towards the park. JJ had his back to me so he didn't see me approaching. As I got closer to him, he was anxiously looking left and right, trying to spot Darren. Just before I entered the park I took the decoy phone out and rang JJ. His phone rang and he answered immediately. I hung up and went straight to my text's with JJ. I scrolled up the chat to the video he sent earlier that morning and took a seat beside JJ on the bench. "Excuse me mate," I said to him. "Do you know where this place is?" Before JJ had a chance to look at my phone I pressed play on the video. JJ looked just in time to see a video of himself masturbating. His eyes darted up towards mine.

"Where did you get that?" He asked.

"So this is you JJ? Where do you think I got it?"

"I don't know, somebody sent it to you as a joke or something."

"Who are you here to meet?"

"Oh fuck! I knew it was a setup. I fucking knew it. You bastard." As soon as the words rushed out of JJ's mouth he made a sudden leap from the bench and tried to make a run for it.

I reacted in time to grab him by the shoulder and stop him from moving away from me. He was strong and gave everything he had to try and run. I wrapped my other arm around him and managed to anchor him to the spot. The decoy phone went tumbling to the ground.

"Relax, for fuck sake," I told him. "Even if you got away I know where your restaurant is. Now sit down and don't do anything stupid."

JJ slumped back onto the bench. He was hysterical. Tears were streaming down his face and it sounded as if he was hyperventilating.

"I'll ask you again," I said, as I picked up the decoy phone and sat beside JJ. I studied our immediate surroundings to see if JJ's outburst had attracted any attention. But it seemed to have gone unnoticed.

"Who are you here to meet?"

"A friend." He answered.

"How old is your friend?"

"What's it to you?"

"Not much really, only I know you're here to meet a thirteen-year-old kid named Darren, and you have a hotel room booked for you and him, don't you my good man?"

"He told me he was eighteen!"

"Bullshit! Let's get this clear if you haven't already guessed. There is no he, there is no Darren. You were talking to me the whole time. I have all the conversations saved and printed, and I have every picture along with the video you sent this morning."

"That's entrapment."

"Entrapment! First of all, you began the conversation with Darren. Plus, it could only be entrapment if I were a Guard."

"So who are you then?"

"That's not important."

"Oh, Fuck off."

JJ stood up from the bench. I mirrored his every move. "Run away if you want. I'm not going to chase you. I have everything I need to ruin you."

JJ exited the park and began to walk along the Queens Road towards the Sandycove Beach direction. I followed. It was time to let him know why I confronted him.

"You've got a lot to lose JJ. Your business, your reputation, your future. Have you ever been arrested before?"

"You're not a Guard so you can't arrest me."

"That may be true, but I could turn all this information into the Guards and let them take it from here. You groomed a minor! Do you realise how much shit you're actually in? We're talking prison, we're talking Sex Offenders Register. You'll lose everything. Your business, your house, friends, family, everything."

"Who are you and what the fuck do you want?"

"Who I am doesn't concern you. What I want is €10,000. That buys my silence. Pay me in cash and consider all this history. You can go back to your life like it never happened.

Nobody will ever know."

"You're trying to fucking blackmail me?" he fired at me while abruptly halting his stride.

"Call it what you want, but who can you turn to? The Guards?"

"I'll go to my solicitor about this."

"And tell them what? That you're a pervert?"

"No. I can tell them that I'm being blackmailed!"

"Prove it."

"What do you mean prove it?"

"Prove that I ever asked you for money. I've got all the chat logs, pictures and a video of you. You've got shit on me. You wouldn't even be able to prove that I exist."

"Oh fuck off! This is all too much."

"You're right. It's a lot to take in. I'll give you some time to think about it. But trust me, €10,000 is your only way out. If you try to ignore me I'll send everything to the Guards. Ok, I won't get my money, but I'll take pleasure in ruining your life JJ. Keep your phone on. I'll be in touch in a few days."

As I turned and started walking along the seafront back towards the DART station, JJ took a much-needed seat on a bench facing the sea again. I doubt the rhythm of the waves gave him any kind of solace. He was doubled at the waist with his hands inserted in his jacket pockets. His head bowed down, staring at his feet. I couldn't blame him, he certainly had a lot to think about. The trap was set. I made it home and immediately obliterated any trace of Darren from the internet.

Wednesday, December 16th I texted JJ.

"You've had time to think. What are you doing?"

"I'll pay you. But I have to be sure it never gets out!" He replied.

"Fine. Once all is paid up I've no interest in ratting you out. Have the cash ready for Saturday. Wrap it up in Christmas wrapping paper, head into the City Centre for 7:00 PM. I'll give you further instruction then."
"Fine." Was his only response.

It's astonishing how quickly these 'men' who were once all bravado and sending text's and pictures to kids become little boys themselves. The power had changed hands and JJ felt it as much as I did.

Saturday, December 19th I devised a plan to pick up my cash. It was six days before Christmas. Everybody was busy buying last minute presents that nobody wants for people they don't like. I used this to my advantage. My plan was to meet JJ in a very public and highly populated spot. The GPO (General Post Office) was the best place I could think of. There are always hundreds of people passing up and down O'Connell Street. It would be easy to meet JJ, get what I need, and disappear into the crowds and make my way home. At about 3:00 PM I texted him...
"7:00 PM tonight. I'll tell you where to meet."
"Yea. I'll be there." He replied.

I needed to keep my wits about me, after downing two whiskeys I put the bottle away. At 6:00 PM I threw my backpack over my shoulder and got the 27 bus into town. Sitting in traffic just outside Christ Church, I gave JJ his instructions.
"Meet me outside the GPO. When I approach you, I'll open a bag. Place the 'gift' inside. When I walk away, you walk the opposite way. As long as every cent is there and you don't try anything smart, you'll never hear from me again. Text me when you're at the GPO."

I got off the bus on Dame Street where the Christmas shoppers were out in their droves. There's a certain buzz around Dublin at that time of the year. The atmosphere is frantic. I stepped into a steady flow of pedestrians making our way down Dame Street and onto Westmoreland Street. You'd be taking your life into your hands if you dared to step outside of the current you were walking in. One wrong move and you could easily be sucked into the crowds marching in the opposite direction. The claustrophobic feeling became a bit too much by the time I made it to O'Connell Bridge. I crossed the road and made it to the island that separates O'Connell Street. It was still busy but came as a welcome relief compared to the frenzied herd I freed myself from. I continued walking on the island and passed the G.P.O. Crossing over towards the corner of Cathedral Street, I stood just beyond a taxi rank and waited for word from JJ. I figured that if he got the DART into town from Dun Laoghaire, he'd either stop at Tara Street or Connolly Station to walk to the GPO. If he was walking from his restaurant based on the south side, there'd be no reason for him to walk up as far as Cathedral Street. Both scenarios eliminated almost all possibilities that he would spot me before I wanted him to. I waited at my post, trying to blend in as much as possible. A little after 7:00 PM, I got a text from JJ. It simply read... "I'm Here."

Way to be specific. He could have told me which pillar, which corner, but no. Just that he was at the meeting spot. From the corner of Cathedral Street, it was impossible to see anyone through the crowd, so I made my way back to the island and walked slowly towards the G.P.O. As I scanned the six pillars at the front of the G.P.O I spotted a man standing directly under the statue of Cú Chulainn. The first thing that stood out was a tweed farmers cap. The wearer had his head bowed as if he didn't want anyone to notice him. Both arms were tucked behind his back as he rested against the glass. I was sure it was JJ. The traffic was at a standstill, it was safe enough to cross the road towards JJ.

It was an odd sight seeing JJ standing at the feet of Cú Chulainn. One a fallen Warrior, who tied himself to a standing stone so he could die on his feet. His enemies would only approach after they saw a Raven landing on his shoulder, making sure he was dead. The other, a pervert, a man who tried to lure a child into a hotel room, who believed he was paying €10,000 for his freedom. I slid the backpack off my shoulder, unzipped it and walked towards JJ.

"You got it?" I asked.

Without saying a word, JJ removed 'the gift' from inside his jacket. As instructed he wrapped it up to look like a Christmas present. It was red shiny paper. He placed it in my backpack. I zipped it up, walked away and took a left onto Henry Street. I blended into the crowd as planned, and continued onto Mary Street. Dodging my way through the crowds, while sliding my bag off my shoulder, I carefully manoeuvered it to my front. While still walking, I unzipped the main compartment to inspect 'the gift'. I tore a small corner of the paper and from the incision, the satisfying glow of €50 notes brought an immediate smile to my face. The parcel itself wasn't very big. I couldn't wait to get home to count the cash and make sure it was all there. I continued down Mary Street and took a left onto Wolfe Tone Street. There were no taxis around, so I figured it would be best to make my way out towards the Quays and get one there. That plan was about to be interrupted.

I passed Wolfe Tone Square and was about to take a left onto Upper Abbey Street when something struck the back of my head. It hurt like hell and I fell to the ground clutching the freshly split wound. I felt the heat of my blood gushing onto my hands. Laying on the ground, I was kicked and punched so many times I lost count.

"Get the bag, search his pockets," a voice said.

There were three of them in total. I desperately tried to defend myself, but it was hopeless. They had my bag, my personal phone the decoy phone and my wallet. In the split seconds between the kicks and punches, I was trying to see who the attackers were. Could it be JJ getting his money back? But if it was, he'd have to tell at least two other people exactly what was going on. What felt like forever was probably no more than twenty or thirty seconds. Beaten and bleeding I watched the three figures running away, they took a right onto Upper Abbey Street. At the corner, one of the muggers turned around as if to inspect the damage they inflicted. A wool hat and a scarf covered most of his face, but his blue puffy jacket was open. As he turned to run again I couldn't believe my eyes. A red bum bag fastened around his body, hanging over one shoulder. Junkie! The fuckin' scumbag and two of his buddies had just taken my €10,000. I didn't care about the decoy phone, that was being discarded anyway, but they took my own personal phone and my wallet. That killed me.

While struggling to get back to my feet a lady approached...

"Jesus love are you alright?"

"I'm ok," I said. "They took my bag and phone."

"I'll call the Guards."

"NO." I snapped back immediately. My response seemed to startle her.

"I'll call an Ambulance then."

"It's alright thanks. I'll just get a taxi home."

"You should go to the hospital love, your poor face is in bits." With that, she pulled a tissue from her handbag and gave it to me. I knew that I was bleeding from my nose and the right corner of my mouth. I could feel the blood trickling down my face.

"I'll get a taxi home. I'll go the hospital tomorrow if I need to."

"Well ok love, but I think you'd be better going now. Are you sure you don't want me to call the Guards?"

"It's ok thanks, there was only a few presents in the bag, nothing that can't be replaced, and the phone was ancient, no use to anyone. Thanks for your help. I appreciate it."

"Take care of yourself love. And Merry Christmas."

"Thanks again, and the same to you."

I continued with my original plan and made my way to the Quays to try and hail a taxi. With my right hand clasping the back of my head and my left hand holding my rib cage, I staggered up through Jervis Street and finally made it to the Quays. Trying to hail a taxi, at Christmas while visibly bleeding was no easy feat. Eventually, a taxi pulled up, the driver kept all doors locked as he rolled the passenger window down and shouted out to me in a thick Dublin tone.

"What happened you?"

"I was mugged up the road, the fuckers took my phone, wallet, everything."

"Ah for Jaysis sake, get in! Get in!" With that, I heard him unlock all the doors, and I got in the car.

The driver offered to take me to hospital or to the Guards after telling him what happened. I declined both offers and told him I just wanted to go home.

"Ye can't have a thing these days without some fuckers wanting it! They'd rob the eyes outta yer head!". The driver shared his wisdom.

"I know yea, there were three of them. I didn't see them coming."

"Fuckin' three of them! Very brave men when they're in their packs. Bastards!"

When he pulled up outside my house I told the driver I'd have to go inside and get some cash to pay him.

"It's alright son. I think you've been through enough for one day." He said.

"I can't let ye' do that mate."

"It's grand, it's grand. Sure I was finishin' up in any way."

"No, no. Wait there and I'll be back in a sec."

"Merry Christmas son. Look after yourself."

I got out of his car and walked towards my house. As soon as I opened the front door, the taxi beeped its horn and drove away. It was good to see there are still some decent people around. With the remnants of a bottle of whiskey for company, I went over and over what happened in my head a thousand times that night. Did junkie spot me and follow me? Did someone see me counting the cash on Mary Street? Was it a coincidence? Did JJ pay junkie and his buddies to jump me? Was it an opportunistic mugging? Either way, junkie and his buddies had my €10,000. I'm sure they thought all their

Christmases came at once when they opened the present. I figured there was only one place that all that cash was going, straight into Junkie and his buddies veins. With a bit of luck, they'd overdose and wouldn't even see Christmas. Fuckin' scumbags. All my hard earned money gone just like that. Merry Fuckin' Christmas junkie.

4. Decision Time

My face was beaten and bruised. But nothing was broken. There was no point in going to hospital, my black eyes, cuts and scrapes, would heal eventually. I printed all the conversations between JJ and Darren. Some of them were lost when the decoy phone was taken, all the pictures and the video were gone too. On the drive out of Dublin to post the evidence, I had a lot of time to think. Was it worth continuing? As a lone soldier, it was a huge risk. If I was going to continue snaring I'd need some kind of protection. But of course, that would come at a cost. So was it worth doing all this for €10,000? Stopping in Carlow Town I found a post box and dropped the envelope inside. It was addressed to Dun Laoghaire Garda Station. With the Christmas rush, the information probably wouldn't reach the Gardaí until sometime in the New Year, but at least it'd get there.

In the days leading up to Christmas, I bought some presents for my parents and my Uncle George. Although I had the money to buy them expensive gifts, I couldn't. I had been out of work for almost eight months, if I aroused any kind of suspicion, they would have questioned how I could afford such luxuries. My black eyes and the wounds on my face had healed slightly since the attack. But it was still unwelcomely obvious that I was involved in some kind of trouble. I contemplated making excuses not to go over to my parent's house on Christmas day, but I knew Ma would know there was something wrong. And besides, she would have been heartbroken not to at least see one of her kids on Christmas. My sister Emily had just emigrated to New Zealand earlier that year with her husband James. It was best to face the music.

Christmas morning was welcomed with a hangover. Cans of beer and too much whiskey the night before had drained the energy from me. While still lying in bed I thought of the pervs I snared and how their day was going to plan out. Did Marty still have a family around him? Was Dr.Octave going to spend the day with his mutt? JJ probably still thought he was off the hook. So maybe he was having his usual Christmas, whatever that was. Eventually, I peeled myself off the mattress, gathered up the presents, and got ready to make the short walk to my parent's house. I got there at about 1:00 PM and rang the doorbell. I have a key but never use it. Knowing that Ma was going to immediately start asking about the scars on my face, I already had my answers well rehearsed. She swung the door wide open and greeted me with her usual smile. She instantly covered her mouth with her hand and said...

"Jesus. What happened to you?"

"It's nothing Ma, I'm alright."

"Come in before someone sees you. Wait 'till your father gets a look at you!"

She knew as well as I did that Da was going to go off on one. I'd get smart and put him in his place. Then we'd hardly speak for the rest of the day. It was Christmas tradition. I walked into the house and headed straight for the kitchen. The heat hit me as soon as the kitchen door opened. Pots and pans were sizzling and bubbling on the cooker. The smell of the turkey and ham baking in the oven was amazing. Nothing beats the feeling of a home cooked Christmas dinner. Da was sitting at the kitchen table watching the telly and had already started drinking.

"Howya son." He said as he was turning to look at me. "Ah for Jaysus sake, you're a bit long in the tooth to be fightin' in pub's now aren't you?"

"I learned from the best." I shot back at him.

The traditional Christmas atmosphere was back with a vengeance, even Ma's best carving knife wouldn't cut through it. Da turned back to the telly, and Ma started to probe.

"What happened love?"

"I was mugged, in town a few days ago. Three junkies jumped me."

"Were they big?" Da sarcastically asked.

"Oh leave it out Jerry." Ma snapped back. "There was bloody three of them. What was he supposed to do."

"Junkies? Sure a fart would knock them over!"

"Oh give it over. Ignore Superman over there, he's already on his third can. You know how brave he gets with the drink."

I answered all Ma's questions about what happened, what time it happened at, and what the muggers took. Every last detail. I felt guilty lying to Ma by telling her that I went to the Guards and to hospital. I'd never hear the end of it if I told her I didn't report it or got myself checked out. Satisfied that she had all the information she needed about the incident, Ma changed the subject.

"Any word from Laura?"

"No Ma. Nothing. It's over, she's not coming back."

"It might be just a phase love."

"It's not. I heard she's livin' with him now."

"And to think that bastard was your groomsman."

"What's done is done, I don't want to talk about it."

Dinner was served at about 3:30 PM. Uncle George decided not to join us at the table. He said the chairs give him a backache. He'd been living with Ma and Da ever since Aunt June passed away. Although I call him Uncle George, he's actually Ma's Uncle. An old gent in his eighties, I had a lot of time for George. I always made a point of sitting with him for a while any time I was in Ma's.

"Any sign of a job yet?" Da asked before I had time to pick up a fork.

"I'm workin' on it." I answered.

"What's it been now? Five, six months?"

"Somethin' like that."

"Don't know how you still have a roof over your head."

"Let me worry about it."

Ma interrupted the conversation before an argument erupted.

"Emily and James are settling in well. James starts his new job in January and Emily is still with the phone company."

"Good to hear," I answered. "Tell them I was asking for them."

"She said she'd ring at some stage today. You can talk to her when she rings."

I don't mind talking to Emily, she's my younger sister and I look out for her as best I can. But what she's doing with that James fella I'll never know. He's one boring bastard. He works in insurance, and that's all he ever talks about. I can't stand people who spend their free time talking about their job. Like there's nothing else to talk about other than work. Give me some glimmer of hope that you actually have a personality.

Dinner was all but finished when the phone rang. Ma left the table to answer it. She was delighted to hear Emily's voice on the other end of the phone. That left me and Da sitting at the table in silence. It was the perfect time to go into George. What used to be the sitting room was converted into a bedroom for George. He was too frail to make it upstairs. I knocked on his door before entering. The curtains were pulled closed, the room was dark and lit only by the flickering of the telly. George looked up at the door when I entered, he re-aligned his glasses to see who it was, and then all I heard was "Ah howya youngfella." There was a genuine joyfulness in his voice. I hadn't seen him in a while. A zimmer frame sat directly in front of George, but he made no effort to stand. He threw his left arm out, inviting me in for a hug.

"It's great to see you George." I said, mid-embrace.

"You too son, you too." He replied as he moved some debris off the sofa beside him and gestured for me to sit.

"You look like you were in a spot of bother, everything alright youngfella?"

"Ah, it's nothing, just a few scratches. I'm grand thanks."

"I hope you gave as good as ye got! What have I always told you...'If you can't beat them...'"

"...die trying." I finished the sentence for him.

George had been quoting me that line since I was about twelve. God knows where he got it from, but I liked it. We exchanged the customary smile and nod we always do after we recite his motto.

"And how about you? I heard you were in hospital a few weeks back?"

"Ah yea it was nothing, the aul breathing again. I woke your mother up about three one morning with me wheezin'. Needless to say, your father wasn't best pleased. He tells me I'm interruptin' his retirement!"

"Ah take no notice of him, you know what he's like."

"I've known him for over forty years, and to be fair he's not a bad man. There's just one thing I don't like about him."

"What's that George?"

"He's an arsehole!" He delivered that line with such a smirk on his face I couldn't help but burst out laughing.

"You're a wise man George!"

George and my Da never got along. I don't know why. It was just one of those things. Maybe George was too optimistic for my Da's liking. Da is a card-carrying pessimist, and George the polar opposite. A divide that was only widened once George moved into my Da's house. Jesus, I can only imagine the things Da might have said to poor aul George.

"How was dinner?" I asked.

"Lovely as always, your mother outdid herself."

"You couldn't make it all the way out to the kitchen table to have it could ya?"

"Ah you know yourself, sometimes you're just better in your own company," he winked.

"Here, I got ye this for Christmas, but don't tell the rest of them." I made him promise, as I handed him a bottle of whiskey. I didn't bother wrapping it. I knew the paper would be too much for his rheumatism.

"Ah Jaysus, thanks a million youngfella." He took the bottle and placed it carefully on his lap. He rummaged around beside him for a few seconds until he lifted a glass.

"Here, hold that a second," he said, as he reached for another.

He pulled up a yellow mug and muttered to himself "That'll do."

He opened the whiskey and pointed the bottle my way, I held out my glass for him to pour, and pour he did. He gave us both a generous measure and said "Happy Christmas youngfella," as we clinked the glass and mug together.

"Are ya alright for a few bob?" George asked. For as long as I can remember, George always asked if I needed money. He was by no means a rich man but always offered to help whenever he could.

"I'm grand thanks."

"Well, you know where to come if you're stuck!"

"Thanks, George. I appreciate it."

I felt terrible after George offered me money. He probably thought I was struggling to get by, little did he know I had almost €8,000 in a shoebox under my bed. Money I blackmailed from paedophiles. I know George would have got a kick out of it if he knew the truth, and I could have trusted him to keep it to himself. But the less people that knew the better, and besides, I wasn't sure if I was going to continue hunting or not.

We sat sipping our whiskey and watching whatever came on the telly. We must have sat there for nearly an hour. When my drink was gone, George offered me another. I declined and told him it was time to head home.

"Alright, son." He said as he steadied himself on his zimmer frame and slowly rose to hug me. He threw his arms around me and patted me on the back.

"It was great to see ya youngfella. You should come by more often. Gimmie a break from that grumpy bollix."

"Ah now it's Christmas," I said. "There's no need for that sort of language."

We hugged and said our goodbyes and I made my way back into the kitchen to say goodbye to Ma and Da. Emily had just got off the phone.

"You couldn't have said Merry Christmas to your sister?" Da said before I could even start to tell them I was leaving. "Have you spoken to George today?" I asked him. "Did you wish him a Merry Christmas?" My question had the desired effect. Da shut his trap and turned back to his telly. "I'm off Ma," I said. "Thanks for dinner. There's a present for both of you in that paper bag over there." I pointed to the bag I left behind the kitchen door when I first arrived. "Ah, there was no need for that love." Ma answered as she started scrambling to find the gift she had got for me. "That's yours. It's not much."

"Thanks, Ma. And thanks again for dinner. I'll see ye before New Years. See ye Da."

"See ye." Was his semi-audible response.

I left Ma and Da's and walked home. That night I did what most of the country do on Christmas night. I had a few drinks and fell asleep in front of the telly.

The next few days were spent pondering my next move. Do I take the risk and keep going alone? Or give up? I had my fun, made almost €20,000, but also got my head kicked in, losing €10,000 in the process. I was in two minds at that point. But then I saw it. Browsing the internet not looking for anything in particular, I came across an article about Marty. He'd been arrested. His house had been searched and all computers and mobile devices were seized. Over 3,000 indecent images involving children were recovered from Marty's hard drive's. Marty thought his €10,000 got him off the hook. He didn't think to start deleting or destroying his hard drives. Bad news for him, excellent news for me, the Guards, and any child Marty was likely to contact. To think that I was responsible for this scumbag's arrest was a rush. But that rush was short lived. Since his arrest, a niece of his now aged in her twenties came forward to the Guards and accused Marty of historical sexual abuse. He was accused of 'Sexual Assault in the third degree of a minor aged between nine and twelve years'. My evidence then came into play, the report continued...

'Gardaí received an anonymous tip-off that led to the accused's arrest. Mobile phone and Internet chat records were sent to the Gardaí that allegedly show the accused grooming a minor with the intent of meeting for sexual intercourse.'

Fucking scumbag. He pled Guilty to every charge, and his sentencing hearing was due to take place in February. The article didn't say anything about his wife, his kids, or more importantly...me. Not once did it say he was blackmailed, conned or threatened. Nor did it mention anything about €10,000. Maybe Marty kept tight-lipped about the whole situation, or he told the Guards but they didn't want that information to be public knowledge. Either way, it didn't matter. I got exactly what I wanted, plus that bastard would face prison time. My heart went out to his niece. She'd been more than likely scared to death to tell anybody what happened to her, fearing no-one would believe her. I can imagine how many nights she cried herself to sleep, drank herself to the brink, or even contemplated ending the struggle. But finally, Marty would face the consequences of his actions and by the looks of things he was staring down the barrel of ten years plus. I knew right then that what I was doing was justified. It was time to start hunting again.

5. Q and Dumb-Dumb

Something had to change. Although I liked the idea of being in a crowded place when the cash was exchanging hands, it had its faults. I was still alone, and if anybody brought some friends with them, they could easily just beat the shit out of me and take the cash back. I wasn't sure if that's what happened with JJ, but I highly doubted it. Why would JJ associate with junkies? I put it down to an opportunistic mugging. Next time I'd be sure to stick to the main streets where there were plenty of people around and make my getaway a lot quicker. Meeting the perverts in a rented car had its advantages. But still, I was alone, a sitting duck waiting to be pounced on. I needed protection, but I didn't want 'the bodyguard' to ask too many questions. The fewer people that knew what was going on, the better. So far it was only me, the Guards, and the paedos. I racked my brain thinking of someone who would watch over the transaction and then make sure I got to a taxi safely. And if the situation turned nasty, they could intervene in an altercation and get me out of there with the cash. I couldn't go to any friends, it was too close for comfort. Besides, most of them were all married and had families of their own. Even trying to get a hold of them was tough enough. But there was one person that came to mind, someone who I knew for a fact could take care of himself. With one look he'd make you think twice about confronting him. It was 'Q'.

Q got his nickname because of his appearance. He was as bald as a Monk. People started to call him 'Cue-Ball' and over time that was shortened to 'Q'. I heard he'd been bald since his early twenties. He started to lose his hair and decided to shave it all off to speed up the process. His eyes were cold, dark and dead, they had the ability to cut you to pieces with just a glance. If that wasn't enough to scare you, the powerful arms that hung from his broad shoulders should. He stood at about 6'4, and it would be a braver man than I that would dare to take him on. There were rumours that Q had spent some time behind bars for beating the living shit out of some bloke who insulted his girlfriend. But nobody dared to ask him the truth. The story got more elaborate depending on who you asked, some say he put a guy in hospital, others say Q killed a man. Nobody knows why, or even if he ever spent time inside. Stories like those seem to leech themselves onto men as menacing looking as Q. I first got to know him when he worked as a bouncer in 'The Dublin Underground', a small bar near St.Stephens Green. Me and the boys used to spend our weekends drinking there. Sometimes Q would let us stay back for a late drink after closing time, and on occasion, he'd join us for a pint. I remember him as a nice lad, the kind of guy you could spend hours talking to but realise you didn't know very much about him. Q gave nothing away, that was the way he was. I've also witnessed Q taking care of business on more than one occasion, but one incident sticks out in my mind. Two college kids drank a little more than they could handle and started to get messy, thinking they were invincible. They were grabbing the waitresses and giving abuse to the barmen demanding that they should be getting a student discount. Q approached them from behind, and without saying a word he lifted them both by their belts. He carried them off to the fire escape and slammed the door shut behind him. God only knows what happened to those poor bastards, but one thing was certain, we never saw them in The Underground again.

In the week between Christmas and New Year, I took a trip into town to see if The Dublin Underground was still open, and more importantly, if Q still worked there. A strange nostalgic feeling came over me as I sat on the bus making my way to the Underground. If I could turn the clock back about fifteen years, I'd have been sitting on the upper deck of the bus with five or six of my close friends. We'd be dressed in our best sitting underneath a plume of cheap aftershave and cheaper vodka. Drinking and laughing our heads off until we got to Dame Street. But there I was, alone, about to see if I could enlist a bodyguard to watch over me when I collected hush-hush money from a paedophile. After a short walk from Dame Street to South Williams Street, I rounded the corner onto South Kings Street, where the luminous sign for The Dublin Underground still shone. It was made to look like a tube station in London. A red circle with the words 'The Dublin' written on the upper semi-circle and a blue rectangle going across the middle of it with 'Underground' written on it. Both the red and blue parts of the sign lit up. So many memories came flooding back once I saw the sign. I couldn't help but smile to myself. The pub itself was a lot similar to an Underground station. A case of black granite stairs led you to the front door where most punters paid in. But back then, regulars like me and the boys were waved in by the bouncers. Once inside, white tiled walls covered with vintage photographs of The London Underground led you down a wooden staircase and straight onto the dance floor. We had our favourite table just to the left of the bar. It was the perfect seat. Only a few steps to get a drink and any girl that wanted to use the toilets had to pass right by our table to get to them. We'd try our best chat up lines on them, once we had enough liquid confidence. But we'd fail 99.9% of the time to ever talk to any of them.

Two large figures, both dressed in black, topped off with wool hats and earpieces, stood either side of the main entrance. The smaller of the two was to my right and he was busy playing with his phone. The light from the phone illuminated his face enough for me to see he had a goatee beard. It wasn't Q. The larger bouncer was staring directly at me, studying me. His gaze showed no sign of letting up as I got close enough to recognize his face. It was definitely Q. Although the lines in his face had grown a little deeper since the last time I'd seen him, there was no mistaking it. The sheer size of this beast cannot be forgotten easily. I extended my right hand to shake his, the other bouncer still hadn't looked up from his phone.

"Hey Q, it's been a long time." I said as he shook my hand with a puzzled look on his face.

"How's it goin' man," he replied. I could tell he was trying to figure out who I was.

"I know your face alright, but the name... you're gonna have to remind me."

Q used to know my name, but with the years that had passed without seeing each other, it was obvious he had forgotten it. I suppose in Q's line of work you see so many faces and hear so many names, it would be next to impossible to remember everyone.

"Frankie," I told him. Frankie was one of the lads in our group. He, like so many other tradesmen around that time, had left Ireland for Australia to find work. I hadn't seen or heard much from him in about five or six years. I knew Q would associate the name with my group of friends and I could only hope that he wouldn't know me well enough to know I wasn't Frankie.

"Ah yea, you used to drink here a good while back, there was five or six of ye that used to come in..." He bought it!

"That's right, some good times spent in here I tell ye, Jesus the memories came right back once I saw the sign!"

"I'm surprised you can remember anything that happened here. You and your mates used to fall out of the place two or three times a week! Yez' were never any trouble though, just the kind of customers I like."

"Yea, me and the boys practically lived here for nearly five years...Jaysus, d'ya remember when Johner's Ma drove in to get him one Sunday. We were in watchin' the football and we stayed the whole night. About eleven o'clock Johner's Ma came bargin' in to drag him out of the place. He had an Interview the next mornin' and she wasn't happy about him stayin' out with us. Fuckin' gas."

"Ah Jaysus yea, yez' didn't let him live that one down for many a year!! How are the boys anyway?"

"Ah they're grand, haven't seen a lot of them lately, all married and behavin' themselves. You know how it goes."
"That I do. And how have you been?" Q asked me that while staring me directly in the eye and nodding his head down towards mine. He was gesturing at the black eyes and cuts on my face. It was basically his roundabout way of asking 'What happened to you?'
"Well, that's kinda what I want to talk to you about."
"Go on..." Q said.
"Can I talk to you in private for a sec? It won't take long."
    Q turned to the other bouncer.
"Dom, I'm goin' over there for a minute to chat to an old mate. Give us a shout if ya need me".
    For a second I thought Q addressed the other bouncer as 'Dumb'. It would be a fitting name. He didn't strike me as someone who was exactly 'with it'. He was in his own world, and from then on, all I could call him in my own head was 'Dumb-Dumb'. In response to Q, Dumb-Dumb didn't say a word. He lifted his head from his phone for all of about three seconds, nodded in agreement, and then went back to his phone. Q and I walked away from the entrance a little bit. Not far, just enough to be out of earshot of Dumb-Dumb and the smokers who were huddled together outside.
"Right" I started. "I'll run this by you and if you're interested, great. If not, no worries. I'll walk away and it'll probably be another few years until we see each other."
"Alright." Q responded. It was the kind of answer someone gives you when they're intrigued. They say enough to let you know you have their attention, but not too much to interrupt what you're about to say next.
"I pick up parcels from people. I meet them in a public place, get what I need and walk away. Last time I did this, as you can clearly tell, I was mugged. The parcel was taken along with my phone."
"Ok."
"What I'm looking for is someone I know I can trust to basically look over the transaction. Keep an eye on me

while I collect the parcel and make sure I make it to a taxi safely afterward. If anything goes wrong and the person I'm collecting from turns nasty, that's where you step in. You intervene long enough for me to get away. Once I make it to a taxi with the parcel your job is done. If anyone asks, you were simply a good samaritan breaking up a scuffle between two people. You don't know any Frankie and you won't know the person I'm collecting from. If this interests you..."

"Hang on a second," Q interrupted. He held his hands in front of him as if telling me to slow down.

"What's in the parcel?"

"I'd prefer to keep that to myself."

"Drugs?"

"No, it's nothing like that."

"And what about the Guards?"

"If there's any sign of the Guards, you walk away. At least then I know I'm not going to take another beating. I'll face the music myself. I won't mention anything about you, sure what do I know about you really? All I know is your nickname."

"How much?"

"€500 per pick up. I'll text you on the day, meet you and give you the money. Then you make sure you're where I tell you to be while the transaction is taking place. After all is done, follow me until I get a taxi. And that's it. €500 for ten minutes work."

"I'll think about it."

"Of course. I might not have another pick up for a few weeks. But let's swap numbers and we'll take it from there."

It was right there, I realized a big mistake. Since the mugging, I only replaced my personal phone. I didn't bother buying a decoy because I wasn't sure if I was hunting anymore. This meant I had to give Q my own personal number. Maybe not such a big deal. But it would have been better to give him a decoy number. Q and I exchanged numbers, shook hands again and I left. I walked away feeling good about the meeting. What probably takes Q a week to earn on the doors could easily be made in a few minutes. I knew he'd give it some serious thought. I'd give him a few days to mull it over before I'd make contact again.

In the meantime, a new profile was set up, 'Kims_wayornoway'. Kim was thirteen and from Donnycarney, Dublin. Stock photo, backstory, decoy phone. It all started to become a bit of a routine. I didn't make a lot of progress in the days leading up to New Years. The only person chatting to Kim was a twenty-two-year-old student from Cork. The conversation was bordering on sexual. I'd say within a day or two I could have had him hooked, but there was no point. Having looked at all his social media profiles I found no indication that he was from an affluent family. No big house, fancy car, no photos of him on expensive holidays. I doubt he could have afforded a train or bus ticket to Dublin, let alone €10,000, so I blocked him. Sure it would have been great to get him on the Gardaí radar, but I wasn't prepared to do it for nothing.

The New Year was welcomed with the usual 'New Year, New Me' bullshit. I never liked New Years. Everyone blowin' smoke about how their gonna do this, change that, lose weight or go back to college. Please. Within two weeks everyone will settle back into their usual routine. Work, telly, bed. Work, telly, bed. Continue that pattern until you get to the weekend, then you drink like there's no tomorrow. Any free time you were supposed to have is taken up by nursing a hangover. Then you wake up, promise yourself you'll 'never do it again' and slide back into your weekday routine and start all over. I rang in the New Year with a bottle of whiskey. Drinking wise, it was an early start that day. I can't remember if I was even awake at midnight.

Within the first week of January 2010, I started fishing for a paedo again. I got a few bites, but they didn't go anywhere until Vinnie.KK came along. As his screen name suggested, Vince was from Kilkenny. Nothing stood out about Vince, on his profile, he came across as being so ordinary. He said he was forty-two, a farmer and had an interest in politics. There were pictures of him campaigning in a local election in his hometown. I can only guess that his political career ended there as there were no photos posted after the election. Vince looked so squeaky clean that if anyone ever accused him of trying to groom a child, even a stranger would have a hard time believing it. Maybe that was the picture Vince spent years creating. A perfect alibi. If anybody accused him of anything, no matter how deplorable, nothing would stick because Vince was so well respected within his community. Or perhaps the temptation of chatting to a thirteen-year-old got the better of him. Either way, he contacted Kim.

The conversation went along pretty much the same pattern as the first three. Vince started off being a 'friend', then got closer over the next few days. Phone numbers were exchanged and then the conversation got more and more sexual. Vince started asking Kim to send him more pictures. He wanted to see more than the profile picture. I made the excuse that Kim's phone was old, cracked and beaten up so badly that the camera didn't work anymore. Vince seemed to buy it.

"I'd love to see more pictures of you. You're so pretty. Do you have any other profiles?" He asked.

"No. This is the only one."

"Would you send me some pic's if you had a different phone?"

"Yea. Only if you sent me some.x"

"I can send you a new phone!"

"How?"

"Give me your address and I'll post it to you."

"Don't. If my parents find out I'm talking to someone online they'd kill me!"

"But don't you want a new phone?"

"Yea. But you can't send it to my house!"

"Come down to meet me and I'll buy you whichever phone you want!"

There was no way I was going to make the trip to Kilkenny to nab the bastard, so I made the excuses that a thirteen-year-old would make...

"How can I go to Kilkenny without my parents knowing? I'd never get away with it!"

"I'll come and meet you in Dublin then!"

"Yea. That's a better plan. I can fool my parents for at least a few hours."

"Great. Don't tell your parents you're meeting me. And don't let them see your new phone."

The meeting was set for 6:00 PM, Fusilier's Arch, St.Stephens Green on Friday, January 8th. I told Vince to buy a phone and have it ready to give to Kim. That way there would be no denying why he travelled to Dublin. In the days leading up to the meeting, Vince texted Kim non-stop. He sent a picture of his erect penis to Kim with the caption...

"Now you know what I have. You owe me a naked pic! xx"

I was nervous about the meeting, but not as nervous as the previous ones. My gut instinct told me that Vince would want to bury this whole incident as quickly as he could in order to maintain his faultless persona. With all the chat logs and his penis picture printed, it was time for the confrontation.

Grafton Street was comparatively empty to what it would have been a little over two weeks before. The buzz and excitement of Christmas shoppers had been replaced by the heavy feeling of the January blues. The atmosphere was compounded by a lone busker standing at the top of the street slowly strumming a guitar. His husky, monotone voice droned through an unfamiliar song at the speed of a ballad. I dropped some loose change into the busker's open guitar case before I walked past him and reached St.Stephens Green. I stood facing Fusilier's Arch and assessed the surroundings. The groundskeeper was busy locking the gates beneath the Arch. With the entrance to the park now closed, there was no reason for anybody to loiter around. I continued walking along Stephens Green until I was a safe distance from the meeting point. It was a sharp January evening. I zipped my jacket up as far as it would go and tucked my chin in behind it. Constantly checking the time, I anxiously waited for the decoy phone to vibrate. 5:50 PM nothing. 6:00 PM nothing. 6:10 PM still nothing. I was getting apprehensive. I sent Vince a text and asked...

"Where are you? :-("

I paced up and down the street trying to keep warm and desperately trying to look as if I belonged there. The decoy phone eventually vibrated with a phone call, it was Vince. But I couldn't answer it. I let it ring out and hoped he'd text me...

"Sorry babe, running late, just parking up now. Be there in 5 mins x," was his text

immediately after I ignored the call.

"Great! What are you wearing? Just so I know it's you!" I replied.

"Green jacket, black and gold wool hat x"

Armed with a description I made my way back towards the Arch. A lone figure, wearing a green jacket and black and gold hat stood against one of the three concrete pillars to the right of the Arch. He held a white paper bag with the carphone warehouse logo printed on it. I assumed Kim's new phone was in the bag. I called Vince from my decoy phone as I crossed the road. The man at the pillar hurriedly reached into the pocket of his green jacket and answered his phone.

"Hello, Kim, you there?" I heard him ask, as I walked within earshot of the man who all but confirmed himself to be Vince. Everything about him was clean, smart and respectable. From his brown shoes, smart attire and his freshly shaved face. He looked like he made an effort to impress Kim. I stood directly in front of him, trying to make eye contact. He gave me a quick glance, turned and walked away. I followed. While his back was facing me I put my decoy phone on speaker.

"Hello? Kim?" Hearing his own voice echoing behind him, Vince stopped and turned around to face me.

"Has the penny dropped yet?" I asked.

"Do I know you?" Vince replied.

"No. But you know Kim right?"

"No. Whats goin' on?"

"Don't fuck around. You're Vince from Kilkenny and you're here to meet Kim."

"I don't know what you're talking about."

"Of course you don't! There is no Kim, you've been talking to me the whole time. You groomed a child online and arranged to meet her here. You bought her a new phone so she could take pictures of herself and send them to you. Is the phone in the bag?" Vince made a pitiful attempt to conceal the bag behind him.

"I'm not here to meet anyone."

"Bollix. You just answered your phone. That call was from the number I gave you. You thought it was Kim. A thirteen-year-old child for Christ sake."

"It wasn't me!" Vince muttered.

"Here." I said as I removed the chat logs from my backpack and handed them to Vince. "I have every conversation and the picture of your erect penis that you sent to Kim. That is your penis Vince?"

"Yea." He replied faintly.

"Yea. And the phone you bought for Kim is in the bag?"

"I wasn't going to do anything."

"You told her not to tell her parents where she was tonight. You also told her to hide the phone from them."

"It's no harm. I'm not like that!"

"No harm? What were you going to do with the pictures she sent you?"

"Nothing. It's not what you think!"

"You're sending pictures of your penis to a thirteen-year-old child. You drove from Kilkenny to Dublin to meet her. Do you know how bad this looks!"

"She was never in any danger."

"Oh fuck off! Shut up and listen for a minute. It's as simple as this. I have all this information on you, I could bring it to the Guards right now and have you arrested. Instead of doing that I'm offering you a way out. Pay me €10,000 in cash within one week and nobody has to find out about it. You don't pay me, everything goes to the Guards. You will be arrested, everything will be reported online and in newspapers everywhere. Do you want that? €10,000 and it all disappears. The choice is yours."

"Where am I supposed to get that cash in one week?"

"That's your problem. You have one week. Keep your phone on, I'll be in touch. Ignore me and everything goes to the Guards."

"Wait, hang on a second. I can explain." Vince was pleading as I turned on my heels and walked back towards Grafton Street. There was no point in wasting any more time on him. I said what I wanted to say and got out of there. What happened next was his decision. The busker who provided the soundtrack for the confrontation was still strumming his guitar. His voice faded to a whisper as I continued along Grafton Street. Reaching Suffolk Street I hailed a taxi and headed home. Over a large whiskey, I deleted any trace of Kim from the internet.

The next morning, January 9th, I decided to text Q. I felt he had enough time to think about my offer.

"Hey Q. It's Frankie. Have you thought about what we discussed the other night?"

"Heya Frankie. Yea I've thought about it. We're in. We'll do it."

WE? What the fuck did he mean by we? I hoped that he meant 'we' as in him and I. But no...

"We?" I asked.

"Yea, me and Dom. We'll do it, as discussed." It dawned on me then that he wanted Dumb-Dumb in on the action.

"I was actually only pitching the idea to you..."

"I'm not doing something like this alone. It's both of us or nothing."

"If you want Dom there that's fine. You can split your money with him." I already knew the answer I was going to get.

"Bollix. It's €500 each or nothing." So my €500 suddenly turned to €1,000. But I had no other choice. I could have run the risk of going it alone again and getting mugged, or pay the extra €500 to Dumb-Dumb. The thought of paying Dumb-Dumb was infuriating. I knew I'd be paying him to stand around and text on his phone, but screw it, it wasn't my money anyway.

"Ok. Cool. I'll text you in a few days and let you know where to meet. Cheers."

Wednesday, January 13th, I texted Vince to see what his decision was.

"Vince, you've had time to think...what will it be?"

"I have the money." Was his response. Music to my ears.

"Good. Meet me back at Fusilier's Arch this Friday at 6 PM."

"Ok."

A very simple conversation. We were all set. I just had to get Q and Dumb-Dumb on board. I texted Q.

"Hey Q. I have a meeting at 6:00 PM on Friday. Can I meet you about half 5 and we sort it out?"

"Hey, Frankie. Yea sound. Where will I meet you?"

It was better to ring Q and tell him where to meet me. I didn't want too much information in a text in case his phone fell into the wrong hands. We arranged to meet in a cafe on South Anne Street, just off Grafton Street, at 5:30 PM on Friday. I would pay Q and Dumb-Dumb there and tell them where the transaction was taking place. It was a risk, I was €1,000 down. If Vince didn't show up I was screwed. But at least I'd still be able to send his information to the Guards.

Friday, January 15th. After buying a new backpack to replace the one that was stolen from me during the mugging, I got to the cafe at about 5:15 PM. I sat with a pot of tea, looking out the window facing South Anne Street. I watched all the people passing by on a busy afternoon. It's extraordinary when you stop and think about each individual. I'd like to think that the vast majority of those people were good, hard-working, decent human beings. But amongst the crowds, you have your scum. I was certain that in all the people I watched walking past, there must have been at least one who had molested a child. Maybe they were caught and charged for it, maybe not. Maybe their victim or victims are too scared to talk. Even as adults they fear that nobody will believe them, they're embarrassed to tell the truth. I felt like the only one trying to weed these fuckers out to let everyone know exactly what they are.

A heavy hand fell on my shoulder with a thump, and a booming voice from behind said "Howya Frankie."
"Jesus fuckin' Christ." I said as I turned to look up at Q.
"Sorry, did I frighten ye?" Q asked with a smirk on his face.
"No. You're grand." I was miles away.
"Frankie, this is Dominic. Dominic, Frankie." Q took charge of the introduction.
"How's it goin' Dominic. Nice to meet you." I said.
"Alright." Was his only response. This was my first proper meeting with Dumb-Dumb. I basically ignored him the first time I went to see Q because he was the only person I wanted to talk to.

They sat down with me, ordered some coffee and we got down to business.
"I've explained everything to Dom, he knows the score," said Q.
"Good stuff. I'm meetin' yer man at the entrance to Stephens Green at 6." I said.
"You's stand either side of the Arch and keep an eye out for me. Q I'll ring your phone when I'm about to walk up. Don't answer it. It's a signal to let you know I'm coming."

When the plan was all set I placed a sealed envelope in front of Q and Dumb-Dumb. It was better to conceal the cash rather than hand €500 to each of them in public.

"Who's yer man you're meetin'?" Asked Dumb-Dumb. I was shocked that he actually put a sentence together. "You don't need to know," I told him.

"What are you gettin' off him?" Dumb-Dumb completed sentence number two.

"That's not important," I answered. "All you have to do is watch over the transaction and make sure I get a taxi after it. That's all."

"It's easy money, Dom," Q told his partner. "We'll be done in a few minutes."

Dumb-Dumb nodded and went to his pocket for his phone. Thank Christ. It would have taken all night to answer all of Dumb-Dumb's questions had he kept it up. Me and Q made some small talk while we finished our drinks. Dumb-Dumb didn't make another sound. At 5:50 PM, Q stood up and said "We better make a move", and with that he and Dumb-Dumb started to leave.

"I'll ring ye when I'm on the way." I said to Q.

"Sound, see ya later," he replied.

I paid the bill in the cafe and waited to hear from Vince. Knowing that Q and Dumb-Dumb were watching over me was comforting. If anything happened they were there to make sure I was ok. But they couldn't protect me from the law. If Vince wanted to fess up and make a deal with the Guards, he could. Double cross the blackmailer. But I doubted he would want to drag his good name through the mud. Just before 6:00 PM I got a text from Vince...

"At the park."

I rang Q to give him the signal, left the cafe and headed towards St.Stephens Green. At the top of Grafton Street, the Luas had just pulled in. Scores of people disembarked the trams providing excellent cover as I examined the meeting point. I first spotted Q standing to the right of the Arch, he held his phone in his hand pretending to pay attention to it, all the while he was looking out for me. Dumb-Dumb stood at the pillars to the left of the Arch and to my surprise he wasn't on his phone, he just stood there with his arms folded. I spotted Vince's green jacket at the pillars to the right of the Arch, almost exactly where I met him a week ago. Q's eyes were locked on me as I made my way over to Vince.

"Give me the envelope." I instructed.

"How do I know that you won't get the law involved?" Vince asked.

"Your gonna have to trust me."

"But I didn't do anything."

"I'm not here for a conversation. Pay up or I go straight to the Guards." With that, he pulled a white folded paper bag out of his jacket and handed it to me. While placing the package into my backpack, I turned and went to walk away. Vince grabbed my arm and said.

"Hang on a second. I need to know that everything will be destroyed."

"Let go of me fuckin' arm," I told him. I didn't feel threatened, and toe to toe I could probably take him. Q obviously saw what happened and before there was anymore conversation between me and Vince, Q and Dumb-Dumb were standing directly behind him.

"Everything alright?" Q asked. Vince turned around and saw Q and Dumb-Dumb staring down at him. He immediately let go of my arm. I walked away and crossed the road back towards Grafton Street. Q and Dumb-Dumb followed. Vince was left standing by the pillars in shock. I got into a taxi and headed home. Q and Dumb-Dumb continued walking onto Grafton Street and soon disappeared from sight. In my kitchen, I inspected the package Vince gave me. The white folded paper bag had the carphone warehouse logo printed on it. Was this poetic justice? Did Vince really use the same bag that once contained a phone he bought for a thirteen-year-old child? All that mattered to me was what was in the bag. I counted the cash. €10,000 in €20 notes. It was perfect. I had protection and €9,000 profit. I texted Q.

"Cheers for that earlier. I'll be in touch."

"No worries," he replied.

I'm sure he and Dumb-Dumb were delighted with themselves. €500 for half an hour of their time.

The next day I printed all the information I had on Vince, including the picture of his penis. With everything sealed in an envelope and addressed to his local Garda Station in Kilkenny, I took a drive out of Dublin and looked for somewhere to post the letter. Somehow, I ended up in Co.Roscommon. After dumping the decoy phone in a bin on the street, and posting the letter, I booked into a hotel for the night. It was good to switch off.

6. Business as Usual

The money earned from the previous snares allowed me to take some time away from interacting with paedophiles. This took me into February 2010. Marty's sentencing hearing was taking place. He pled guilty to every charge, which meant his niece didn't have to give evidence at a trial. He received a total of eight years in prison and was listed on the Sex Offenders Register indefinitely. He was sentenced for the three thousand indecent images found on his computer. The sexual assault of a minor and the information I sent to the Gardaí about him grooming a child with intent. The bastard got off lightly. The Judge in the case did make a remark that was incredibly satisfying. "Had it not been for the anonymous tip-off that the Gardaí received, you would be a free man. There is no place in society for men who use innocent children for their own sexual gratification." I was delighted that Marty was behind bars. And the best part was, he paid me €10,000 for the one way trip.

When it was time to start hunting again, I tried snaring in a different format. Rather than setting up a profile on a chat room and waiting for someone to make contact, I downloaded an infamous dating app onto a new decoy phone. This app was notorious for allowing people to meet up for a one night stand. It catered for gay, straight, bisexual, trans everything you could imagine. You simply input what you're looking for on your profile and it directs you to like-minded people. The first profile I set up on the app was a girl called 'RebeccaInRed'. As usual, a stock photo and backstory were ready and Rebecca's profile stated she was eighteen. When anyone liked the picture and started to chat, I made it clear that this girl was fourteen. Technology has done a lot of wonderful things, but I was genuinely shocked at the number of adults willing to talk to who they believed to be an underage girl. I had a choice of who to hook and chose them carefully. I looked closely at their social media profiles, their age, what car they drove, if they wore jewellery. Anything that indicated they had money was a bonus. They were more likely to afford €10,000 'hush-hush' money.

Over the course of the next five months, I snared three perverts using three different profiles on the app. I made sure to delete the profile and dump the decoy phone after every snare and start afresh with a new decoy phone for each hunt. The first was a married man with three kids 'Charlie4Fun'. After three days of chatting with Rebecca on the app, he had arranged a meeting. As usual, the first confrontation was in a public place and I went alone. It was risky, but I didn't want anyone bar me and the pervert to know what we were talking about. That fucker tried to blame all the messages on one of his sons. He said his son was fourteen and borrowed his phone a lot. He must have been messaging girls and chatting them up. When I questioned him why he showed up to meet this girl, he didn't have an answer. We both knew he was screwed. He begged me not to take his money, he said he had been saving a long time to take his family on holiday. "Please. How am I going to explain taking that amount of money out of a joint account?" He pleaded.
"Would you rather explain everything else to the Guards?"

My statement had the desired effect. I told him he had one week to get the money. I met Q and Dumb-Dumb on the day of the cash handover and paid them just like the last time. They stood as lookouts while I collected the cash. It all went according to plan. He paid up and I made another €9,000 profit. All his information was then sent on to the Gardaí.

The second profile was a gay profile. I had about six men all willing to talk to a thirteen-year-old boy called Aiden. I chose my victim and honed in on him. 'TomIsHere' was in his early fifties and worked as an Architect. He gave me the impression he lived a good life. We chatted for a few days and then he wanted to meet. I coaxed him into sending me some pictures by saying that I 'wanted to see more of him' before we met. He obliged and sent three pictures of himself stark naked. I had the evidence I needed to hang him. I swear this fella nearly had a heart attack when I confronted him. He stood there looking at the pictures he sent and couldn't think of a thing to say. He then began to try and destroy his phone. He threw it to the ground and repeatedly stomped on it in a desperate bid to destroy the evidence. I allowed him to work himself into a sweat before saying...

"Destroy the phone all you want. But I have everything printed. I have pictures of you naked! You also told me where you work."

"Fuck off you bastard!" Was his only reply.

"Nope. Look, pay me €10,000 cash within one week or I'll send everything I have on you to every email address on your companies website as well as the Gardaí."

Tom offered no response. He slumped to the ground leaning against a wall, puffing and panting heavily. I leaned down towards him and gave him his final instructions.

"Now that you've destroyed your phone, I'll email you where to meet me. If I don't get what I want within a week I'll fuckin' hang you!"

On the decoy phone, I set up a temporary email address in order to contact Tom. We arranged to meet for the money to exchange hands. Q and Dumb-Dumb were all set. We waited for about forty minutes, but nothing. The bastard stood me up. I followed through with my threat and sent the pictures and the chat logs to every person I could find on his companies website. The same information was passed on to the Guards. That fucker cost me €1,000 for nothing.

The third profile was female again, 'Denise_Dublin' thirteen. His screen name was 'True_Rumer'. It turned out his real name was Noel, he was forty-seven and originally from Co. Longford. Noel must have been going for some kind of record. He was my fastest ever snare. Within a few hours, he wanted to meet. He was a high-end car salesman and drove a sports car. He used his car to try and impress the decoy. That and two unsolicited pictures of his penis. It was after the second day of talking on the app that I agreed to meet him. He immediately turned bright red when I showed him the pictures he sent. He was sweating and visibly shaking. He apologised over and over again, thinking I was the girl's father. Once I made it clear there was no girl involved he began to relax a little.

"I suffer with depression!" He told me.

"And? That gives you a license to arrange a meeting with a minor?"

"No. Of course not. I have social anxiety and take medication too."

"What are you telling me this for? Do you think it changes anything?"

"I don't know! I haven't been myself lately!"

"If you're looking for sympathy your barking up the wrong fuckin' tree! It's as simple as this, pay me €10,000 within one week and it's history. Fuck me around and everything goes to the Guards."

He paid up three days after our first meeting, five days after our first contact. Again Q and Dumb-Dumb oversaw the exchange which went without incident. I made €9,000 in five days, I wish all my clients were like Noel.

It was mid-July 2010 and I had already made €27,000 so far that year. It would have been more had 'TomIsHere' not stood me up, but all was going according to plan. I set up another female profile on the app. 'Heather' was fourteen and from Dublin. I had a few people talking to her but it didn't seem to be going anywhere. But then one person texted Heather and wouldn't stop. His profile picture was a close up of a tattoo on his arm. I clicked on his profile to see if he had some pictures of himself. I couldn't believe my eyes when I realised who was talking to Heather. It was Dumb-Dumb.

Dumb-Dumb called himself 'TheDominator' on his profile and it said on there that he was thirty-four. Maybe this was why Dumb-Dumb was on his phone so often. He was very upfront and open with his messages. I told him immediately that Heather was fourteen, his initial reaction was "So?" He went on and start bragging about being a bouncer at the Underground. How he kicked the shit out this guy, knocked out that guy. All bravado bullshit. He asked Heather where she goes with her friends on the weekend, and if she's ever been to the Underground. "I can get you and your mates in no bother." He told her.

That really worried me. Could he let a group of fourteen-year-olds into a bar? And more importantly, if he did, what did Q have to say about it? He sent Heather multiple pictures of his tattoos. Most of them were of Oriental origin. Chinese Dragons and writing. The ink was fresh on some of the pictures he sent, which led me to believe that the money I paid him had been spent on tattoos. I pretended to be impressed and asked him what they meant. But truthfully I never understood why people would get Chinese writing tattooed on themselves. Do you think Asian people go around with 'Peace', 'Love' and 'Serenity' tattooed on themselves in English? I think not.

The conversation continued over the next few days and Dumb-Dumb started to get explicit. He asked Heather about her sexual experience. How many partners she's had and if she's ever tried anal sex. That was the first time anal sex was suggested to any of my female decoys. Trust Dumb-Dumb to be the one to mention it. He went on to ask Heather to meet him one particular Thursday night. He said that if she went to the Underground at about midnight, he'd be able to get off work a little early if it was quiet and have a drink with her. He also made it clear that if Heather agreed to meet him, she would be more than welcome to go back to Dunboyne to spend the night in his. It really baffles me that these perverts don't think beyond meeting a person online. Heather said she was fourteen, how was she going to disappear for a night and not have her parents notice? Ok, it was in July so there would be no school the next day, but it's as if it doesn't matter to some of the paedos. All they want is to get the person they met online to meet them, have sex with them, and what happens after that doesn't seem to come in to play.

There was no chance that I could snare Dumb-Dumb. One, I highly doubted that he would have €10 to his name after getting the Chinese phonebook tattooed on himself. Two, it was way too close for comfort. Dumb-Dumb knew me, and if I tried to get any money from him, the game was up. I cut off all ties with Dumb-Dumb on the app after he invited Heather to the Underground. Having printed all of the chat logs and taken a drive, all the information was sent to Dunboyne Garda Station. Things were going to change from that point onwards, but I wasn't quite sure how. Maybe Dumb-Dumb would tell Q everything, maybe he'd keep it to himself. Only time would tell. I had to keep things on track. If Dumb-Dumb was still going to snare with me, fine. I had to keep tight-lipped about what was going on and keep conversation with Q and Dumb-Dumb to a minimum.

After three successful snares in seven months, it was time to take a step back from hunting. The money earned gave me everything I needed and wanted but also didn't draw too much attention. If I had a snare every month, there was a risk of attracting some kind of attention from the Guards. I decided that two more snares in 2010 would be enough. All in, I would be looking at a total of €45,000 profit. It's hardly the kind of money that would allow you to live in luxury, but it certainly kept the wolf from the door.

I never came across any articles about Dr.Octave or JJ, so I searched online to see if I could find anything. It turned out that Octave was already on the Sex Offenders Register. His comment "I can't go through all that again," came to mind. He pleaded guilty to grooming a child with intent and was sentenced to eighteen months in prison with that last six months suspended. He also failed to disclose the fact he was a sex offender to the taxi company he worked for and was fined €5,000.

J.J was a first offender and basically got off with a slap on the wrist. His legal team argued that he was a man of excellent character and well respected in his community. They also made the point that if his business stopped trading, twenty-two people would be unemployed. J.J was given a six month suspended sentence and placed on the Sex Offenders Register for three years.

September 2010 I began to hunt again. I stayed away from the dating app and went back to the chatrooms. In comparison, the chat rooms are a lot more old-fashioned. It's much easier to connect with people on the app, but it was best to switch between the two. There was less chance of being caught that way. I set up a decoy profile in the usual way and got my backstory ready.

'Elaines_World2000' was thirteen and from Sutton. It took me a few days to get anybody hooked but it happened eventually. 'Denis.Mac' was fifty, married with two children and from Waterford. He told Elaine he worked as a foreman on a construction site. The conversation took the usual route. Find out a bit more about each other, become 'friends', steer the conversation towards sex, send pictures, arrange to meet. It was so routine by that stage.

Denis believed that he was going to meet Elaine and take her virginity. He reminded me of Marty by the way he was talking to Elaine, constantly calling her 'sweetheart', and 'princess'. The meeting was set for Friday, September 17th at 6:00 PM. Denis would get the train from Waterford to Pearse Street Station. They would meet there and then go to the hotel that Denis booked. Elaine would get back on the DART and be home before 10:00 PM. She was to tell her parents that she was working on a school project at her friend's house. All was well thought out and planned. But Denis never thought he'd come face to face with me, rather than a thirteen-year-old schoolgirl.

Friday, September 17th I arrived at Pearse Street Train Station, evidence in toe, at about 5:45 PM. I could see on the notice board that the train from Waterford was due in at 6:10 PM. With time to spare I downed a pint of

Guinness and whiskey chaser in a bar on Lombard Street. I was in contact with Denis throughout the day. He told me how excited he was to meet Elaine and that he had the condoms ready so that he wouldn't get her pregnant. He also said that he had some vodka with him in case they fancied a drink. I asked him what he was wearing so I could identify him immediately. He said he was wearing blue jeans, a light brown jacket and that he was carrying a red sports bag.

At 6:05 PM I walked to the intersection where Lombard Street meets Westland Row. I was on the opposite side of the road from Pearse Station, ensuring I had a good view of the main entrance which sits below an elevated railway line. 6:10 PM I got a text from Denis. "Train just pulled in, I'll see you soon xx" "Great, I'll meet you under the bridge by the main entrance." I replied.

With the train having arrived the volume of people exiting the station increased. I tried my best to look out for a man in blue jeans, a light brown jacket, and a red sports bag, but it wasn't easy. I walked from the corner, down Westland Row looking over towards the Train Station. I was studying as many people as possible trying to make sure I didn't miss him. As I was passing the main entrance, a man fitting Denis's description caught my eye. He had his phone in his hand and it looked like he was texting. He stopped and put his red sports bag down right underneath the bridge. I continued walking down Westland Row and checked the decoy phone.

"I'm under the bridge, you're late :-/ " Read the text from Denis.

I crossed the road at the pedestrian lights past the railway bridge and walked back towards Denis. He stood against a wall under the bridge, smoking. His salt and pepper hair was parted at the side and neatly combed. He had perfected the art of smoking a cigarette without using his hands. He took three or four drags of the cigarette that hung loosely from the corner of his mouth. Holding the

smoke in his lungs for a few seconds before exhaling it out the opposite corner of his mouth. His face
had a dehydrated complexion. No doubt the result of decades of hands-free smoking. I stood right beside him and toyed with the decoy phone. I was like anybody else around there at that time, waiting to meet someone who just got off the train.

"Waiting for someone?" I asked Denis.

"Yea, yea. Yourself?" He replied. The cigarette still hung from his mouth. His left hand was holding his phone while the right hand typed a text message.

"Yea. Who are you waitin' for?"

"Ah, just me daughter. You?"

"How is Elaine these days?

    With that question, Denis removed the cigarette from his mouth and gently tapped the ash on the ground. He discretely slipped his phone into his pocket and continued...

"Her name's not Elaine."

"No? Well according to my records, you're here to meet Elaine who told you she was thirteen. You're gonna bring her to a hotel to take her virginity and make sure she gets back to Sutton by 10:00 PM."

"I don't know what you're talking about."

"Of course not Denis." I pulled out the chat logs and handed them to him. "So this isn't you?" I asked him as I pointed at his profile picture. No response.

"I have it all here in black and white. You have groomed who you thought was a thirteen-year-old girl and travelled from Waterford to Dublin to have sex with her. Do you have the condoms and vodka?"

"Who are you?" He asked.

"I'm Elaine. I'm the one you were chatting to all along. Elaine's phone number you were texting is mine too. What do you have to say for yourself? What will your family have to say about this? How about your employer?"

"I didn't do anything wrong," Denis mumbled as he threw his cigarette to the ground and crushed it beneath his foot.

"Not yet. But what if I was a thirteen-year-old girl? We'd be on our way to the hotel you booked! You groomed a child with the intent of having sex with her. You're looking at prison time for this Denis, do you realise that?"

"I wasn't going to do anything with her, I only wanted to talk."

"Talk my arse. It's all here Denis. You talk about taking this girl's virginity, talk about bringing condoms so you don't get her pregnant, talk about bringing vodka. Would you rather talk to the Guards? Pearse Street Garda Station is just up the road..."

"Who are you if you're not a Guard?"

"I'm the only one left on your side, Denis."

"What does that mean?"

"It means I'm your only way out of this mess. €10,000 in cash will make this all go away. It will stay between me and you, nobody else will know. You have one week from today to pay me. Fuck around and I send everything I have on you to the Guards. I don't care if you go to prison for this. I really don't. So it's up to you..."

"How am I supposed to get €10,000 just like that?"

"Beg, steal or borrow it. I don't care. You have one week. Keep your phone on. I'll be in touch."

As I was walking away from Denis I saw him fumble into his pocket for another cigarette. He was visibly shaking. At least he had the comfort of a hotel room and a bottle of vodka to get himself together. The trap was set. It was up to Denis what happened next. I'd give him a few days to think about it and see what he wanted to do.

Tuesday, September 21st I texted him.

"You've had enough time to think about our discussion. What will it be?"

"I'll pay. How do I get the money to you?"

"Cash only. Friday, get the same train at the same time to where we last met. I'll text you then with further instruction."

"Fine."

So Denis was going to play ball. Now all I had to do was text Q and get him on board. I had no idea if Dumb-Dumb was still on the scene.

"Hey Q. I've got a meeting on Friday. Are you available?"

"Hey, Frankie. Not sure. Haven't heard from Dom. He hasn't shown up for work in a few days."

"Ok. Can't you meet without him?"

"I dunno. Meet me tonight and we'll have a word about it."

"Ok. I'll ring you when I'm in town."

So Dumb-Dumb had disappeared. I could only assume that he was arrested. I doubt they would have kept him in custody for more than a few hours. So it looked like Dumb-Dumb was on the run. Silly boy. With the brain capacity of an empty shoe, I was sure it wouldn't be long before he got caught.

That night at about 8:00 PM I got the 27 bus into town. Q and I didn't text about a meeting point, but I assumed he was working at the Underground. A short phone call to him confirmed my assumption. There were two bouncers on the door of The Underground as I approached. Q was one, the other was a stranger. Q introduced us, "Frankie, Tony, Tony, Frankie." We shook hands and exchanged our "Nice to meet you," greeting. Q told Tony that he was having a word with me inside and to radio for him if Tony needed help at the door. Q and I descended the staircases to the bar. I ordered a whiskey on the rocks, he had a coffee. We took a seat beside the staircase, Q's choice. He could keep an eye on everyone coming in, and he had quick access to the main entrance if Tony radioed for help.

"So what's the story with Dom?" I asked.

"I've no idea. One minute he was here, the next he vanished. I can't get through to his phone or anything."

"Strange one..."

"Yea, very odd alright. I know his mother lives in England. So maybe some kind of family emergency or something?"

"Oh right. Hope everything's ok."

I wondered what Q's reaction would have been if he knew the truth. 'I'm a paedophile hunter and Dom tried to meet up with who he thought was a fourteen-year-old girl. I sent all the info to the Guards, that's why Dom has disappeared.' I'd like to think that Q would be disgusted with Dom and praise me for my actions. But being involved in hunting paedophiles gives you a different perspective of how peoples minds work. You never know what people are actually thinking.

"So, back to business," I said. "The meeting on Friday, can you make it?"

"I'm not sure I want to work on something like this alone."

"Ok. But Q, you've seen the people I meet, they're hardly menacing. All of the previous meetings have gone without a hitch. Except for the one fella that didn't show, but even then, I still paid you."

"I get that, but the risk is higher. What if I ask Tony? I know him a few years, I know we can trust him."

"I'm sure Tony's a great bloke, I take your word for it. But the less people that know the better."

"I understand that but, it's better for me to have a backup in case something goes wrong. It's a dangerous business you're in. People die for what you're selling."

That last remark indicated that Q still thought I was a drug dealer.

"I'll tell you what. I was down €1,000 for these meetings before Dom disappeared. I'll pay you €1,000 for each meeting. Double your money for the same job."

"Yea, alright. I'll do it." It's funny how he didn't need time to think about that offer. Money talks.

"Cool. I'll text you Friday. The meeting will be up around Pearse Street/Westland Row. I'll meet you up there beforehand, pay you and tell you where I need you to go."

"Dealing right beside the cop shop? You sure that's a good idea?"

"It'll be grand. Sure any sign of the Guards you jog on."

"Fair enough. I'll talk to ya Friday so."

We shook on the deal and Q went back upstairs to Tony. I stayed and had a few more drinks. I thought about what Q said about 'dealing' very close to Pearse Street Garda Station. But it was going to be a quick exchange, no more than one minute. I didn't believe that Denis would hand himself into the Guards and do a deal by ratting me out. He had too much to lose. Pay €10,000 and get back on the train to Waterford and all will be forgotten. My instinct told me that was Denis's mindset. I'd find out on Friday. I left the Underground and said my goodbyes to Q and Tony, and got a taxi straight home.

Friday morning September 24th I texted Denis...
"You're coming to Dublin tonight yea?"
"Yea. Arrive same time as last week."
"Have what you owe me in a large envelope. I'll text you with instructions on where to meet me."
"Ok."

The 77a took me to Erne Street in the City Centre by about 5:00 PM. I put my backpack on under my jacket wearing it back to front so that the zip to open the bag was on my chest. It made sense. It was the safest way to carry the cash after the exchange, out of sight of any opportunist muggers. I had arranged to meet Q in a small cafe on Lombard Street. Near the intersection of Pearse Street and Westland Row at 5:30 PM. The meeting was set with plenty of time to spare, just in case he was running late. But €1,000 made sure he was right on time. I passed Q the envelope containing his payment and told him to stand at the corner of Westland Row, just where I stood before my first confrontation with Denis. As normal I'd ring Q when I was approaching to alert him to keep an eye out for me. 5:45 PM I texted Denis.
"Come out of the Station and turn right. At the intersection, there is a small island in the middle of the road where the pedestrian lights are. Text me when you're on the island."
"Ok". He replied.

6:00 PM Q left to take up his post on the corner of Westland Row. I waited for a text from Denis. 6:15 PM my decoy phone vibrated.

"On the island." It read.

"On my way. When I approach hand me the envelope. I walk one way, you walk the other. I'm not alone. You are being watched. Any funny shit and I send everything to you know who!"

I rang Q to give him the signal. Walking towards the meeting point, a lone figure stood idol on the pedestrian island. He stuck out like a sore thumb. Everyone was using the island as a temporary stop to cross the road. But Denis just stood there. He looked either lost or very suspicious. Q was standing on the opposite side of the road. Once he spotted me he followed my every move. Crossing Lombard Street towards Westland Row I unzipped my jacket and the backpack in anticipation. I waited to cross towards Denis with five or six other people. Denis spotted me and reached into his jacket. The lights changed, I repositioned myself to walk as close as possible to Denis. There was about six feet between us when he removed a white envelope from his jacket and held it at waist height. While passing, I took the envelope from him and zipped it safely into the backpack under my jacket. I continued onto Westland Row, passed Q, and hailed the first available taxi. Q blended into everyone walking on the footpath and soon disappeared from view. The exchange was a complete success. Not even a word needed to be spoken. I got home and counted the cash. €10,000 in a mixture of €50 and €20 notes. €9,000 profit. Beautiful. I packed up all the information on Denis and addressed it to a Garda Station on Patrick Street, Waterford. The following day, after a short drive to Kildare, the package was on its way to the Gardaí. Little did I know that encounter was the last of my 'normal snares', everything was about to be turned on its head. I should have stopped there and then and tried to get my life back together. But hindsight is a wonderful thing.

7. Money Mayhem

I had planned to do one more snare before Christmas. If I set up a new profile around the end of November 2010, it would give me the opportunity to get another €9,000 before the end of the year. Mid October I got a call from Q. He wanted to meet me but didn't tell me why. That got me thinking. Did he get word from Dumb-Dumb? Did he figure out exactly what I was doing and wanted a bigger cut? We arranged to meet in The Underground at 3:00 PM on Saturday, October 16th. I felt comfortable meeting him there. If he was going to challenge me on what I did to Dumb-Dumb, he was hardly going to get angry in the place he worked. I arrived at the Underground at about 2:50 PM. There was no sign of Q outside, too early in the afternoon to need a bouncer I guessed. Making my way down the staircase, I could see that it was quiet. There were three or four people sitting at the bar but the rest of the place was virtually empty. Q sat in one of the booths in the right-hand corner of the room. He wasn't alone, there was another man sitting across from Q.

The stranger sat with his back to me. Who the hell was this? I already told Q that I didn't want anybody else involved in our agreement. Did he drag me in here to try and convince me to hire his buddy for €1,000 per pickup? We could have had this conversation over the phone. Q saw me at the end of the staircase and beckoned me over to the booth.

"Frankie, thanks for coming in," Q said as we shook hands.

"Yea no worries man," I replied.

"This is Henry, a good friend of mine," Q said as he introduced me to the stranger.

"How's it going Frankie, nice to meet ye," Henry said in a thick Northern Irish accent.

"Nice to meet you too Henry."

"I'll get you a drink," said Q. "What are you havin'?"

I ordered a whiskey on the rocks and Q went to the bar. "Have a seat, Frankie," Henry said. He was sitting in the middle of the seat, with a half pint of beer in front of him. It would have been awkward to attempt to sit beside him. I slid into the seat opposite him. There was a half-empty cup of coffee on the left-hand side of the table, obviously Q's. I moved to the right of the seat, leaving enough room for Q to sit beside me. Henry was a slim figure, about mid-forties. His brown/grey hair was well groomed and his clean shaved face accentuated his prominent square jawbone. He was well dressed in a shirt and trousers. Two large gold rings decorated his right hand and a loose gold bracelet hung from his left wrist. On anybody else, they would have looked tacky, but they suited Henry. He had money and wanted you to know it. We made some small talk until Q returned with my whiskey. Q sat beside me, so we were both facing Henry.

"Alright, let's get down to business," Henry started. "My Security Company run the doors on a number of pubs and clubs in Dublin. We've just signed a contract to represent seven more clubs starting in the New Year. What I'm looking for is a dealer to have exclusive access to our clubs. Sell their merchandise with no competition and split their profit with us. Q tells me that you're the kind of person I'm looking for. Someone who won't run their mouth and can keep personal business to themselves. Would this be something that you'd be interested in Frankie?"

Dumbfounded, I had to take a second to absorb the information. So Q still thought that I was a drug dealer. He'd been talking to Henry who I assumed was his boss, and he was looking for a dealer to have exclusive access to the clubs he provided Security for. The Dealer would sell 'their merchandise' in those clubs and split the profit with Henry. It was genius when you think about it. The very people who are employed to keep drugs out of clubs let particular dealers in. They sell what they have in there and move on to a different club. After everything is done, the dealer splits the profit with the 'Security Company' all the while the owners have no idea what's going on. It was cunning and smart. I liked it. The only problem, I wasn't a dealer. I had to play along with the conversation because if I told them I wasn't in the drug business, Q would start to ask questions about what I was actually doing.

"Maybe," I answered. "You want someone for the seven clubs in the New Year?"

"No, not only them but all the pubs and clubs we represent," Henry replied.

"Including this place," Q piped in.

"So your lads let me in, I sell what I have and move off to the next place?" I asked.

"Exactly Frankie," Henry said. "You do this every Thursday, Friday and Saturday night and you'll easily make yourself a few grand."

"What's the split," I asked Henry.

"50/50. It may not seem all that good at first but think about it. We run the doors to nearly thirty venues around Dublin. That's thirty venues packed with people looking to score cocaine and pills and whatever else you want to sell. Plus it's a monopoly. Our lads know every dealer out there, they can spot them a mile off. We keep the other dealers away, you and your crew have exclusive access. This means that you can inflate the price of your goods, and the punters will have no choice but to pay." Henry's bracelet clattered off the table as he emphasised every point he made with his hand gestures.

"It's an interesting proposition, and one that I will definitely think about." I lied.

The one question on my mind that I didn't dare to ask was 'what happened to the last dealer?' If they run the doors to almost thirty clubs, they've been doing this a long time. Why did they suddenly lose a dealer and his 'crew'? Maybe he got banged up. Or worse.

"Certainly Frankie, that's no problem at all. But let me know sometime next week. You can let Q know and he'll tell me."

"Sound."

"Aye, sure thanks for coming down to meet with us, and I hope we can do business in the future. It's big business and an opportunity like this doesn't come along very often, so I hope you make the right decision." With that, Henry finished his drink and stood up from the booth. "I'll see ye later lads. Nice to meet ye, Frankie." The three of us stood up, shook hands and said our goodbyes. It was a brief meeting. But I liked Henry. Very direct, he got to the point and left. Much like me when I confront a paedo. Q took Henry's seat at the booth, we were now facing each other.

"So what do you think," Q asked.

"Yea. It's an interesting one."

"You'll make a fortune. Nearly thirty pubs and clubs in Dublin. You'll make a few grand every night."

"Yea, how do you know Henry?"

"Ah, I met him years ago. Nice fella. He runs a Security Company like he said. I started working for him about five years ago."

"And you let dealers in?"

"Yea, it's been going on donkey's years."

"But what's in it for the bouncers?"

"Henry looks after us. We all know the score. Henry gives us our cut so you don't have to worry about it."

"Ok. A lot to take in."

"Yea sorry," Q delivered with a laugh. "I should have warned you first. But I didn't want to give too much away on the phone. You know yourself."

"Yea. No worries."

"So how many lads have you got?"

"Lads?"

"Yea. How many lads sell for ye?"

"Ah, I keep it small. I have a few lads here and there that I work with the odd time. But less is more in this game."

"Yea. So you reckon you'll do it?"

"Dunno man. It's a risk. But it sounds like one worth taking."

"I know. Sure think about it and let me know yea?"

"Yea sound. Cheers Q."

Q left and I sat alone in the booth finishing my drink, trying to make sense of the proposition. I'm not a drug dealer and never was, but I did know some people in that line of work. I could have gotten them in to sell and take a cut. I'd never even have to touch the drugs myself, and still come out with a tidy profit. But it was way over my head. My love affair with pills ended a long time ago. I wasn't about to get back into that. My decision was made there in that booth, but I wouldn't tell Q for a few days. Let them believe that I did give it some serious consideration. The nagging question of what happened to the last dealer still bothered me. Had the relationship gone sour? If so, why? I then began to think that Henry could have had an ulterior motive. Maybe he was trying to get information on a rival. He could have been trying to figure out where I sold my merchandise, maybe he wanted to know who 'my lads' were. In the end, I was never a dealer, they had me all wrong, but it was a good thing. Q thought I was picking up drugs every time he watched over a transaction, he was way off and would never question exactly what I was doing. I had another drink in the Underground and headed home.

Monday, October 18th. Ma texted me.
"Hiya love, just letting you know George is in hospital. He has the flu."
I rang her right after I got the text. Poor George's breathing was acting up again. He was wheezing heavily that Sunday night and Ma called an Ambulance. He was still in St. James's Hospital. I hate hospitals and avoid them whenever I can. But I promised myself I'd go up to George, he'd done so much for me over the years it was the least I could do. Later that day I jumped on the 123 bus to go and see him. I entered the hospital and was immediately hit by the heat in the place. I was merely a few feet in and had to stop to take my jacket off. Other than whiskey George and I also share a love of chocolate.

In the shop in the main foyer of the hospital, I picked up some of George's favourite chocolate bars. Maybe they'd cheer him up. With a set of complex directions from the information desk, I set off to find George. After walking through long meandering hallways, up flights of stairs and getting on two lifts, I still found myself lost. With thanks to nurses and other hospital staff, I finally found Georges ward. He shared the ward with five other people. I'm sure he hated that, he was a very private person. His bed was the first one on the right as you entered, just beside the toilet, so at least he didn't have to walk far. George looked weak as he lay in the bed, he had an oxygen mask attached to his face. His speech was slow and the gushing hiss of the mask made it difficult to hear him.

"Howya youngfella. Good to see ya son." He delivered with a smile, as he raised his hand to wave at me.

"Howya George. How are ya?"

"Ah, I've been better. Me next clean shirt will do me." An old expression, when people think they are about to die. His next clean shirt would be fit to bury him in.

"Ah now George, don't be talkin' like that." He gave me a faint laugh. "I brought you up some chocolate. Fatten ya up a bit."

"Ah, thanks son. Throw it in the locker there, I'll have some later."

Looking around the ward I could see that George was the only patient in there without a telly. Everybody else had a portable telly on a stand next to their beds.

"D'ya not have a telly here George?"

"Ah no, it's too expensive."

"Expensive me arse, I'll get ya one."

"No, no, son, don't be wastin' your money." I ignored him and asked a nurse how to get a telly. She called someone from the nurses station and said he'd be right down. A man arrived a few minutes later with one of the portable telly's. He set it all up and asked me how long I wanted it for. I wasn't sure how long George was supposed to be in. So I gave him €100 and told him to make sure George always had a telly and I'd pay any bill that was owed next time I was up.

"Whatcha do that for? There was no need."

"It's grand George don't worry about it." I knew that telly was Georges best companion since Aunt June died. At least watching telly might give George some sense of normality and take his mind off where he was.

"Will I bring ye up some whiskey next time I'm up?" I joked.

"No, no I'm not in the mood son. Any luck finding a job?"

"No, nothing yet. But I'm sure I'll find something."

"Jaysus, does nobody need a carpenter anymore?"

"Haven't a clue. The construction game is still on its knees."

We sat watching telly and chatted away for almost two hours. I didn't feel the time slipping by. It was nice to see George again, although I promised him last Christmas that I'd visit him at my Ma's, it was a promise I didn't keep. Too busy catching paedophile's I suppose.

Towards the end of my visit, I could see George becoming fatigued. He fought to keep his eyes open and his head constantly nodded towards his chest. I felt like he was trying to stay awake just because I was there. It was best to let him get some rest. When he startled himself awake from another attempted slumber, I told him I was heading home.

"I better go, George, before they kick me out!"

"Ok son. Thanks a million for the telly."

"Don't worry about it, and don't forget that chocolate in the locker."

"Indeed I won't, thanks again son."

I stood up and patted George on the arm. My hand moved down towards his and gently squeezed it.

"Listen, George, I was thinkin' over the last while and I want to thank you for everything you've done for me over the years. The car, the job, everything."

"It was a pleasure son. I knew you wouldn't let me down. Ever since you were a little fella you always kept your promises. Everyone thought I was mad buying you that car, but I knew you wouldn't let me down, and you didn't."

"Thanks George. I wouldn't have made it this far without ya."

"I'm sorry to see you're going through a hard time at the minute, but trust me, son, it'll pass."

"I know it will."

"All the best son, and thanks for comin' up. It was great to see you."

With my eyes welling up I left the stuffy hospital. It was great to see George. There was plenty of life in the old dog yet. I was sure that he'd bounce back and be home before Christmas.

Wednesday morning, October 20th I woke up to a phone call from Q.

"Hey Frankie, have you thought about the situation?"

"Hey Q. Yea I thought about it. Unfortunately, there's no way I can take Henry up on his offer." Q seemed disappointed. I went on to tell him that it was way over my head and that I have a few clients that I sell to and that gets me by. I didn't want to get into something that I couldn't manage so had to politely decline the offer. Q quite bluntly ended the conversation by saying "I'll let Henry know," and that was that. My fictitious career as a drug dealer was a very short-lived one.

In the hallway later that morning, three letters sat waiting for me. The bills didn't worry me anymore because I had more than enough cash to cover them, but one sent shivers through my body. The envelope was stamped in blood red ink which read 'Mulraney Solicitors Strictly Private and Confidential.' A million thoughts started racing through my mind at once. Did JJ's threat about going to his solicitor come back to haunt me? If so, how did he find me? I sat at the kitchen table and tore the envelope open. Reading the first sentence, all my fears and worries began to unravel. The letter was from a solicitor representing Laura, my ex-wife. It was inviting me to a mediation meeting to try and sort out the legal end of separating. She had to wait four years before filing for a divorce so the mediation would have led to a separation agreement. It would have stated that we were legally separated before we could get divorced. But fuck her, she can wait. If she didn't cheat on me with one of my close friends and fucked off to live with him, we wouldn't be in this mess. She hadn't contributed to the mortgage since the day she left and she wanted me to spend more money on a solicitor to do this separation agreement. Talk about kicking a man when he's down. I tore the letter into pieces, binned it and thought no more about it.

By the end of November and the start of December 2010, it was time to start hunting again if I wanted my €9,000 before Christmas. I wasted almost a week in the chat rooms trying to hook a paedo, it was time to change tactic and get back to the dating app. Decoy phone bought, picture downloaded and profile set up. 'StacySez' was thirteen and from Santry.

As per usual, some people talked to Stacy and when they found out her age they disappeared. But it was only a matter of time before one stuck around. Enter 'AllThatYouWant'. He said his name was Stephen, he was forty-one and described himself as a businessman. I told him that Stacy was thirteen and he didn't seem to care. There was no picture on Stephen's profile, but I kept him hooked anyway. We made friends and exchanged numbers. Over the next few days, Stephen texted Stacy and asked all kinds of things. About school, her friends, what she wanted to do when she was older, etc. Then the conversation took its usual route to sex. Was Stacy a Virgin, how many boyfriends had she in the past, what kind of underwear she had. The type of questions that an adult should not be asking a child. But by that stage, I had become accustomed to such questioning. Stephen asked Stacy if she had any experience with an older man, I told him she didn't. He then asked if she would consider meeting an older man. I told him "yes" but on one condition, he had to send me a picture. Stephen seemed hesitant, but I eventually talked him into it. He sent a photo to the decoy phone, it wasn't exactly clear but I could make out some distinctive features. He had almost shoulder length curly blonde hair, I could only assume it was dyed. He had small beady, rodent-like eyes that sat either side of a prominent but thin nose. His face was gaunt, and I guessed he had a figure to match. I did press him for more photos saying I couldn't make that one out, but again he was reluctant. Why so shy I thought? The conversation continued either way.

Stephen got more and more sexual over the next few days.

"We could meet at a hotel in town sometime," He told Stacy.

"Really? What for?"

"What do you think?"

"I don't know!"

"It's my birthday next week. I'm meeting two friends in town."

"Ok. I hope you have fun."

"Come with me and meet my friends."

"Why?"

"Why not? Bring some of your friends too and we can have a party."

"But my friends are the same age as me."

"I know, it's fine babe, my friends like younger ladies too. I'll bring some drinks. It will be fun!"

"I'm not old enough to drink."

"I know that, but I wont tell anyone if you don't!"

"I've never drank before."

"It's ok babe, just one or two will be fine. It will help us relax and have a great night."

"I don't know. I'd be really nervous."

"You'll be fine, trust me. I'll take care of you. Consider it your birthday present to me!"

"Ok then."

"Great, and see if you can get your friends to come too!"

It looked like Stephen was getting quite the party together. He wanted to meet what he believed to be a thirteen-year-old girl, introduce her to his two friends and see if Stacy would bring some friends too. Absolute scumbag. But all I could think about was, that if all this was true, I could kill three birds with one stone. €30,000 in one sting. €1,000 to Q as normal and a total profit of €29,000 right before Christmas. The allure of that amount of cash was too much to ignore. I arranged to meet Stephen on Thursday, December 16th. I told him that Stacy had a half day off school and could meet him in town. He agreed to meet and told Stacy to stay in her school uniform. He asked if she was bringing some friends, I told him no. He made sure that Stacy didn't tell anyone who she was meeting or where she was going. He also instructed her to delete every conversation that they've had on both the dating app and text message. He told Stacy that he would leave a key to the hotel room at reception for her and if anyone asked who Stacy was meeting, she was to say it was her father. If she was real, a thirteen-year-old child would walk into a hotel room and be confronted by three grown men.

That situation wasn't going to work for me. There was no chance I was going to enter a hotel room to confront three paedophile's, it was far too risky. I couldn't get Q to come with me because it would blow my cover. The only option I had was to try and convince Stephen to meet Stacy on the street and make him think he's going to walk her to the hotel. Again Stephen was reluctant. What exactly was he trying to hide? I made the excuse that Stacy didn't know the City Centre very well. He gave me directions to the hotel from O'Connell Street, I knew exactly where it was but I had to make him believe that Stacy didn't have a clue. I knew that I'd get him with one final text on the matter...

"I don't know where the hotel is. I'm not going!" There was no way he was going to let an opportunity like this slip through his hands.

"Ok. Ok. Meet me at the Spire at 1:30 PM on Thursday."
He texted.
"Ok. How will I know it's you." I was looking to see if
he'd give me a description of his clothing or something.
"Ring me when you're there. I'll answer. But don't come
over to me."
"Why not? I'm there to meet you!!!"
"But some people don't understand it, babe. I could get
into a lot of trouble."
"Oh. Ok."
"When you see me, follow me to the hotel. Walk behind
me, and not beside me."
"Ok cool."
"Can't wait to see you x"

Stephen was the most elusive paedophile I had dealt
with since I first start snaring. 'Delete all conversations.
Don't come over to me. Walk behind me to the hotel.' He
knew the risk involved in meeting a thirteen-year-old and I
was convinced this wasn't his first time doing it. Armed
with only a blurry photograph of Stephen I searched online
to try find out more about him. After hours of torturing
myself trawling through any article that mentioned the
word 'Paedophile'. I finally found exactly what I was
looking for. A portrait photograph of a man with curly
blonde hair, a gaunt face, and distinctive rat-like eyes
accompanied the headline 'Child Rapist'. Reading the
tabloid 'exclusive' written in 2006, I found out a lot more
about 'Stephen'. His real name was Alan and there was
some truth in the fact that he was a businessman. His
father owned a chain of high-quality hotels and spas all
over the Country. He is a very wealthy man, and his three
son's (Alan included) all had a hand in the day to day
running of the family business. The case in question
related to a girl who at the time was fifteen years old. She
accused Alan of rape. The incident was said to have
happened on the grounds of one of the family's hotels in
Co. Galway. The unnamed girl had isolated herself from a
family wedding as she did not want her parents to see her

smoking. Alan confronted her and told her that he wouldn't tell her parents he had caught her smoking if she 'did something for him in return'. It was reported that the girl had performed oral sex on Alan at a fire escape in the hotel. Alan then allegedly threw her to the ground and raped her while covering her mouth with his hand.

The alarm was raised the following morning after the girl's mother noticed her acting out of character. When mother confronted daughter she told her what happened and the Gardaí were called. Alan was arrested at his home seven miles from the hotel. And of course, he denied everything. I searched and read a number of articles relating to the case. Some reported that Alan had bite marks on the palm of his right hand when he was arrested. Others concentrated on the rumour that CCTV footage had been lost or tampered with. Right before the case was due to go to trial, all charges against Alan were mysteriously dropped. To me, it was so obvious what had happened. Daddy didn't want his son to be sentenced for raping a child, it was bad for business, so he got his chequebook out. Disgusting. I looked at the family's hotel website and there was no mention of Alan. I had no idea if he was still involved in the family business or not. Four years on and Alan was attempting to meet what he believed to be a child in Dublin.

Thursday, December 16th, the morning of the meeting. I printed out every conversation between 'Stephen' (who I then knew was really Alan) and Stacy. I boarded the 27 bus into town at about 12:30 PM. That snare was going to be different. Alan was going to be a tricky one, I could feel it. Getting off the bus at Dame Street I could tell the City Centre was busy, but not overcrowded. It was a little early for Christmas shoppers to flood the streets. I walked through Temple Bar, over the Ha'Penny Bridge, and onto Liffey Street. At about 1:15 PM, while making my way towards Henry Street, I texted Alan from the decoy phone. "Hey, The Spire right?"

"Yes. Ring me when you're there. x. x." Came his immediate response.

"Ok. ;-)"

Turning onto Henry Street I was met with the sight of street vendors stalls lining the entire right-hand side of the street. Everything from festive lights, decorations, tinsel, wreaths, sweets, and toys were on display, ready to find a new home. I soaked up the atmosphere walking towards the Spire. Cries of 'wrapping paper five for fifty', 'selection boxes three for a fiver' and 'get the last of the tinsel here, best prices in Dublin' filled the air. Adding to the ambience of the city. It really is a sight to behold, especially at night, when Dublin is illuminated by the festive lights that hang overhead on practically every street. The Spire grew in stature the closer I got. A one hundred and twenty-one-metre silver pin sticking out of O'Connell Street. Dubliners christened it 'The Stiletto in the Ghetto' when it was first erected. A nickname it has yet to shake. It's a perfect meeting spot. Even people unfamiliar with Dublin, like Stacy, couldn't miss such an enormous landmark. Just before 1:30 PM from the corner of the G.P.O I sent Alan a text.

"Are you there?"

"Yes. Ring me." He replied.

The pedestrian lights changed and I made my way to the island splitting O'Connell Street. I wasn't worried about Alan spotting me. There were plenty of people around, and besides, he'd be too busy looking for a girl in a school uniform. I rang his number and scrutinized my surrounds, looking for anybody answering a call. "Hello, Stacy?" I heard Alan answer. But I couldn't reply. I ended the call, placed the phone in my pocket and waited.

The decoy phone vibrated in my pocket with a call. I examined every person in my line of vision while pacing on the island, making sure I got a glimpse of every angle of the circumference of the Spire. But nobody stood out. I continued walking until I reached the Christmas Tree that sat almost directly opposite the main entrance of the G.P.O. Pretending to take pictures of the tree, I took a minute to ready myself. I couldn't let that bastard get away. With some short, sharp breaths of crisp December air in my lungs, I headed back to the meeting point. I rang Alan again and placed the phone in my pocket. Striding towards the Spire, a tall, gangly character in a black jacket and black baseball style hat caught my eye. He was standing across the road at the corner of North Earl Street. The mysterious figure reached into his pocket and answered a call on his phone. There was no telling if it was Alan unless I got a closer look.

At the traffic lights, I desperately tried to blend into the pedestrians crossing towards North Earl Street. I cut across the flow of people traffic towards the corner where the man in the baseball hat stood. My movements attracted his attention. He looked up from under the peak of his hat and gazed directly at me. His dark, beady eyes were nearly enough to stop me dead. I knew it was Alan. He jolted from the corner and began to make his way up North Earl street, I followed. To no surprise, another phone call to Alan was ignored. He shot a look over his left shoulder to see if I was still in pursuit. Quickening his pace as he zig-zagged through leisurely Christmas shoppers gave him no distinct advantage. His height made him easy to track. I was within touching distance, it was time to reel him in. "It's very rude not to answer your phone ALAN!" He stopped in his tracks. Having told Stacy his name was Stephen, he knew I had done my homework to find out his real name.

"Who the fuck are you?" He asked as he turned to face me. Alan towered over me, but I didn't feel intimidated. He was so scrawny it looked like a gentle breeze would knock him over.

"I'm Stacy. I'm here to meet you and your two friends." I replied.

"You have the wrong man."

"Cut the bull shite. I have every text you sent to Stacy right here." I handed him the chat logs.

"Who are you though?"

"What does that matter? I know who you are, and we both know what you're here for."

"Fuck off you prick." He said as he turned and attempted to bolt away. I grabbed his bony arm and spun him back around.

"No, I won't fuck off Alan. How about I tell everyone in earshot exactly what you are? Do you think you'd make it out alive?" The increased volume of my voice drew some attention. Some people started to stare, others were looking to see where the commotion was coming from.

"Ok. Ok. Keep your voice down." Alan relented.

"Take off the hat, I want to be certain it's you." He lifted his hat for a split second. I could see the curly vibrant blonde hair swept beneath it.

"Are you the Gardaí?" He asked.

"We'll get to that."

"Who the fuck are ye?"

"I'm someone who stops people like you getting their hands on teenage girls. Is there really two other fuckers waiting in a hotel room?"

"I can't deny it now can I?"

"No, you certainly can't you sick fuck. And this isn't the first time you've done something like this is it Alan? Delete the text's, follow me to the hotel, don't tell anyone. How many kids have you raped?"

"It's not rape if they come to meet me."

"Don't play that shit with me. A child of thirteen cannot consent to sex. You know that as well as I do ya fuckin' perv. What do you think happens to these kids after you rape them? It fucks up their life. And for what? For you to get your kicks?"

"Look, what is this all about?"

"All about? Jesus Fuckin' Christ, how long do you have? But fuck it, if you want me to get to the point, I will. You're staring at prison time for this and you know it. I want €30,000 cash and all this goes away. Nothing goes to the Guards, it all just disappears. It's €10,000 a man for you and your two buddies."

"How am I supposed to pay that?"

"Don't start. Daddy did it once and now he'll have to do it again unless he wants to see you go to prison."

"Don't bring my father into this. Who the fuck are you to demand €30,000?"

"It's none of your business who I am. Have the cash for me in one week. That's plenty of time to go begging to Daddy. Keep your phone on, I'll be in touch. Try anything smart and everything goes to the Guards."

With everything said and done, I headed back towards O'Connell Street and made my way home. I would have loved to be a fly on the wall in the hotel room where the other two perv's were waiting for Alan. They were expecting him to return with a thirteen-year-old girl in her school uniform. Instead, they got a dejected Alan, explaining that each of them owed €10,000 to keep their little secret. I wonder if they turned on each other. Did the other two say they had nothing to do with it and it was all up to Alan to pay? Did Alan then threaten to give their names to the Gardaí if they didn't chip in? Three paedophiles with a major dilemma on their hands. I gave Alan some time to mull it over.

Over the weekend I did some Christmas shopping. I bought some token presents for Ma and Da and got Uncle George his customary bottle of whiskey. He was still in hospital, Ma wasn't sure if he'd be home for Christmas. By Monday, December 20th it was time to see if Alan had enough time to contemplate his next move.

"What's it going to be? Pay me what you owe me or spend Christmas behind bars?" I sent to him in a text.

"We're paying, ok? How do I get the money to you?" He replied.

"Cash only. Wrap it up and make it look like a Christmas present. Head into town on Thursday for 6 PM."

"You hardly expect me to walk around town with €30,000 wrapped up as a present!"

"Wrap it. Bag it. Head to town for 6 on Thursday. I'll text you from there. This is your instruction, not a negotiation!"

I rang Q to see if he was available on Thursday. He told me that all would be fine as long as the meeting was somewhere near the Underground. He was working that night. That suited me, Grafton Street at that time of year was the perfect location for the meeting. Hundreds of people frantically getting some last minute shopping before Christmas. It would be easy to take the cash and blend into the crowd, but there were some negatives. I could have been outnumbered. There were three perverts and if all three showed up to the meeting it could have been trouble. But I had Q. He would easily take on two men at once giving me the chance to fight the other and get away with the cash. But, Grafton Street is pedestrianised, there was no sure route to get a taxi quickly. All things considered, it was worth the risk. Meet somewhere on Grafton Street that wasn't too far from the Underground. Take the cash from Alan and head back up towards St.Stephens Green, keep walking until I found a taxi. Q would follow and then go back to work as soon as I was out of there. If only everything went as smoothly as planned.

Thursday, December 23rd, everything was in place. I had arranged to meet Q at the Underground at 5:30 PM and told Alan to make his way to Grafton Street at 6:00 PM and wait for further instruction. I zipped Q's money into my old backpack, put it on back to front and concealed it under my jacket. The 27 bus was packed, standing room only as I made my way to Dame Street. I got to the Underground at about 5:20 PM and Q was already on the door.

"Startin' early today Q?"

"Ah we have to, Christmas drinkers, you know yourself. How have you been Frankie? Been a while."

"Ah grand. And you?"

"Yea, not bad. You certainly left Henry scratchin' his head."

"Yea? Not a happy bunny was he not?"

"He couldn't understand why you didn't take him up on his offer."

"Ah, I think it was over me head, you know?"

"Fair enough, you woulda cleaned up thou."

"Maybe so, did he get someone else in?"

"Yea, they haven't a clue what they're doin'. What they're sellin' is shite as well."

"I'm sure Henry will sort it out."

"You can say that again."

"Anyway, this meeting. I'm going to meet him at the Phil Lynott Statue on Harry Street. You know it yea?"

"Of Course I do."

"Stand across from the Statue at about ten to 6. I'll be comin' up from South Anne Street. Keep your eyes peeled yea."

"No worries Frankie."

"Here," I said while unzipping my jacket, then the backpack. I reached in and pulled out the envelope with Q's money inside.

"Merry Christmas."

"It will be now." Q winked as he tucked the envelope into the inside pocket of his jacket. "See you in a few. Ring me when you're on the way yea."

   Leaving the backpack open, I zipped up my jacket and headed up South King Street. I turned onto Grafton Street, and made my way through the hundreds of shoppers, towards South Anne Street. The walking pace slowed as collective voices sang 'Silver Bells.' Just beyond the corner of Harry Street, a choir had gathered, attracting a semi-circle of onlookers that huddled around them. Five or six people in high visibility vests shook buckets of loose change as they collected money for the Dublin Children's Hospital Foundation. I veered off to the right just before the crowds came to a complete standstill. On South Anne

Street I ducked into the same cafe where I first met Dumb-Dumb. It was crowded and hot to the point that the front window fogged up with condensation. I stood at a small ledge with a pot of tea and realised a big mistake. I couldn't take my jacket off in case the backward backpack drew any unwanted attention. The nerves kicked in. It felt like one-thousand butterflies on acid were having a rave in my belly. Thinking I could scald them away with hot tea was a bad idea. All I managed to do was work myself into an uncomfortable sweat. I'm not sure if it was the fact that I was collecting €30,000 on that snare, the number of people around or maybe I felt something was wrong. But I was more on edge than ever.

5:45 PM I texted Alan.

"Where are you?"

"Trinity College." He replied.

"Make your way to the Phil Lynott Statute on Harry Street. Text me when you're there. You will be watched. Don't try anything stupid."

5:55 PM I texted Q.

"You there?"

"Yup." He replied.

"He's on the way. I'll ring you shortly."

I could do nothing but play the waiting game. Steam sputtered from the coffee maker almost constantly, adding to the already dense, heavy heat that filled the cafe. The sweat was rolling down my back which made my t-shirt stick to my skin.

6:02 PM I got a text from Alan.

"I'm here."

"On my way. When I approach, hand me the present. I walk one way, you go the other."

The sharp bite of winter was a welcome relief as I left the cafe. Approaching Harry Street I rang Q to give him the signal. The crowd huddled around the choir had grown to the point that barely anyone was able to make it up or down Grafton Street. The percussion sound of half empty collection buckets were keeping time with 'Silent Night.'

It was as if the choice of song was a deliberate contrast to the commotion within the human traffic jam. I apologised, bumped and battered my way through the crowd and eventually made it across to Harry Street. I immediately saw Q standing to my left but he didn't notice me. His head was moving from left to right searching for me to no avail. Alan stood directly behind the Statue of Phil Lynott as if trying to hide in the shadow of one of Ireland's most gifted and well-respected musicians. He wore the same baseball hat as last time. His arms were folded and he clutched a brown paper bag in his right hand. There was no time to try and get Q's attention, I zipped my jacket down and walked towards Alan.

"Give me the present." I instructed him.

He reached into the brown paper bag and pulled out a package wrapped in blue wrapping paper. I took it from him and placed it in my backpack as quickly as possible. I zipped up my jacket and the backpack almost simultaneously turned and walked towards Grafton Street. Q finally spotted me as I crossed his path. Before I could disappear into the crowds I felt someone forcefully grab my left forearm. Thinking that it might be Alan or an angry pedestrian I may have bumped into in my eagerness to get to Grafton Street, I pulled my arm free from the grip and attempted to walk away again. Before I could take another step, my right arm was grabbed by two hands which pulled me backwards.

"Detective Harrison, Pearse Street Garda Station, this is Detective O'Leary can we have a word please Sir." Harrison discreetly held a golden badge at about waist height. O'Leary was the one with a tight grip on my arm. Q darted towards me as soon as he saw someone making physical contact. But at first glimpse of the badge, he walked past me and out of view. I couldn't blame him, he did exactly what we planned.

At a guess, I'd say Harrison was in his late-fifties. He was heavyset with a plump, red face to match. His greying ginger hair was swept over to one side. O'Leary was not much older than me. He was slim and dressed smartly. His well-polished shoes seemed to gleam even in the crisp December air. I was turned and marched back over to Alan.

"That's him. He's trying to blackmail me out of €30,000." Alan told the Detectives.

"What did you put in the bag?" Harrison asked.

"Nothing." I replied. My head was spinning. I couldn't make sense of the situation.

"Open it up and show me." Harrison said.

"Christmas presents, that's all."

"Then why conceal them in a bag under your jacket? Why not put the bag over your shoulder like a normal person?" Harrison said as he zipped my jacket down.

"What's your name." O'Leary asked.

"None of your business." Was the only answer I could fire back.

"Do you have any ID on you." Harrison quipped.

"No." I replied. My voice had quivered to a whisper. The acid tripping butterflies invaded my stomach again with a vengeance. It felt like both my legs were flailing under me but my calf muscles were tense at the same time. It was a horrible sensation.

I couldn't understand what was going on. Alan must have gone to the Guards even though I could prove he arranged to meet a thirteen-year-old girl and pass her around to his friends. Or maybe he went begging to Daddy and he called the Gardaí? But why would they risk this story getting out?

"Open the bag and show us what's in it?" Harrison said.

"I told you It's my personal belongings."

"It's my €30,000 more like." Said Alan.

"Ok. Ok." O'Leary directed at Alan. "We'll get to the bottom of it. I need you to back off for now and we'll get the details later."

Harrison grew impatient and had enough small talk. He unzipped my backpack, reached in and removed the present. He held it in the palm of his right hand and tore the paper off with his left. I could see the orange glow of the fresh, crisp €50 notes neatly lined up beside the blue tint of the €20's.

"How do you explain this?" He said while cradling the newly exposed cash in front of me with both hands.

It was then or never. An idea hurtled itself to the forefront of my mind from the whirlwind of thoughts flying around in my head. It was a split-second decision made on a whim. With one action I broke free of O'Leary's grip and brought my hand up under Harrison's hand's with all the strength I could. Time seemed to stand still as the €30,000 flew from Harrison's hands and scattered into the air. The adrenalin took over and I ran towards Grafton Street. I was the only one heading that way as swarms of wide-eyed, flabbergasted shoppers rushed to try and grab as much of the cash as they could. The furiosity of the stampeding crowds intensified to the point where it drowned out the choir. Harrison and O'Leary stood no chance of giving chase. I barged and fought my way through the crowds until I had enough space in front of me to pick up some speed.

I didn't dare to look back while running. I made it to the top of Grafton Street and continued along the side of St.Stephens Green Park. I took a right onto Cuffe Street and headed towards the intersection at Wexford Street. Just before the intersection, I took the laneway to my left which led me to Montague Court. I was familiar with all the small streets and laneways in the area. I spent many a day mitching from Synge Street school and hanging around that part of town. Alone in the laneway, I slowed my running to a brisk walk. If by some miracle, Harrison and O'Leary made it out of the crowds in one piece, I was sure that the pot-bellied Harrison would have run out of steam very quickly. O'Leary looked fit, but running in immaculately polished shoes could not have been easy. I took a right onto Protestant Row and then a quick left onto Wexford Street. It was busy and full of life. Most people had probably finished work that day for the Christmas

Holidays. The streets were full of tanked up revellers who paid little or no attention to me. The traffic was at a standstill. Had I managed to hail a taxi on Wexford Street I would have been sitting there for ages, giving plenty of time for anyone who might have been chasing me to catch up. I waded through the busy street and took my first right onto Camden Row. Another right-hand turn led me into Liberty Lane. It was empty and pitch dark. I decided to stop there for a minute to catch my breath. Resting on the pavement beside some large steel wheelie bins I tried to gather myself. My personal phone vibrated with a text from Q.

"What the fuck happened?"

There was no time to reply. I thought it was best to dump the decoy phone there and then. After wiping it down as much as possible and while holding it using my sleeve, I stood up and put the phone in one of the bins. Heading towards Lower Kevin Street, I tripped on something and almost lost my balance. I looked down to try and figure out what it was, but the darkness made it difficult. I took out my personal phone and investigated with the flashlight. There was a pair of legs sticking out between two large wheelie bins, I moved the light up the legs and onto to torso. There lying in front of me was an opened blue bubble jacket with a red bumbag clasped diagonally around the body. Hypodermic needles, a cigarette box and a bag of white powder had fallen from the bumbag and rested on the person's chest. Moving the light up the body to illuminate the gaunt face, I could see it was junkie.

His right arm was still in the sleeve of his bubble jacket, his left arm was exposed. A shoelace was tied tightly around his bicep and the needle was still in his vein. His head lay back on the pavement, eyes wide open and his mouth gaping. I put my hand on his neck to check for a pulse, but the second I made contact with him, I could feel that he was stone cold. I guessed he was dead at least a few hours. It was a weird coincidence. The one laneway in all of Dublin where I stop to catch my breath after avoiding certain arrest, I stumble upon junkies dead body. My mind couldn't help but be brought back to nearly exactly a year ago when junkie and his buddies jumped me and took my €10,000. As I lay beaten and bleeding in the street, the muggers ran off. It was time for me to do the same. There was nothing I could do anyway. Merry Fuckin' Christmas junkie. I made my way to Lower Kevin Street and got a taxi. It was a strange feeling passing Kevin Street Garda Station knowing that the Guards would love to have me in custody. But I couldn't help but smile about it. The second I got in the door I opened the bottle of whiskey I had bought for George. I'd pick him up another in the morning.

What was going on? I snared a paedophile and hit him and his two friends for €10,000 each. They go to the Guards and made a deal? How on earth were the Guards going to deal with scum like that? It should have been straightforward. Alan goes to Daddy, and Daddy gives him the money, then I hang him. He could rat his mates out all he wanted after that, it had nothing to do with me. The most important thing was that I got paid. But no, €30,000 literally went up in the air. I should have been glad to get away like I did, I didn't know at that time how deep I was in. Over numerous glasses of whiskey, the night's events replayed over and over in my head but none of it made sense. The telly was bound to distract my mind. Flicking through the stations I saw a breaking news bulletin...
"Cash rains down on Dublin's busiest Shopping Street." Holy shit. It was national news. The news channel had their reporter and camera crew standing near Harry Street. The Guards had it cordoned off. The report started.
"It was here a few hours ago that Dubliners watched in shock as an estimated €100,000 rained down on this busy Street and nobody seems to know why."

The news station began to air a number of video clips taken on mobile phones at the scene of the incident. In one clip the cash is still falling from the sky The person had been recording the choir when their attention was averted to the commotion on Harry Street. People were scrambling over each other grabbing for the money. It was bedlam. In another video, I could see Harrison trying to fight his way out of the crowd. "Get outta me way," he cried as he tried to battle his way out, but the current was too strong and he soon disappeared. The reporter continued...

"Earlier this evening we were able to track down one lady who witnessed the whole scene unfolding."

They cut to footage shot earlier in the evening, interviewing a local woman. She stood talking to the reporter casually leaning on the handle of her shopping trolly. She had short grey curly hair and glasses as thick as the end of milk bottles. I could tell by her accent that she was local, a real Dub.

"Can you tell us what you saw today?" The reporter asked as she shoved the microphone into the old woman's face.

"Sure I was standing there talkin' to me friend, and next of all we hears a load of screamin' n shoutin'."

"Did you look to see what it was?"

"Well I didn't have to look too far, it was nearly on top of us."

"And what exactly did you see?"

"The money. It started fallen from the Heaven's."

"And can you describe the scene?"

"Yes love, everyone was goin' mad tryin' t grab the money n all, fallin' over one n other left, right and centre."

"Did you manage to get any yourself?"

"No no love. I wouldn't take what wasn't mine." She delivered with the most unconvincing smile.

"And what do you make of the people who got injured today? Do you have any thoughts on that?"

"Yes love. They weren't quick enough." With that line, the old woman patted the reporter twice on the arm and pushed her shopping trolly away smiling to herself. I had probably made that aul one's Christmas.

The news bulletin cut back to the live report...

"As the dust settled, a number of Ambulances were called to the scene to deal with the aftermath of the excitement.

Cuts, bruises, twisted wrists, and ankles were some of the minor injuries treated at the scene. But some shoppers scuffled for the cash and in more than one situation, fights broke out and blows were exchanged. Gardaí have released the following statement.

'At this time we do not know the details which led to this incident. A full and thorough investigation is underway and anybody with information is encouraged to contact their local Garda Station.'

The statement was amazing. Talk about putting your best foot forward. If they actually told the truth it would have read...

'We tried to catch an online paedophile hunter who pretends to be a child and lures perverts into a trap. He then blackmails them for money and sends all the information to us. But he outsmarted us and got away.'

It was all over the news, all over social media, everyone was talking about it.

I woke up on the sofa early Christmas Eve morning. Most of the whiskey was gone. A combination of nerves and excitement meant I kept pouring until I fell asleep. The telly was still on and every news channel was still talking about what had happened the previous night. Their estimation of €100,000 reduced to €50,000, but the interest in the story showed no sign of slowing down. One thing was very clear as I read story after story about the incident online. I had to keep a low profile for the foreseeable future.

8. The Aftermath

I tolerated the news regurgitating the same old information for about a half an hour before going to bed to sleep off the remainder of my hangover. Later in the afternoon, I walked to the local supermarket to replace the bottle of whiskey I had bought for George. Inside the main entrance, the newspaper stand was the first thing to catch my eye. Every single newspaper had the story of the 'Falling Money' on the front page. "The Grafton Street Grushie" read one headline. "Free Cash for Dublin Shoppers" read another and "Money Mayhem" were among my favourites. I didn't buy any of the papers, it was best to let the interest in the story trickle out. Come New Year's Eve it would all be history. I bought the whiskey then walked a short distance to get the 123 bus which goes straight to James's Street Hospital.

On the lower deck of the bus, I couldn't help but overhear two women deep in conversation two seats in front.

"Did ye see what happened on Grafton Street last night? Crazy wasn't it?"

"Jesus yea, the money? I wish I was there!"

"Why? Sure it was all a hoax! The money was all fake. It was just some company advertising something."

"I don't believe ya!"

"I'm tellin' ye. My Tommy was in there shoppin' with his girlfriend. They managed to grab a few notes and took them home. They're all fake, I saw them with me own eyes."

"Ah, Jaysus. I thought it would have got me through the Christmas!"

"Not at all. I don't know what all the fuss is about."

In less than twenty-four hours the amount of cash was halved, and now the remaining half was fake. Bad news travels fast as they say. I walked into the hospital and made my way to Georges ward. Ready to greet him and watch his eyes light up when he saw me, I was instead met by the blank stare of a frail old lady. Confused, I asked one of the nurses where George was. She directed me to one of the private wards on the opposite side of the corridor. George lay in the bed fast asleep. Not only did he have his own room, but he also had his own bathroom. Why the sudden change I thought? Maybe he was more comfortable being alone. The rented telly followed him over and it was on with the volume down to a whisper. I sat on the chair beside him and waited to see if he'd wake up. But it looked like he was out for the count. While hiding the whiskey in George's locker, out of view of the nurses, I noticed that the chocolate bars I had brought up last time were untouched. Maybe George forgot about them.

While sitting with George, Q texted me. I still hadn't answered his text from the night before.
"What the fuck happened last night? Where are you?"
"Things didn't go to plan. I made it out alive anyway." I replied.
"Whats the craic with all the money? Everyones talkin' about it?"
"Not too sure myself to be honest. It went tits up, but no harm done."
"Alright so."
"I'll be in touch in a couple of weeks. Have a good Christmas."
"Same to you pal."

To pass the time while George was sleeping, I decided to walk down to the shop in the hospital and indulge in one of the newspapers. Back up in Georges room, I had a read of the six-page article. There wasn't much detail at all to talk about. The Gardaí were reluctant to give too much away to the press, so most of the article was speculation. Stories ranging from a drug deal gone wrong to a lonely millionaire sharing his wealth filled most of the articles. The rest consisted of first-hand accounts of eyewitnesses. Stories of people being knocked over, trampled on, phones being lost and blood being drawn. All in all, it wasn't very interesting. Exaggerated drama to try to sell more papers. I flicked through the rest of the paper and happened to see an article about a body that was found in the City Centre. In comparison to the six-page article that the 'Money Mayhem' story got, the small write up about someone losing their life was about a square inch.

The body was found in Liberty Lane, so I knew it was junkie. The article continued to say that the identification of the man is yet to be confirmed. The sentence 'Gardaí are investigating the significance of a mobile phone found close to the scene,' hit me like a ton of bricks. The phone was the one I dumped in the steel wheelie bin right before I tripped over junkies legs. I wracked my brain trying to think of what information could still be on it. The dating app, so all conversations and texts between Alan and Stacy could be recovered. Q only had my personal number, so at least that ruled him out. The phone itself was bought in a supermarket, so it had no contract. I never connected it to my home broadband so it couldn't be traced back to me. The stock photo worried me. If the Gardaí were to trace who bought the photo from the stock website, it could be trouble. But it would take them a while to sift through everyone who purchased that particular photograph. Even if they did, how could they prove what that person used it for? Only time would tell if I had wiped the phone free of all fingerprints.

After about an hour of sitting with George, he showed no signs of waking up. Not wanting to disturb him, I felt it was best to head home. I was sure I'd see him again soon. Before leaving the hospital, I gave €100 to one of the nurses and asked her to pay the TV rental company to make sure George always had his telly. At home, I couldn't stop myself from looking at the news. The incident on Harry Street still dominated the headlines. More theories were presented and eyewitnesses interviewed. It was hilarious. I doubted a lot of the individual accounts. Some of them had the time wrong, some had the exact location wrong. People were obviously having a laugh and getting their fifteen minutes of fame by being interviewed. But one woman gave an accurate description of me. She was dressed in a white shirt and black waistcoat, giving me the impression she worked in a bar or restaurant close to where the money was scattered.

"Did you see who caused the mayhem?" Asked the interviewer.

"Yes. He was a man in his early thirties, short dark hair and wearing a dark waist length jacket." The woman answered. She was very sure of what she had seen.

"What drew your attention to him?"

"He was trying to walk away very quickly when I saw another man grabbing his arm. The man that grabbed his arm was an undercover policeman. I saw him flashing his badge."

"So the Gardaí were at the scene?"

"Yes. They were waiting for him."

"Can you tell us what happened next?"

"They stood talking for a minute or so, and then the money went flying into the air."

"And what happened to the man that the Gardaí stopped?"

"He ran like the wind. I saw him heading towards Grafton Street but he soon disappeared. There was chaos after that, everybody rushing to grab the money."

"And what happened to the Gardaí?"

"I'm not sure. I lost sight of them in the crowd."

The news channel were delighted with their new lead. They were the first to report that the Gardaí were already on the scene waiting to make an arrest. Plus they were the first to get a description of me. But it wasn't exactly specific, all they had to go on was 'a man in his early thirties with short dark hair and a waist-length black jacket.' It could have been anyone.

Christmas Day, I rolled out of bed about noon and didn't bother having anything to eat. I knew the mountain of food Ma would prepare would be enough to feed me for a week. I wrapped the presents I bought for Ma and Da and headed over to their house at about 3:00 PM. Poor

George was still in hospital, we had hoped he'd be well enough to come home for the day but the doctors advised against it. Ma answered the door with her usual smile. Her greeting wasn't interrupted by the shock of seeing my bruised and battered face like it was the previous year. In the kitchen, Da was in his usual spot at the table, drinking and looking at the telly.

"Howya Da, Merry Christmas."

"Howya son, same to you."

That was about as much as we said to each other. Ma followed me in and started her usual round of questioning. 'How are you? Any sign of a job? Are you seeing anyone? Any word from Laura?' Having answered her barrage of questioning, I was rewarded with a cold beer. I sat at the table beside Da, he had his back to me, fixated on the telly. The news came on with yet another story about the incident on Grafton Street.

"That was crazy wasn't it?" Ma said.

"Yea. Mad." I answered.

"What is the World comin' to, people throwin' away money like that?"

"It was a drug deal. You'll find that out if you listened to the shaggin' thing." Da snapped as he increased the volume on the telly.

'News just in. CCTV footage has emerged relating to the incident that happened off Grafton Street on December 23rd.'

"Oh Jesus look. It's him." Ma said as she desperately searched for her glasses. My blood ran cold.

'A man believed to be involved in the incident can be seen fleeing Grafton Street and heading towards St.Stephens Green. The same suspect was traced up as far as Cuffe Street before CCTV cameras lose him. He is described as a white male of slender build, with short dark hair and a waist-length dark jacket.'

The picture on the screen zoomed into a close up of me running at the top of Grafton Street. The image was blurred which made it next to impossible to identify me. Thank God for terrible CCTV cameras. Having located her glasses, Ma put them on and walked towards the telly to get a better view.

'Anyone with information is encouraged to contact their local Garda Station.' The report continued.

"How did he manage to get away from the Guards?" Ma asked.

"He was probably as high as a kite and hadn't a clue what he was doing!" Da answered.

"Have you been up with George Ma?" I asked, in a desperate attempt to peel Ma away from the telly.

"Yes, love. Every day since he went in." Ma answered as she finally removed her glasses and sat at the table.

"I was up with him yesterday, but he was asleep."

"Did you leave the whiskey?"

"Yea, I got it for him for Christmas."

"I saw it there and figured it was you. You know you're not supposed to bring any drink up."

"I know Ma. But a little tipple every now and then won't hurt him."

"I'll tell him you left it for him when I'm up today."

"Any more word on him comin' home?"

"Home?" Da interrupted. "You must mean this house. Sure George doesn't have his own home anymore, remember?"

"Oh give it a fuckin' rest ye grumpy old bastard!" Ma snapped back. It's always easy to tell when Ma loses her temper, she wouldn't dream of swearing at any other time. "God forbid it was ever one of your lot that ever needed a bit of compassion. Well, they can all fuck off with themselves! Not like they ever done a thing for us!" Having put Da firmly in his place, Ma turned to me and spoke in a much milder tone...

"There's no sign of George coming HOME yet love. We just have to wait until the infection clears."

"Grand. I'll drop up to him again, he might be awake next time, it's good to talk to him."

The news report had a detrimental effect on my appetite. I fought against my own body as I tried to eat the seemingly endless amount of food Ma had piled on my plate. It was a battle that didn't go unnoticed.

"Are you feeling ok love?" Ma asked.

"I'm grand Ma. I had a big breakfast, that's all."

"You can take the rest home with you if you want to leave it till later."

I struggled through the rest of dinner, not wanting to insult Ma. At the same time, I didn't want to trigger her suspicion that something was wrong. Emily was expected to call later that evening. I waited around until about 7:00 PM, but there was no word. I gave Ma the bag with her and Da's present in it. It wasn't a lot, I couldn't spend too much of my blackmailed money on them, as I was still unemployed as far as they could tell. With a hug and a kiss, Ma gave me a small gift as we said goodbye.

"Merry Christmas Da." I said as I left the kitchen.

"Good luck son." Was Da's reply, while barely budging from his seat, still glued to the telly.

I walked the short distance home and fixed myself a whiskey as soon as I got in. In front of the telly just like the year before, I gave a lot of thought to where I was as a paedophile hunter. Around this time last year, I found the article about Marty. That was all I needed to read to convince myself I was doing some good. Marty was enjoying his first Christmas behind bars. I was lucky to be a free man myself. But it was a rush. I was one step ahead of the Guards and it felt good. Ok, they were closing in. Alan, Harrison and O'Leary would all be able to positively identify me. But they'd have to catch me first.

9. Joe?

Towards the end of January 2011, I decided it was safe to hunt again. I bought a decoy phone, set up a new profile on the dating app, downloaded a stock photo and named the decoy account 'Ella_Eire.' Ella was thirteen and from Raheny. As usual, it didn't take long for people to talk to Ella. Most blocked the account from contacting them when I told them Ella was thirteen. But I knew it wouldn't be long before someone would take the bait. 'Joe-D' took a shine to Ella straight off the bat. I told him that Ella was thirteen and he didn't care. On his profile, it said he was sixty-one, from Drogheda and was 'Married and looking for NSA (no strings attached) fun.' Unsurprisingly there were no photographs of Joe on his profile.

We chatted on the app for an hour or so and Joe asked Ella for her number. We exchanged numbers and Joe contacted Ella by text after that, the app became obsolete. Joe and Ella got to know each other and I found out what he did for a living. Joe said he was a school teacher. He taught in a Secondary School in Drogheda, a mixed school with pupils in the age range of twelve to eighteen. To think that a teacher who is surrounded by young girls all day was texting what he believed to be a thirteen-year-old sickened me. I found it very strange that someone in his position would openly join a dating app looking for extramarital affairs. He ran a huge risk of getting caught, but maybe his sexual fantasies meant more to him than his reputation.

"I love the dress you wore in your profile pic on the app. Do you have more pictures?" Joe asked.

"No. I haven't seen a pic of you yet..." I replied.

"Give me two minutes..."

The next text that came through was a picture of Joe's erect penis.

"Have you ever seen one of these before? How do I measure up haha!" Read the caption accompanying the photo. I kept him hooked by telling him that Ella had little or no experience with men and that she was a virgin. That information had the desired effect as the texts continued to flow in.

Over the next two days, Joe constantly texted Ella. He continually begged and pleaded with her to send him pictures in various states of undress. In one particular conversation about swapping pictures, I could sense that Joe was growing a little suspicious. I had to buy some time to think about how to reel him in, so made an excuse to end the conversation.

"I have to go now. I have GAA practice tonight!" I told Joe.

"Ok love!" He replied. "Will you do me a favour?"

"What is it?"

"Seeing as you won't send me any photos. I want you to send me something else!"

"Like what?" I asked.

"Your knickers! lol," I had to roll the dice. My next text was either going to lead to a meeting or make Joe head for the hills.

"Come to Dublin and get them yourself! x"

The meeting was set for Saturday, February 5th at 4:00 PM. We agreed to meet at Heuston Street Station. Joe said he booked a hotel in the area. Ella was to tell her parents she was staying at a friends house. I tried to coax Joe into sending me a picture of his face, but he refused.

"You've seen more of me than I have of you! Send me more pics and I'll send you one!" He answered.

"But you've seen my face and I haven't seen yours!"

"We'll just have to wait until Saturday, my dear!"

Saturday morning, the day of the meeting, Joe sent a video message to Ella. It was a forty-second clip of him laying on his bed masturbating. His breathing became heavier as the video went on until he climaxed and ejaculated all over his pasty white, hairy, mound of a belly. A schoolteacher sending a disgusting video like that to who he believed to be a young girl was infuriating.

I printed out the chat logs and had the photos and video on the decoy phone. Sitting on the 27 bus at about 2:30 PM I got a text from Joe.

"Just on the train. Can't wait to meet you."

"Great, can't wait to meet you too. Did you get the condoms?" I replied. I wanted to make sure he admitted exactly what his intentions were.

"Yes, hun. Have them here, no baby for you haha. x"

"What are you wearing? Just so I'll know it's you?" I asked.

"I have a black sports bag and I'm carrying a blue umbrella also. I'll ring you when I get there. Won't be long now. x"

Having never seen Joe's face I knew he was going to be difficult to spot. But at least the umbrella and the sports bag gave me something to look out for. I got off the bus at Dame Street a little after 3:00 PM. With plenty of time to spare I wasted no time in heading for a drink. My nerves were virtually nonexistent on that snare. Keeping my anger at bay would be far more challenging than it had been before. After downing three whiskeys it was time to get the Luas to meet Joe. As the carriage snaked its way through the city, edging closer to Heuston Street, my decoy phone rang. It was Joe. I ignored the call and waited for an inevitable text.

"Just off the train. I'll meet you outside the Station."

"Great. Be there in 5." I replied.

I mingled with the scores of people exiting the carriage while doing my best to observe the people outside Heuston Station. To the right of the main entrance stood a short fat man of about 5'4 puffing on a cigarette. He was completely bald on top, excluding the streaks of hair combed over from one side of his temple to the other in a desperate attempt to conceal his baldness. Thin silver-framed glasses sat perched on his stubby, pug nose. His wrinkled skin looked compressed. Almost as if his face had been pierced and it was slowly deflating and drooping downwards. A black sports bag sat on the ground in front of him and a blue umbrella leaned against the wall behind him. He looked like he hadn't a care in the world, I was convinced it was Joe.

Approaching the stubby smoker, I could see that he was smoking a thin cigar, the white filter rested on his lips as he took a drag. He arched his head upwards and bellowed the thick, off-white smoke into the February sky. I could smell it from at least fifteen feet away. From the decoy phone, I called Joe. The serenity of the carefree smoker was immediately replaced by erratic fumbling as his phone rang loudly from his pocket. He answered with a huge grin on his face while studying the people around him.

"Hello, sweetheart. Have you just got off the Luas?" The high-pitched tone of Joe's voice was almost comical.

"Yes, I have darling." I answered. I hung up the phone and was standing right in front of Joe.

"I'm Ella. Nice to meet you, Joe."

"What, what is this?" He asked. His voice sounded like he hadn't hit puberty yet.

"I'll tell you what it is Joe. You're a sixty-one-year-old man trying to meet a thirteen-year-old girl for sex. That's what this is."

"No, I'm not. You have the wrong man."

"Like fuck I do." I held out the chat logs so Joe could see them.

"You contacted this girl on a dating app. Every message you sent her is right here. I have a picture of your penis, and a video of you ejaculating."

"It wasn't me. I swear!" Joe said as he snatched at the chat logs as if trying to conceal them from view.

"What the fuck are ye doin'?" I shot at him. Joe was clutching and grappling at the chat logs. He turned his body into mine in an attempt to pry the chat logs from my hand. I didn't need to hold onto them but wanted to keep Joe in close proximity. Suddenly Joe twisted back towards me. His pudgy, knotted left fist made a swing towards my face. He caught me on the right side of my jaw. It didn't hurt too much, but I needed Joe to calm down and stop making a scene. I grabbed him by the collar of his jacket and pinned him to the wall. The printouts scattered on the ground around us.

"Calm the fuck down!" I warned him as he stared back at me from his tiptoes.

"Here, here, here. Is everything alright over there?" A voice questioned from behind.

"Grand thanks, mate. Just a bit of personal business!" I answered. The last thing I wanted was some busybody putting their nose where it wasn't needed.

"Tell him why you're here if you want to." I snarled at Joe. I loosened my grip on his collar and Joe shrunk back to his original stature.

"Everything's ok thanks." Joe said to the questioning passerby. I turned around in time to see the stranger roll his eyes to heaven and walk away shaking his head.

"What the fuck are you playing at?" I directed at Joe.

"Who are you? What's all this about?" He answered in high pitched astonishment.

"Oh fuck off, the game is up. You're a school teacher. Surrounded by adolescent girls all day. Now you've travelled to Dublin to have sex with a thirteen-year-old. You have a hotel booked and you have condoms with you. Correct?"

"She was on an eighteen and over dating app. I presumed she was at least eighteen."

"The whole conversation is scattered all around you! It clearly states that she is thirteen and you don't have a problem with it. What is your explanation? You like children, and I bet this isn't the first time you've done this considering what you do for a living."

"You have it all wrong. I was never going to have sex with her."

"Bollix. Then why have you got an overnight bag?"

"It's all a big mistake, you have it all wrong."

"I'm not buying that for a second. If a thirteen-year-old girl showed up today, you'd be on your way to a hotel right now. Fuck this, I've had enough talking to you, you fucking scumbag. Do you want to deal with this at a Garda Station?"

"No please, I'll lose everything." He interrupted me.

"Fine. Then this is how it's going to be. You pay me €10,000 cash and nobody ever finds out about it. It stays between us."

"I don't have that kind of money just lying around."

"You have one week to find it. If you don't pay me, everything goes to the Guards. That video alone will destroy you! You'll lose your job, your wife, everything. Think about it. You have one week."

Joe was a shaking, fumbling mess as I walked away. He was trying, in desperation to pick up every page of the chat logs and roll them into a ball. From the back seat of a taxi, Joe cut a desperate figure. He sat on the ground beside his bag puffing another little cigar at record speed. Devastation in motion.

The following Monday, February 7th I texted Joe. "You've had time to think, what will it be. Pay up or go to the Guards?"

"I'll pay." Was his only response.

"Come to Dublin this Saturday afternoon with the cash. I'll tell you where to meet me from there."

"Ok."

It was the first cash transaction since Harrison and O'Leary nearly caught me. I was bound to be apprehensive. The thought of paying someone to pick up the cash did cross my mind. But the risk of having that person run off with the money was too great to ignore. It was best to keep things as they were. I'd arrange to have Q there to look over the transaction, get the money and get out of there as soon as possible. I texted Q that afternoon.

"Q. I have a meeting this Saturday. You available?"

"Yea no worries. Working at 7, before that is fine."

"Great. I'll be in touch."

I considered setting up another profile, but my original plan of one sting every two months made more sense. The stories about what happened on Harry Street before

Christmas had eventually died down. There was no point running the risk of drawing too much attention to myself by setting up too many decoys in quick succession. Friday, February 11th, I sent a text to Joe to make sure he didn't get cold feet.

"You're coming to Dublin tomorrow yea?"

"Yes." Was his only reply.

"We're meeting at 6:00 PM. Have the cash in a large sealed envelope. When you get off the train at Heuston, get the Luas to Abbey Street. I'll direct you from there."

"Ok."

I arranged to meet Q in Temple Bar that Saturday at 5:00 PM. His €1,000 was sealed in an envelope as usual as I got the bus at about 4:00 PM into town. I didn't make the mistake of putting my backpack on under my jacket. I was meeting Q in a bar, so there was no point in having it strapped on me ready to conceal the cash. Dame Street, 4:30 PM, I picked a small pub that wasn't playing Irish music. That shite drives me crazy. Its only purpose is to draw in the tourists and make them pay over the odds for a sub-standard drink. I sent Q the name of the bar. The place was dead. From a worn-out bar stool I ordered a whiskey. Staring into my glass, the satisfying crack of the melting ice almost filled the empty room. The upcoming exchange began to play on my mind. What if Joe went to the Guards? What if Harrison and O'Leary are there again? How much shit would I be in? Would I go to prison? My thought process was rudely interrupted when two enormous, bear-like hands grabbed either side of my rib cage.

"YOU'RE UNDER ARREST," A voice boomed behind me. I turned around with my heart in my mouth, and to my relief it was Q.

"Jesus fuckin' Christ man, are you trying to give me a heart attack?" I shot at him. The shock hit me with such force that I felt a little dizzy.

"Ah Jaysus Frankie, you're very jumpy." He said with a huge grin on his face.

"Sit down, what do you want to drink?"

"Get us a coffee. I'm workin' later." I ordered Q his coffee, got another whiskey for my nerves, and waited for his questions.

"So what happened before Christmas? It was fuckin' mad."

"Things didn't go to plan."

"You can say that again. Cops n all were there. What was the story with the money? Was yer man paying you?"

"I don't mean to be rude Q, but you get paid to make sure I get out of there alright. Any sign of a badge you walk away. That's exactly what happened last time and it's what we agreed. The fewer details you know, the better."

"Fair enough Frankie, but it was crazy. It was all over the news." The barman came over with our drinks. I cut Q with a look that told him to shut up while the barman was in earshot. He paused the conversation until the barman was gone.

"I saw you on the news on Christmas Day." He continued.

"I saw it myself, you couldn't make out it was me though."

"No. You were blessed."

Thankfully the conversation drifted away from the Christmas incident onto less important matters. I hoped Q would say something about Dumb-Dumb. I was dying to know where he disappeared to and if he had made contact. I didn't want to ask directly in case my questioning triggered suspicion. Q never mentioned Dumb-Dumb, so neither did I.

"Here. Your cash." I said, passing Q the envelope.

"Cheers. Where are you meeting this one?" Q asked while tucking the envelope into the inside pocket of his jacket.

"G.P.O. He's gettin' off at Heuston around now and getting the Luas to Abbey Street. Should be meeting him around 6."

"Sound. I'll shoot off now and see ye up there. Give us a ring when you're on the way. Talk to ya later man."

"Grand. See ya up there Q."

It was 5:35 PM. Plenty of time for another whiskey while waiting for updates from Joe.

"Where are you?" I texted him.

"On the Luas. Will be at Abbey Street shortly." He replied.

"Text me when you're there. I'll let you know where to go."

"Ok."

Sipping my drink, I began to overthink the situation again. Joe could have got a deal. Harrison and O'Leary would have done all they could for him in order to get me. But I eventually calmed down by convincing myself that Joe had too much to lose. He was sixty-one and nearly retired. €10,000 was a small price to pay for my silence. He had much more to lose by turning himself in, and besides, the lump sum he was bound to receive upon retirement would reimburse his hush-hush money.

"Just off the Luas on Abbey Street..." Joe texted.

"Walk over to the G.P.O. I'll ring you when I'm on the way. When I approach, hand me the envelope, I walk one way you go the other. I'm not alone, you're being watched. No funny business."

"Ok." He replied.

I stood up from the bar, downed the half glass of whiskey, grabbed my jacket and backpack and went to the toilets. I didn't want to risk putting the backpack in place and then putting my jacket over it in public. Although the bar was empty, that procedure could have still raised the eyebrows of the staff. In the small, cramped stinking men's toilet, I put the backpack on backwards. It was unzipped ready to place the envelope inside, my jacket concealed the backpack. Ice-cold water splashed on my face and caressed on the back of my neck shocked me into a new state of alertness. From the shiny cobblelock streets of a Temple Bar recently drenched in a downpour, I made my way to the G.P.O. Although the night was young, there were still plenty of drinkers getting a head start on what was undoubtedly going to be another busy night in the Capital. I continued onto the pedestrianised Fleet Street which leads onto Westmorland Street. Crossing over O'Connell Bridge, I made sure to be on the opposite side of the road from the G.P.O. I wanted to get a clear view of Joe before approaching. A phone call to Q gave him the familiar signal. From the base of the Statue of Jim Larkin, 'Big Jim' as all Dubliners know him, I surveyed the G.P.O and its surroundings. The Statue stands proudly on the island in the middle of O'Connell Street. Jim was a Trade Union Leader. A man that stood up for the normal working man, condemning poverty and injustice and urging people to stand up for themselves and their rights. And there I was right under him. About to meet a paedophile who thinks his €10,000 was about to buy my silence.

From my vantage point, I could see the whole front of the G.P.O, but there was no clear sign of Joe. I called his phone. It rang a few times before he answered, and when he did, there was complete silence. Why answer your phone and not speak? Very strange. I didn't say a word either and hung up. Something didn't feel right. The decoy phone received a text from Joe.

"I'm at the G.P.O front entrance. Where are you."

Cat got your tongue, Joe? Why was it ok to text and not talk? I rang his phone again. He answered, but didn't say a word.

"Joe?" I asked.

"Yes," A voice replied. The voice was deep and husky, a direct contrast to Joe's.

"Are you alone Joe?"

"Yes." He replied again.

Why the short answers, was he afraid to talk too much in case I realised it wasn't Joe on the other end of the line?

While on the phone to 'Joe' my personal phone vibrated with a text, I didn't check it. I was too concentrated on trying to find out what was going on.

"Describe what you're wearing. I can't see you." I told the voice. At least that way, whoever it was couldn't give me a one-word answer.

"Tell me what you're wearing, it's easier."

Ok, so why would the hunted one need to know what the hunter is wearing? All they had to do was describe where they were, and what they were wearing, wait for someone to approach and hand over the cash. Something was definitely wrong. I scanned the front of the G.P.O and saw a man of roughly my build talking on his phone. He was standing by the first pillar of the G.P.O as you approached from O'Connell Bridge. He wore a grey wool hat, a dark jacket, and a scarf sat untied over his shoulders. "Grey wool hat, dark jacket, untied scarf. At the first pillar." I told Joe.

As soon as that sentence was out of my mouth, the man that I described was thrown to the ground by two plainclothes Gardaí. Before they even had his handcuffs on, three unmarked squad cars were on the scene with lights flashing and sirens blaring. It was time to get out of there. I walked from the base of the 'Big Jim' Statue to the road and jumped in a taxi heading towards O'Connell Bridge.

Sitting behind the driver, I glanced over at the G.P.O again. Harrison and O'Leary looked bemused standing right beside the arrested man who was now on his feet. The poor bastard was probably just talking to his wife when all of a sudden he was thrown to the ground and arrested. I'm sure the Detectives couldn't understand why they didn't catch me that time. "Crumlin," I said to the driver while bending down and pretending to tie my shoelace. It was better to stay out of view. As we drove up Wellington Quay I rolled the window down, hung my arm out the window and dropped the decoy phone onto the road. It cracked and smashed to pieces under the wheels of the taxi. The text I got while talking to 'Joe' was from Q, it simply read...

"Cops here. Stay Away."

He had obviously spotted either Detective. Hopefully, he got out of there, exactly like last time. Not a bad day's work for Q, €1,000 to send one text. How on earth did Harrison and O'Leary know I was going to be there? The only logical explanation was that Joe handed himself in. But why? He had so much to lose. The only other thought that crossed my mind was, maybe it was Q? Maybe he got spooked after what happened at Christmas and decided to talk. But he didn't have much to talk about. He thought I was a drug dealer. But how does that explain the text he sent me? Was it a cover-up? So many questions were going through my head and I couldn't think of one feasible answer. Things were strange, very strange. But when the truth was eventually uncovered, it was more shocking and unexpected than I could have ever imagined.

10. Beginning of the end

After a disturbed night of sleep, I was still trying to figure out what happened. There was no point in sending Joe's information or the chat logs to the Guards. They already knew everything about him. But how were Harrison and O'Leary so hot on my heels? I couldn't figure it out. They were good, I had to hand it to them. But once again I gave them the slip, which only inflated my confidence. Had I casually strolled over to the G.P.O there's no doubt I'd be in deep shit. But rather than arresting me and getting the man they wanted, they grabbed some random stranger who knew nothing about what was going on. I'm sure Harrison and his team were furious. They would have loved to have me, I could feel it.

That afternoon Q rang me.

"Frankie?"

"Yea." I answered.

"Look, I haven't a clue what's goin' on, but I've seen enough. I'm out."

"What do ya mean you're out?"

"Two close shaves within two months! I can do without the drama ye know?"

"What drama? You walked away both times with a grand in your pocket!"

"I know, but there's something else goin' on. You're not tellin' me the whole story!"

"You don't need to know Q. Stand there and keep an eye out! That's all you have to do."

"Frankie, I had enough. I don't know what you're up to, but the net is closin'."

"Come on man, it's easy money!"

"I'm out. All the best Frankie. It was good to see you again."

"If you're serious, get rid of your phone, that way you're completely gone."

"Dumpin' it the minute I hang up. Good luck!"

"Cheers Q. All the best."

And that was it. Q was out, he'd seen enough. No amount of persuasion could coax him back, his mind was made up. I couldn't blame him really, ok the money was good and in the last two stings, he made €1,000 for doing virtually nothing. But still, he didn't know the full story. If I was a drug dealer, I wasn't a very good one. What kind of dealer throws his money away in the middle of Grafton Street? He had no way of knowing what was going on, and I guess he didn't want to find out. He'd seen Harrison up close twice in two months, who knows if Harrison had spotted him or not. Either way, he was out, I'd have to keep that in mind for my next sting.

Keeping to my plan of one hunt every two months, I waited until April 2011 to start again. I decided to stay away from the dating app and revert back to the chatrooms. I chose a chat room aimed at gay men. Decoy phone bought, picture downloaded, profile created. 'MansMan_Sam' was fourteen and from Maryland. This wasn't too far from where I grew up and I was able to use my local knowledge in the early conversations about school, etc. 'Cathal_Canz' was forty-seven, from Drumcondra and worked as a retail manager. On his profile picture, his hair was bleached blonde and he dressed in very bright colours. He gave me the impression that he was trying to cling on to a youth that was long gone. He wore thick-framed black glasses, probably more as an accessory than a necessity. His skin was an unnatural shade of orange that made his teeth appear blinding white in contrast. We started talking and I told him Sam was fourteen, gay but nobody knew yet. He replied that he knew exactly what it was like and that he was gay before it was socially acceptable to be gay. We continued talking on the chatroom for about an hour. Cathal told Sam that he was just out of a twelve-year relationship and that he was really cut up about it. He said the thing he missed most about his ex-partner was the intimacy. I knew exactly where the conversation was going.

After a few nights of arranging to meet each other in the chatroom to communicate, Cathal asked Sam for his phone number. After we exchanged numbers, the conversation moved from chat room to mobile. I guess Cathal didn't want any records of the chat being recorded on his computer. From there the chat turned sexual. Cathal asked Sam about his experience, how far he'd gone with a man and how it felt. I gave him enough of what he wanted to hear to keep him hooked. He asked Sam if he wanted to exchange pictures. I told him no, and made the excuse that a girl in Sam's class sent a naked photo to her boyfriend, and it went all over the school. The girl had to change school as a result of the humiliation and ridicule she endured as a result. Sam couldn't risk that happening to him. Cathal bought the story and asked if Sam wanted pictures anyway. Of course, I said yes, the more dirt I got on him, the more likely it was that he'd pay up. He sent three pictures in total. One was a photo of Cathal with no shirt on, taken in a full-length mirror. He gave me the impression he was proud to show off his almost sickly frame. I could see his rib-cage protruding through his skin. I urged him to send more, and he obliged. The next photo was taken in the same mirror where he stood fully naked. And last but not least, a close up of his penis. It was time to meet Cathal.

We arranged to meet on Saturday, April 9th. Cathal told Sam that since his break up, he was living in a rented apartment that he shared with an Italian woman. But since the Italian girl spent her weekends at her boyfriend's house, they could have the apartment to themselves. I told him that it all sounded great, but Sam would have to meet him in town first because he had no idea of how to get to Drumcondra. We agreed to meet on The Liffey Board Walk on Ormond Quay at 3:00 PM.

That Morning, I printed out the chat logs and got myself prepared for the confrontation. Sitting on the bus bound for Dame Street, I sent a text to Cathal shortly after 2:00 PM.

"On my way, can't wait to meet you x"

"On my way too, see you soon. Meet me at the Boardwalk just beside the Ha'Penny Bridge. x". Was his reply.

Stopping off for my customary whiskey, I began to think ahead to collecting the money from Cathal. With Q out of the picture, it all became risky again, especially with Harrison breathing down my neck. I could hire a locker or a safe of some kind, have him drop the money off, and pick it up at a later date? Maybe have him book a hotel room, leave the cash there and a spare key for me at reception? Or go back to my first sting and drive to him? There was going to be at least a few days to come up with a plan, so I let it slip my mind. The imminent confrontation with Cathal didn't worry me too much. He was a skinny, middle-aged man who I assumed would be easily intimidated. 2:50 PM, Cathal texted.

"Here and all. Ready and waiting."

"Be there in 5. What are you wearing so I'll know it's you?"

"Blue chinos, dark jacket. Sure you'd spot my glasses from miles away!"

"lol. ok see you soon xx" I replied.

Forty-seven and wearing blue chinos. It was going to be interesting.

I finished my drink and walked through the always busy Temple Bar. A left turn took me into the narrow laneway of Merchants Arch and straight over the Ha'Penny Bridge. Another left took me onto the Liffey Boardwalk. Cathal loitered nonchalantly in his pathetic blue chinos. He looked exactly as I had imagined. Someone too old to fit in with younger people but too proud to give up trying to. He was about 20 feet away from the entrance to the Boardwalk leaning on the guardrail looking towards the Ha'Penny Bridge. I inched my way up along the guardrail until he was within earshot.

"Nice chinos mate." I opened with.

"Thanks." He replied nervously and tried to busy himself by looking anywhere but directly at me.

"Does your cock not get a bit strangled in them though?"

"Excuse me?"

"In the chinos, does your cock not get a bit uncomfortable like?"

"What a question to ask!"

"Just saying, you should let your cock breathe every once in a while." With that, I showed him the picture of his penis.

"Where did you get that?"

"What? That? And That? And That?" I asked while swiping through the other two pictures that he sent to Sam.

"Who are you?" He asked.

"I'm Sam. You were trying to groom me online thinking I was fourteen."

"I knew it was a hoax all along."

"Right, so that explains the naked pictures?"

"I was going to make sure that Sam didn't make a stupid mistake, I was only going to talk to him."

"A picture paints a thousand words right? You know how bad this looks!"

"I realise it looks bad, but I was never going to do anything."

"So why invite a fourteen-year-old boy back to your apartment when you know your roommate will be out?"

"To talk. That's all. Who are you? Am I going to be arrested?"

"Well, that's up to you."

"What do ye mean?"

"It's your choice if you want to be arrested or not..."

"I don't understand."

"If you want to be arrested now, we'll call the Guards and they will come and pick you up. I have all the chat logs and photos you sent to Sam with me. Or, you can pay me €10,000 cash, and all this goes away."

"So you're blackmailing me?"

"Call it what you want. But they are your only two options."

"How can you even do this. I didn't do anything wrong."

"But you showed up. You groomed a minor online, sent him naked pictures of yourself and now you are here to meet him to bring him back to your apartment in Drumcondra."

Without realising it, the volume of my voice had increased with every accusation I threw at him. People started to look.

"It's not what you think, I'm not like that."

"Bullshit! I'm done talking now so what will it be? Guards or €10,000?" If he said 'call the Guards' I was screwed. There was zero possibility of getting Harrison and Co involved. But it was a bluff. There was no way he wanted to answer to the Guards either.

"How am I supposed to get access to that kind of money? I'm going away on Thursday so that only gives me three bloody days." He confessed.

"Well that was some plan, rape a child on Saturday and flee the country on Thursday." He looked at me as if he had been found out.

"Have €10,000 in cash by Wednesday. If I don't hear from you I'll send everything to the Guards. Understood?"

"I'll try my best."

"You're gonna havta' do better than that. Keep your phone on. I'll be in touch."

I crossed back over the Ha'Penny Bridge and got a taxi that was stopped at the traffic lights. Job done. Confront a paedo on a Saturday and make €10,000 clear profit the following Wednesday. It couldn't have gone better. As the taxi was driving up Wood Quay, one of the phones began to vibrate in my pocket. There was no urgency in answering the call because in all probability it would be Cathal trying to plead with me or convince me of his innocence. It turned out to be my personal phone that was ringing, and even more surprising, it was Da who was calling. That was very strange, Da never rings me.

"Where are YOU?" He snarled without so much as saying hello.

"I'm out Da, why?" I answered.

"Well for some," he said under his breath. I'm sure he never intended on me hearing him saying that, but I heard it anyway.

"Your mothers in bits up here!" Was his next statement. "What? Up where?" I asked.

"Timbuk-bleedin-tu where do you think? James's Hospital. George is dead." I couldn't believe what I heard. George was gone.

"I'll be up in a minute." I managed to stutter to Da.

"James's Hospital please." I said to the driver. The rest of the journey was a blur. We arrived at the hospital and I threw €50 on the driver's lap and didn't bother waiting for change. On my way towards the main entrance, I spotted Da on his way out. He seemed to take an age to exit the large revolving doors.

"Wheres Ma?" I asked him when he finally made it outside.

"She's up at the ward," he said as he eyeballed the taxi I got out of. "How did you get up here?"

"I got a taxi Da, to get up quicker."

"Jaysus, no job but can afford to get taxis everywhere... I'm goin' for a pint. Get upstairs to your mother."

"Yea, see ya later." I said and walked into the hospital. What a cantankerous old bollix. George had just died and all he can do is pick fights and think of himself by going for a pint.

I hurried through the maze of corridors, stairs, and lifts to Georges ward knowing that my Ma was most likely alone up there. I made it to his floor in a sweat. His private room was the second last one on the right-hand side. There was no sense of emergency around the whole floor, no air of panic. Everything continued like nothing had happened. The rented telly was the first thing to catch my eye. It sat outside Georges room beside his tray table and his locker. The door of his locker was slightly ajar and peering out at me was a full bottle of whiskey. It hadn't been touched since I left it there on Christmas Eve. Beside the whiskey were the chocolate bars I got for him on my first visit.

Poor aul George was too sick to enjoy either. The curtain on the window of Georges room had been closed from the inside, stopping anybody from looking in. I opened the door as quietly as possible thinking Ma was in there. My right shoulder manoeuvred its way into the gap, to get a better look inside. I could see Georges bare legs from above the knee down to his toes. They were frail looking and pale. A nurse had her back to me, she was leaning over George as if she was bathing him. There was no sign of Ma. The nurse didn't hear me open the door and didn't know I was there. After closing the door again, I stood outside George's room trying to take it all in. Be strong for Ma was my only thought while trying to stop the tears from flowing. Eventually, the lump in my throat grew until it felt like I had swallowed a golf ball. A nurse spotted me, "Your mother's in the 'Family Room'. Past the nurses' station, first door on your left."

"Thanks." I managed to respond in a forced whisper.

Desperately wanting to comfort Ma, I wasted no time in getting to the family room. It was silent, cold and empty, much like a lot of the people that have occupied it over the years. This is where you go to mourn the death of a loved one. How many broken hearts had those four walls witnessed? Ma was sitting in a white plastic chair, doubled over at the waist, her hands held her head almost at her knees. She was sobbing uncontrollably. I pulled up another chair beside her and put my arms around her.

She didn't realise I was there until we made contact. She raised her head, her eyes were red from crying and she held a tissue in her right hand.

"Heya love, thanks for comin' up."

"What happened Ma?"

"I got a phone call about an hour ago telling me to come up to the hospital, George
took a bad turn."

"What happened to him?"

"Pneumonia, his immune system was too weak to fight it anymore."

"For fuck sake. Why didn't you ring me?"

"Sure what could you have done love?"

"I woulda came up."

"I know love, I know, but there's nothing we can do now. He's in God's hands."

"Were you with him when he died?"

"Yea. I got here just in time. I held his hand and told him to go if he wanted to. He fought all he could."

"Did he say anything?"

"No love he couldn't, he just went, that was it."

"Sorry I wasn't here Ma."

"It's ok."

We sat there for about a half an hour crying and swapping stories about George. Ma told me, as she always had, that I was the apple of George's eye, the son he never had. She repeated the fact that George was eighty-six and he had a good life. George worked on the Docks from the time he was fourteen up until he retired. Although he married Aunt June when he was twenty-two and she was twenty, they never had any children. George lived his whole life in the Liberties in Dublin. An old part of the inner city with a very rich heritage. An area where everybody knew everybody else and looked out for each other. It was only after Aunt June died that George left the Liberties and moved in with Ma and Da. Ma couldn't stand the thought of George going into a nursing home, so she brought him up to hers. I don't know how she ever convinced Da to move George in, but she made it happen anyway. She can be persuasive when she wants to be.

A nurse came into the family room and offered her condolences. She got to know George over the last few weeks and described him as a 'real gentleman'. She asked me if I wanted to see him before he was moved to the mortuary, but I couldn't bear to do it. I'd rather remember him in my own way, not lying dead in a hospital bed. The nurse gave us a number and told us to call it on Monday. It was the coroner's number. We needed to let them know which funeral director to release the body to. When she said the words 'the body' I could have swung for her. He wasn't a body, he was George. But it's just the term they use after somebody dies. I told Ma I'd take her home, there was nothing more we could do at the hospital. She insisted we get the 123 and then walk from the Drimnagh Road home, but I wasn't taking no for an answer. We got in a taxi and headed to Ma's. When we got there, Ma tried to pay the fare because I wasn't working. If only she knew I had almost €40,000 under my bed at home. I paid the fare before Ma got a chance to and we went inside. Seeing Ma in such a state of despair was unbearable, and there was nothing anyone could do. We sat drinking tea in the kitchen talking about George again.

"Everyone thought he was mad when he bought you that car. 'Buying a joyrider a car' they said 'it's a one-way ticket to prison,' but I knew you wouldn't let him down. He pulled a lot of strings to get you that apprenticeship and you needed a car to get to work. He was proud of you love. And I'm proud of you too."

"Thanks, Ma. I couldn't let him down. He spent a fortune on that car and stuck his neck out for me."

"And it put you right. From that day to this you haven't been in an ounce of trouble with the Guards." Jesus if only she knew how close I was to getting caught blackmailing paedophile's in recent weeks.

After copious amounts of tea and stories swapped about George, Ma said she wanted to get to bed before Da came home.

"Ok, Goodnight Ma. I'll be over in the mornin' ring me if you need anything."

"Thanks love. Goodnight."

I walked home poured myself a large whiskey and saluted my Great Uncle. 'This one's for you George. Thanks for everything.'

Over the next few days, I helped Ma arrange Georges funeral. The night before he went to Francis Street church, George was brought over to my parent's house to spend one last night with his family. His coffin was placed in the front room where George spent the majority of his time. Ma cried into my shoulder as the lid of the coffin was removed. As a docker, George wore work overalls every day of the week except Sundays. George loved making an effort to dress well on Sundays. He donned his best suit, tie, shoes, waistcoat, the works. It was the only day he could. He and Aunt June used to come over to our house almost every week after mass. The first thing George would do was dig into his pockets and hand money to me and Emily. He always did that with a wink and a smile making sure my parents never saw him. Seeing him lying in a coffin in his Sunday best was heartbreaking. He didn't look like George. His skin was pale and had a porcelain complexion. He didn't have his glasses on, and I can probably count on one hand the number of times I ever saw him without them.

Friends, relatives, and neighbours dropped by to pay their respects and say goodbye for the last time. It was tough, but nobody had a bad word to say about George. When the last of the visitors left, Ma went to bed. Da, of course, made himself scarce that night by going to one of the local pubs. But nobody missed him, nobody even asked for him.

I stayed with George that night. Laying on his bed without being able to sleep, I talked to George like he was still alive. It's funny how it's only when you lose somebody that you start to question whether you done enough for them. George had done so much for me throughout my life, I wondered if he ever knew how much it was appreciated. But in the end, although we never said it, I loved him, and he loved me. At times like that, it's all that seems to matter. Da came home a little after 1:00 AM and stumbled straight up the stairs.

George's removal mass took place that Tuesday night April 12th at 7:00 PM in Francis Street. There was a good turn out. Locally George was a popular character, his nickname was 'The Gent'. George by nature was always there to help you out if ever you needed him. Aunt June had a stall in the Liberty Market where she sold women's shoes and fashion accessories. Everybody knew June and I recognised a lot of her old friends from the Market at mass that night. Unfortunately, they are a dying breed. Good people who look out for each other and help each other out whenever they need it. A real community spirit that seems to be disintegrating day by day. After the mass we headed to a small pub on Meath street, that was once George's local. It was good to hear people talk about George, every memory was a good one and we even managed to laugh at some of the stories that were exchanged.

I had the decoy phone with me and sent a text to Cathal.

"We're meeting tomorrow afternoon. Have you got what you owe me?"

"Yea. Where and when?"

"I'll text you tomorrow with details..."

It felt horrible setting up the meeting after Georges funeral. But I missed out on €40,000 thanks to Harrison and O'Leary. €30,000 went up in the air on Harry Street and the €10,000 I was supposed to get from Joe. I had to keep the ball rolling somehow. Renting a car to pick up the cash was the best way to meet Cathal. But it was still risky. I had to make an excuse to leave Georges funeral for about an hour or so. The best excuse I could come up with was that I was meeting someone about starting a new job. Having been out of work for well over a year, maybe people would understand.

Georges funeral took place on Wednesday Morning April 13th at 11:00 AM. Before leaving my house, I made sure to bring a small roll of black duct tape with me, knowing that I had to rent a car later that day. Ma asked me to get up and say a few words about George before we left the church. But there was no way I would get through it without bursting into tears. She understood and said no more about it. I helped carry the coffin from the church to the hearse and from the hearse to the grave. George is buried in Mount Jerome graveyard. He is in a grave with my Great Aunt June. The fact that Da was asked to carry the coffin didn't sit well with me at all. He was probably the only person in Dublin who didn't get along with George. Yet there he was giving the man a last mark of respect before he was laid to rest. But there was nothing I could do about it. After we buried George we headed back to his old local on Meath Street. We were there by 2:00 PM but I couldn't drink until later that night because of the meeting with Cathal. I told Ma that I had to go and meet someone at 3:00 PM about starting a new job, she said it was no problem and wished me all the best. With the day that it was, she didn't press me for too much information thank God.

I got a taxi on Thomas Street and told the driver to head to Ballymount. Having rented a car up there before I knew it wouldn't be a problem getting another one at such short notice.

"Make your way up to the Papal Cross car park in Phoenix Park. I'll meet you there at 3." Read the text to Cathal.

"Ok." He replied.

In the rental company, the only car available that suited my needs was a brand new Mercedes S Class. It was the only car left with a '0' in the latter part of the registration. I entered the Phoenix Park via the Chapelizod Road entrance and parked up on Acres Road. It was a risk to tape up the reg plates in broad daylight, but there was no alternative.

While pretending to rummage for something in the boot I tore a small piece of duct tape from the roll. Closing the boot, I placed the tape on one of the '0's in the latter part of the registration and transformed it into an '8'. The procedure was repeated at the front of the car, that time under the guise of looking under the bonnet. After both registration plates were taped, it was time to play the waiting game. 2:50 PM no word from Cathal. 3:10 PM still nothing.

My right foot started to tap against the floor. My fingers drummed on the steering wheel. My eyes were on the clock. 3:20 PM not a whisper. I had to have the car back in Ballymount by 5:00 PM. It didn't make a difference to me if they charged for an extra day's rental if the car was late getting back. But where the hell was I going to keep it? Parking it outside my house would raise too many questions and bring too much-unwanted attention. Getting rid of it the same day made more sense. 3:35 PM the decoy phone vibrated.

"I'm here." Was the text from Cathal.

"On the way." I replied.

Driving the short distance from Acres Road towards the Papal Cross car park, I rang Cathal.

"Turn on your hazard lights. I'm not alone, you're being watched. No funny shit!"

Of course, I was alone, but I didn't need him to know that. In the car park, a purple Honda was parked facing away from the Papal Cross with its hazard lights flashing. Pulling up alongside it, Cathal's thick-framed glasses peered out at me. He was shaking as he passed a large white envelope through his window. I snatched it from him and threw the car into reverse. Not a single word was spoken between us. Cathal must have been wondering why I was dressed so smartly, and driving a brand new car. Blackmailing paedophile's was obviously good business. Driving back to Ballymount I tore the envelope open. €50's, €20's and €10's were scattered inside. It looked right, felt right and smelt right. Back in Ballymount, I dropped the car off and hailed a taxi to take me to my house. Counting the cash in my bedroom, it was all there, €10,000. Beautiful, it was pure elation to get my hands on the cash again having missed out on the money from my previous two snares. I put the cash in the shoebox under my bed, got back in the taxi and headed to Meath Street for the funeral party.

Everybody was well oiled when I returned. Relatives I hadn't seen in years were all there shaking hands and hugging me. They all knew that I wasn't working at the time, so a lot of drinks were sent my way. I didn't refuse them, I couldn't. Where is an unemployed man supposed to get enough money to drink all day at a funeral? If I joined in with them and went round for round, questions would be asked. I couldn't trust myself to keep quiet about blackmailing paedophile's when the drinks were flowing. It was better to let my Aunt's and Uncles give me a drink and chat about George. The same stories about George were repeated about five or six times in the matter of a few hours. George grew up with nothing, worked hard for anything he had and helped out whoever he could. 'The Gent' would be sorely missed.

Ma cornered me and asked how 'the interview' went. "Ah grand yea. He said he'd ring me next week and let me know. Seems like a nice fella." I felt like dirt lying to her. "That's good. If you end up getting the job, you can say George did one last thing for ya."

"Yea, we see what happens."

"Aido and Jumper are here, did you see them?" Ma asked. I was shocked that two of my old drinking buddies would make it down.

With everything that had happened with myself and Laura, I became a bit distant with my friends. It was a tough one to take. I met Laura, fell head over heels in love with her, married her and we bought a house together. We were planning to start a family when all of a sudden she ran off with one of my closest friends, Mark. As you can imagine, it hit me pretty hard and I shut myself off from everyone around me. It made sense at the time, but I had to admit, it was great to see the lads again after such a long time.

It always makes me laugh how Jumper got his nickname. His surname is 'Gann' and in typical Dublin fashion, you either add a syllable or two to such a short surname. 'Gann' became 'Gann-sie'. Geansaí in the Irish language means a pullover or jumper. He had been christened Jumper when we were about twelve, and the name has stuck ever since. Aido was simply short for Adrian, we weren't as inventive with everyone's nickname. Both Aido and Jumper had married in the last year or two. I got an invite to both of their weddings but didn't even reply to them.

"I wasn't sure if Laura would be there with Mark so I thought it was best to steer clear you know?" I apologised.

"I didn't invite them to my wedding." Jumper answered.

"Neither did I." Said Aido.

"Fuck. Sorry lads. It was a bad time for me. Head was all over the place." They shrugged off my apology and told me not to worry about it.

We caught up on the old days, the good days. In our heyday, there were about ten of us in the group. We spent almost every weekend drinking in town, mostly in The Underground. As the years went by the group got smaller. Before we knew it, we had shrunk to me, Aido, Jumper, Mark, and Johner. Mark fucked off with my wife, and nobody has heard much of Johner since he moved to England to find work. We drank into the early hours of the morning. There were some tears towards the end of the night, but all in all, it was a good send-off for George.

When Da has a belly full of drink and an audience around, he feels it's his God-given right to sing every old Irish song ever written. The kind of songs that smell like cigarettes and whiskey. The applause and hoots for 'The Irish Rover' died down and Da cleared his throat to start a new number. The first line of 'Dublin In The Rare Old Times' was familiar enough for Ma to stare daggers at Da. But his eyes were tightly shut, busy delivering his masterful performance. I heard enough, grabbed my jacket and went outside. With my back leaning against the wall of the pub, I fought to keep my balance. The beer and whiskey had taken its toll. Aido and Jumper followed me outside, Ma was close behind them. She threw her arms around me and said,

"Pay no notice to your father, he's pissed."

"Ah fuck him, I'm goin' home," I replied.

Ma went back into the bar. Me, Aido and Jumper got into a taxi.

The journey back to Crumlin was silent, which suited me down to the ground. My house was the first stop. I threw some money to Aido and got out of the taxi.

"I'll give ya a shout next week." Aido said before the taxi door slammed shut. But I didn't believe him. It would more than likely be another two years before seeing the lads again.

The hangover the following day was a bastard. It felt like I had three hearts, and two of them lived in my head. I was sweaty but cold, hungry but full, and tired but couldn't sleep. The kind of day where your body doesn't know which way is up. All I managed to do was crawl onto the sofa and watch the telly.

Much of that Friday was the same. As the saying goes, the older you get, the worse the hangovers are. Saturday, April 15th the hangover finally subsided and my mind cleared a little. I thought about my last snare, the money, and Q. The one snare that he wasn't involved in went without a hitch. Was he working with Harrison? If so, how much did he know? And how did he know? That day, the printouts between Cathal and Sam were printed, sealed in an envelope and ready to post first thing on Monday. My plan was to take a drive, post the letter, dump the phone and check into a hotel somewhere for at least a week. Things had been hectic over the past while and I was beginning to feel it. Almost getting caught twice, Q quitting and George dying. It was all a bit much, some time off was exactly what I needed.

11. Rude Awakening

Monday Morning April 18th, 6:15 AM. I woke up to the sound of someone beating at my front door and windows. Whoever it was caught me off guard, being out of work, there was no reason for me to be awake that early in the past eighteen months. Standing on the landing, a muffled voice from outside delivered the words...

"Michael Mills we have a search warrant for the premises. You can open the door or we'll tear it down. The choice is yours."

I hoped it was Aido or Jumper taking the piss. But after creeping into the spare bedroom at the front of the house to look out the window, the sight of three Garda squad cars and a Garda van waited to greet me. One of the Guards must have spotted me, or some kind of movement at the window because he shouted the order "He's in there, take the door down," to his surrounding colleagues.

I ran back into my bedroom and slammed the door shut behind me. For a split second, the idea of jumping out the window and trying to get away sprang to mind. Even if I managed to land in the back garden without breaking my legs, I'd still have to scale every one of my neighbours garden walls, avoid their dogs and try to make an escape. At 6:15 AM, wearing only my boxer shorts, where the hell was I going to run to? About €45,000 sat in a shoebox under my bed. What the hell was I thinking? How did it make sense? I should have put the cash somewhere else, invested it, gambled it, done something. The game was up. The first blow of the battering ram wasn't enough to break entry, it sent shuddering vibrations throughout the house that tingled on my bare feet. With the second blow, the door gave way.

"Gardaí, we have a search warrant for the premises. If there's anybody in here let yourself be known immediately."

Back on the landing, having flicked the light on, I waited for the inevitable.

The Guards stormed into my house, their footsteps were making their way into the kitchen. They shouted "Clear," as they searched each empty room downstairs. Dull heavy footsteps began to make their way up to me.

"Top of the stairs." I said.

"Lie face down on the ground with your hands behind your head." A voice demanded before anybody came into view.

A knee was firmly pressed between my shoulder blades. My hands were taken from my head and brought down to my lower back. As the handcuffs were tightened on me, one of the two arresting Guards said...

"Michael Mills you are under arrest on suspicion of Blackmail, Extortion and Demanding Money with Menaces under Section 17 of the Criminal Justice (Public Order) Act 1994. You are not obliged to say anything unless you wish to do so. Whatever you say will be taken down in writing and may be given in evidence. Do you understand?"

"Yes." I replied.

"Detective Harrison. Top of the stairs please." One of the Guards shouted as they brought me to my knees.

The stairs creaked under the pressure of a heavy set person slowly ascending. Harrison had a huge smirk plastered on his face as he stared down at me. His shoulders raised and lowered in quick succession as he had a little laugh to himself.

"Is this him?" One of the arresting Guards asked Harrison.

"It's him alright. We have ya now ye little bollix ye. There's no gettin' away from us this time! Let him put some clothes on, but don't let him out of your sight. He's a tricky one. As soon as he's dressed, cuff him up again and bring him downstairs."

The two Guards took the handcuffs off me and told me to get dressed. They came into my bedroom and closed the door behind them. One Guard stood with his back to the door, the other stood by the window. In their own way, they made it clear there was no escape. For some reason, I put a long sleeve shirt on. My thinking at the time was that it would make it difficult for my neighbours to spot the handcuffs when the Gardaí brought me out of my house. But then again, there was a big gaping hole in the front door as it hung off the hinges. Not to mention the squad cars and Garda van parked outside. Once dressed, I was cuffed up again and escorted downstairs. It was all over. I knew I was looking at prison time. Thank God George wasn't there to see me in that kind of trouble again.

In my living room, Harrison sat on the double sofa busying himself writing in a notepad. I was instructed to sit on the single seater sofa, to Harrison's left.
There was no sign of O'Leary.
"We have a search warrant for the premises. All computers, smartphones, and tablets will be seized. You can tell us where they are or let us find them, it's up to you. We will get our hands on them one way or another. Do you want to tell us where they are Michael?" Said Harrison. He spoke clearly and directly. He was a man who didn't like to mess around.

They were going to ransack the place either way. There was no point in trying to hide anything.
"My personal phone is on charge on my bedside locker. Laptop is in my wardrobe. There's another phone in the top drawer of the bedside locker." I told him.

Harrison shot a look towards a Guard standing by the living room door. He nodded and immediately made his way upstairs.
"Why does anyone need two phones?" Harrison asked. He already knew the answer. He just wanted me to say it.
"I'm sure you'll find out." I replied.

I could hear the Guard upstairs searching my bedroom. Wardrobe doors opening and closing and drawers doing the same.

"It was quite a stroke you pulled on Grafton Street last Christmas. Lucky there was nobody killed!" I couldn't help but let out a sarcastic laugh.

"Well, I'm glad you find it funny. It was chaos, people got hurt." Harrison informed me.

"So the money was real? Bit stupid to use real money wasn't it?" I asked.

Harrison had no response, he stared at me with a look of anger on his face. The tension was broken by the Guard who was upstairs. He came into the living room with my laptop, two phones and the envelope full of Cathal's chat logs addressed to Mountjoy Garda Station.

"What do we have here?" Harrison asked. "A letter to the Guards? Very nice of you Michael. You've obviously been up to your old tricks again! How much did you get out of this one?"

"Nothing." I replied.

"Of course not." Harrison said as he opened the envelope. He began to study the chat logs and realised he had another paedo on his hands.

"Which phone is your personal one?" He asked me.

"The one that's charged." I told him.

"And the charger for the decoy phone is...?"

"In the kitchen, on the counter."

"I'm sure everything we need is on the second phone."

"If you say so..." Was my only reply.

It's a nauseating feeling sitting in your own living room in handcuffs while the Guards search every nook and cranny of your house. There were six uniformed Guards in total along with a suited up Harrison. Who wears a suit that early in the morning? Only somebody who knows they have a big day ahead, and I'm sure that day meant a lot to Harrison. He finally got the man who gave him the slip twice before, but how did he find me? The decoy phone I dumped in Liberty Lane, before finding junkies body, came to mind. But all it had on it was an app and text messages. Surely there was no way they could trace my address from that. It was obvious that Alan went and talked to the Guards, but there was no way he could have known where I lived. Was I followed that night after the money was scattered on Grafton Street? If so, why didn't they stop me sooner? And then there was Joe. He must have spilled his guts to the Guards. He never even showed up to pay me off, instead, he had Harrison and Co waiting to nab me. But how did that lead them to my house? It was all too much to take in.

"Detective, you're gonna want to see this," said one of the uniforms as he proudly strutted into the living room. He placed the shoebox on the coffee table right in front of Harrison and opened the lid. It was full to the brim of €50, €20 and €10 notes. About €45,000 in total.

"Well Michael, it looks like you've been a busy boy. Do you realise how deep you're in? You're staring at a fourteen-year stretch. Fourteen years Michael. I hope it was worth it." Said Harrison. I said nothing and let myself slump back into the armchair.

Did the bastard have to repeat 'fourteen years' twice in quick succession? I heard him fine the first time, but it still didn't sink in. It sounded like a lifetime. Eventually, everything was bagged up and ready for removal. My phones, my laptop and the shoebox full of cash. When they were satisfied they had all they wanted we got ready to leave the house. I was led out towards the Garda van by two of the uniforms. Some neighbours were out at their doors chit chatting in dressing gowns, observing the early morning commotion. Mrs. Collins from two doors up was standing by the Garda van as we approached.

"Michael love, what's going on?" She asked. Waiting for the back door of a Garda van to open so you can step in, is the perfect time to have a conversation with a nosy neighbour. The aul bint. You couldn't fart on the road without Mrs. Collins asking what you had for dinner. I didn't answer her either way and right before the back door of the van was slammed shut, Mrs. Collins spouted...

"I rang your mother love, she's on the way."

Oh lovely. George hadn't been buried a week and now my Ma will have to see me like this. It was horrific timing, I felt terrible thinking about the state Ma would get herself in. Da wouldn't be happy either, but then again, he never is.

The journey took longer than expected. I thought we would be traveling the short distance from Kildare Road to Crumlin Village Garda Station. But I was Harrison's catch, so I was shipped off to his base, Pearse Street Garda Station. I was booked into the station. My belt and shoelaces were taken off me, the handcuffs were removed and I was placed in a holding cell that stank of piss. The sound of a turning key locking the bolt of the door into place is gut-wrenching. There I was again, locked away from civilization, with nothing but my own thoughts. Everything runs through your mind when you're alone and facing the consequences of your actions. But it not only effects you, things like this have a domino effect on the people around you. I worried about Ma. She wasn't herself after George died. Emily was a million miles away, I wasn't exactly doing great after my marriage broke drown. And now this. What did she think I was arrested for? Drugs? Being drunk and disorderly? Something to do with Laura? She would have never guessed that I was blackmailing people, it was definitely going to be a shock.

I have no idea how much time passed until the door of the holding cell swung open and two Guards stood in the doorway.

"Where's he goin' again?" One Guard said to the other.

"Interview Room 2." His colleague replied.

"Michael," said the first Guard. "You're goin' to be questioned by Detective Harrison now. Ok?" As if I had a choice.

I sat in 'Interview Room 2' waiting for Harrison. He came in looking relaxed. As if a great weight was lifted from his shoulders. He held a folder in his left hand and a fresh coffee in his right, the smell of it filled the room. He sat and got himself comfortable, he looked like he was preparing to be there a while. He removed a notebook from the folder and was ready and waiting to take notes. "Interview commencing on Monday, April 18th, 2011 at 08:36 AM with one Michael Mills with an address on Kildare Road Crumlin. Ok, Michael, I will reiterate that you are under arrest for suspicion of Blackmail, Extortion and Demanding money with Menaces under Section 17 of the Criminal Justice (Public Order) Act 1994. The Station Sergeant here at Pearse Street Garda Station is satisfied that there is sufficient information to detain you for questioning under Section 4 of the Criminal Justice Act 1984. You can be detained for an initial period of six hours followed by a further six-hour extension. We can apply for further extensions thereafter up to a total of 24 hours, if necessary. You will be given adequate rest periods throughout this procedure. You don't have to answer any of the questions I ask without your solicitor present. If you don't have a solicitor you will be provided with a list of solicitors that will be able to attend the station. If you cannot afford a solicitor you can make an application for Legal Aid at a later date. Is this clear?"

"Yea." I replied. "When can I apply for a solicitor, a free one I mean?"

"You will be able to make that application once you stand in front of a Judge at the District

Court." Harrison replied.

"And when will that be?"

"It depends, it could be as early as this afternoon. Tomorrow at the latest."

"Ok."

"Right Michael lets cut to the chase. You and I both know why you're here. You set up decoy profiles on the internet pretending to be teenagers, you then arranged to meet with people you were chatting to online. Once you met them, you demanded money from them in exchange for your silence. Am I right so far?"

"Not exactly."

"Ok. Can you correct me where I'm wrong?"

"Yea. You used the word 'people', you said I 'arranged to meet people'. They weren't 'people', they were paedophile's".

"Ok Michael. These 'people' were over the age of eighteen and had arranged to meet a minor. Is that better?"

"A bit. They arranged to meet a minor with the intent of having sex with them."

"Ok. We'll get to that. But there is no mistaking the fact that you demanded money from these said people in exchange for anonymity."

"Well, I gave them a choice. Go directly to the Guards or pay me and it all goes away."

"How much did you demand?"

"€10,000." Harrison's eyes raised from his notebook and looked directly into mine. Maybe he was shocked by my honesty, or maybe it was the amount of cash. I could see no sense in hiding anything, they had everything they needed to build a case against me.

"And after this money was paid. What happened then?" Harrison quizzed.

"I sent everything I had on them to their local Garda Station."

"Why Michael?"

"Why not? I got what I wanted from them, why should they get away with what they tried to do?"

"Would you not agree that if you didn't demand money from them, you wouldn't be sitting here?"

"But why would I do it for nothing?"

"Why would you do it at all?"

"Do you have kids Detective?"

"I do. But they're both grown men now."

"Count yourself lucky. Do you realise how easy it was for me to talk to paedophile's online?"

"Not really."

"In some cases, they wanted to meet within a few hours. It's madness."

"But what makes you think it's ok to make a profit from it?"

"Nothing. I figured that people who were caught in that position would have no choice but to pay up. Either that or let everyone know what goes on in their heads."

"Did you honestly think you'd get away with it?"

"Well, I've been going strong for well over a year now. I'm sure I knew you'd catch up with me sooner or later."

"We had two close calls before Michael. We all know what happened on Grafton Street at Christmas, but what about the G.P.O. Why didn't you show up?"

"When I rang Joe it obviously wasn't him that answered, I knew something was up."

"How did you know it wasn't him?"

"When I first confronted Joe he spoke in a very high pitched voice. When he answered his phone that night, his voice was a lot deeper. Plus he didn't say much, he didn't want me to hear him speak. But he obviously spilled his guts to you lads."

"What do you mean by that?"

"He obviously went and spoke to the Guards...That's how you's were there, right?"

"You didn't hear?"

"Hear what?" I should have known the answer was not going to be good.

"You texted Joe on a Monday, February 7th and arranged to meet him in Dublin that coming Saturday the 12th. His wife found him hanging in their garage that Tuesday morning February 8th."

"Oh Jesus," I said as my head lowered into my hands. Joe was dead. Could they pin his death on me? What had I got myself into?

"The Gardaí in Drogheda were called to the scene. They discovered the conversations between Joe and 'Ella' on the dating app. Once they discovered the texts on his phone ordering him to go to Dublin to pay you off, they got us involved. It was a carbon copy of what had happened to

Alan and his friends at Christmas. I knew it was you. That's why we were waiting."

"Did he leave a note?"

"That's all you care about? You want to know if he mentioned you or not?" Harrison fumed. I knew there was no chance of Joe ever mentioning me. He didn't get as much as my first name. He was expecting me to be a thirteen-year-old girl.

"There was no note. But if I can prove you drove him to suicide I will." Although that sentence did cut to the bone, I knew Harrison wasn't confident of pinning Joe's death on me. If he had any clear sign that I drove Joe to suicide, he would have found it by then.

"You had us tackle and handcuff an innocent bystander at the G.P.O. The poor bollix hadn't a clue what was going on."

"I saw that."

"Of course you did Michael, it's all a big joke to you, isn't it? Well let's talk about your arrest, shall we? Let's talk about how we got YOU!" Harrison was agitated, he raised his voice as he was about to delve into the details. I didn't dare to interrupt him. I wanted to know exactly how they finally tracked me down.

"On April 13th of this year, you rented a car from a company in Ballymount, correct?"

"Yea."

"You dropped the car off that same day, didn't you Michael?"

"Yea, and?"

"What did you use the car for Michael? To pick up €10,000 was it?"

"That's nothing to do with you."

"Oh, really? Nothing to do with me? Then why did you tape up the registration Michael?" Harrison removed four photographs from his folder and placed them in front of me.

"This was the car you rented Michael, correct?" Before I had a chance to reply, Harrison continued.

"That Saturday the car underwent a routine service. The rental company noticed the registration was taped and called the Guards immediately. They suspected the car was used in some form of illegal activity, and by Jesus they were right."

It suddenly dawned on me. With my rushing around the day of George's Funeral, getting to Ballymount, picking up the money, dropping the car back before 5:00 PM and getting back to George's wake. I had forgotten to remove the tape from the '0's on the registration plates. Something so simple had finally got me caught. Harrison continued...

"They had a copy of your driving license and your home address. Your information was uploaded to the Garda database and that's where I saw you. I couldn't believe my eyes when I saw your photograph. The same little fucker that I was eyeball to eyeball with on Harry Street. That little bastard that threw the money into the air and made me look like an idiot. I had the search warrant signed immediately and couldn't wait to smash your door down. You weren't so clever this morning Michael. How did it feel to be on your knees on your landing looking up at me? Arrested in your own home?"

I didn't reply to Harrison's last bout of questioning. He got himself worked up, it was better to let him calm down before I spoke again. A minute or so went by, Harrison sipped the last of his coffee and threw the paper cup into a bin. He seemed to have calmed down a bit.

"What happened with Alan?" I dared to ask.

"It's ongoing."

"Since Christmas?"

"Yea. There's more to it than meets the eye. He and his two friends are very sick people."

"You found his buddies too?"

"Yea. You didn't read about it?"

"No. I lost interest in following up on the perverts. But what happened?"

Harrison was either going to give a straight answer or I'd sit back and watch him blow his top again.

"We had Alan on a short leash that night. We needed him there to lure you in and get a positive ID on you. But we still needed to talk to Alan about the whole situation. He only came to us that afternoon, he gave us some information, but it was the tip of the iceberg."

"And what have you found out since?"

"When we brought Alan back to the station for questioning he sang like a bird. He told us about you hitting him for €30,000, he told us about his two friends and where we could find them."

"I figured he'd run to Daddy and get him to pay." I said to Harrison, proving to him that I had done my homework on who Alan really was.

"Alan told us his family want nothing to do with him anymore. There was a case a few years back where he was accused of raping a minor at one of his father's hotels. His father paid off the victim and her family which stopped the case from going to trial. After that Alan's father cut him loose. He gave Alan his share of his inheritance and told him to make his own way in life. Alan didn't like the fact that you were conning him out of €10,000 and thought we were going to help him."

"And what about the other two?"

"They were arrested, their houses searched, phones, computers, and tablets seized. We found links to other individuals in Bristol, Glasgow, London, and Amsterdam. Alan and his friends are part of a paedophile ring. We're working closely with Europol on the investigation. They're looking at serious time."

I didn't know how to take the news. Part of me wanted to dance on the table with delight, another part of me couldn't handle the seriousness of it all. I knew I lost everything, but there was no shame in losing what little I had if it meant paedophiles would be spending 'serious time' behind bars.

A knock came to the door.

"Detective Harrison, can I come in?"

"Yea, yea. Come in." Harrison answered as he stood up to greet his seemingly familiar visitor. The door swung open and was quickly shut again. The slender grey suit of Detective O'Leary slipped in. He immediately shook Harrison's hand and whispered something in his ear. I didn't hear what it was, although they both found it amusing. O'Leary stood and looked at me with a condescending grin on his face. Harrison took great pleasure in introducing us.

"Detective O'Leary this is Michael Mills, Michael, this is Detective O'Leary."

"Nice to see you again Michael," O'Leary said.

"The pleasure's all yours," I replied.

"I got your message when I was in the hospital," O'Leary told Harrison.

"Everything alright?" Harrison replied.

"Great yea. Baby boy 7lbs 6oz."

"Congratulations. Hows Sarah?"

"Ah, she's grand yea. Everybody's doing fine." O'Leary responded.

"You see that Michael. You're keeping Detective O'Leary away from his family. I'm sure he has better things to be doing than sitting here."

"Don't we all." I sarcastically responded.

"Where are we anyway?" O'Leary butted in.

Harrison began to fill in O'Leary on the progress of our conversation. When we were in the Interview room it was clear that they only suspected that I was involved in three paedophile stings. Alan, Joe, and Cathal. There was no mention of any other paedo. Although my suspicion told me that they knew I was involved in more than that. They needed more evidence before they could accuse me of being involved in any more. They had a positive identification of me on Harry Street. Although they didn't see me at the G.P.O for Joe's sting, they were ready and waiting for me. Harrison had the envelope of Cathal's chat logs so they could tie me to that one.

"Right," said Harrison. "I want to get the ball rolling. I believe we have enough evidence here to formally charge you under Section 17 of the Criminal Justice (Public Order) Act 1994. You will be released from the provisions of Section 4 of the Criminal Justice Act and formally charged with an offense under Section 17 of the Criminal Justice (Public Order) Act 1994. I'm confident we will find more evidence on your computer and phones to charge you with similar offenses. I will be requesting that we have time to investigate these crimes thoroughly once we are in front of a Judge at District Court. Do you follow me so far Michael?"

"Yea." I replied.

"Good. Michael Mills at 10:17 AM on April 18th, 2011 you are formally charged under Section 17 of the Criminal Justice (Public Order) Act 1994 of three counts of Blackmail, Extortion and Demanding Money with Menaces on three separate occasions from dates between December 2010 and April 2011. You do not have to reply to these charges, but anything you do say will be taken down and may be used as evidence. Am I right in saying that you are waiting until you stand in front of a Judge at District Court to apply for Legal Aid?"

"Yea. I have no money to pay a solicitor myself."

"Ok. Detective O'Leary informed me when he first entered that your parents are outside and waiting to talk to you."

"Oh, wonderful." I said.

"You will be given an opportunity to speak with them under the supervision of a Guard. I do have to let you know that anything you say to your parents can and will be used as evidence if needs be. Is that clear?"

"Yes."

"Ok Michael. Interview concluded at 10:18 AM on April 18th, 2011. I will do my best to get us into the District Court as soon as possible".

With that Harrison got up and left the room. He looked like he was rushing to get everything tied up so he could have me in front of a Judge that same day. O'Leary stayed with me.

"Your mother was in some state when I saw her outside. I hope she's had time to calm down." He informed me.

"Do me a favour Detective."

"What would that be Michael?"

"Give them ten minutes max. My Ma will be crying and not making sense, my Da will be telling me that 'he knew I'd end up behind bars again'. I've got enough on my plate as it is."

"I'll see what I can do, someone will escort them in shortly. I'll see ye again Michael."

O'Leary left the room and I sat alone contemplating ways of breaking the news to Ma. There was no way of sugar coating it. Break her heart and let the information sink in. Under the supervision of a Guard I couldn't give too much away, so it'd have to be brief. I wasn't worried about Da. His temper went from zero to sixty over the slightest thing anyway. The silence that engulfed the interview room was glorious. My folded arms cradled my head on the table. My eyes were shut tightly as I attempted to mentally escape my surroundings. After such a hectic start to the day, it was a relief to finally sit in solitude. But it was the calm before the storm. The bedlam was bound to re-visit. A creaking hinge let me know that the door was opened. A Guard peered his head in and looked at me.

"In here, follow me please." He opened the door wide with his left hand and gestured the people behind him to follow him in. Ma was the first in, her eyes were bloodshot red and she held a tissue to her face. Da followed suit, his face was stony, expressionless, his eyes were locked on mine.

"Jesus love. What have you got yourself into?" Ma asked as she threw her arms around me. She cried on my shoulder waiting for an answer. Da was still glaring at me. I was waiting for his words of wisdom.

"I hope you're fuckin' proud of yourself now." Da said. As insightful as always. With the greetings over and done with, Ma and Da took a seat at the table.

"Well?" Ma asked.

"Look," I said. "They're holding me on suspicion of blackmail. They say that they have proof I've been conning people out of money."

"What? Conning people how? That's ridiculous!" Said Ma.

"Not really." I answered. "I have been doing it." With a sigh and without giving Ma or Da a chance to speak, I continued.

"I've been posing as a minor on the internet. Once I got talking to people online who arranged to meet this minor for sex, I confronted them. Instead of meeting a minor, they met me. I told them they could either go to the Guards themselves or pay me off to keep quiet about the whole situation."

"What?" Ma gasped. "I don't believe you."

"Well you better start believing, why else would I be here?" I asked. Da said nothing.

"So you were going on the internet to catch perverts?" Ma asked.

"Yea." I replied.

"Jesus fuckin' Christ. It's all because of that Flanagan bastard. I knew you'd never recover from that." Ma stated.

"It's nothing to do with that. That was a long time ago." I tried to reassure her. She burst into floods of tears and was sobbing heavily. The kind of cry you never want your mother to cry. But it happened anyway. I'd seen her like this before. The best thing to do was to keep quiet and let everything sink in.

"And how much were you getting off these fuckers?" Da asked, for two reasons. One to deflect the subject away from Flanagan, and two, he wanted to know how much I was taking in.

"I can't go into detail until I speak to a solicitor. I can apply for Legal Aid once I go to District Court." I answered him.

"You can't go into detail with your own mother and father? Sweet Jesus, that's the fuckin' thanks we get."

"Jesus Da. I can't talk about it in front of the Guard in the room. I don't know what I can or can't say yet, anything I talk to you about can be used as evidence against me. Ok?" He didn't respond to my question.

"How much trouble are you in? Will you go to jail?" Ma asked between sniffles.

"I don't know yet Ma. I won't know anything until I go to Court." I hated lying to her, but if I told her I was looking at fourteen years in prison I think she would have dropped dead there on the spot.

The crying and sobbing from Ma and the angry questions from Da were pleasantly interrupted by a knock on the door. The Guard in there with us opened the door and O'Leary came in.

"I'm sorry to interrupt you folks, but Michael will be transferred to the District Court very shortly. I'm going to have to ask you to finish up." O'Leary followed through with my request. He had given my Ma and Da about ten or fifteen minutes to find out what they needed to and then he put the breaks on the meeting.

"I'm sorry. Sorry about all this. Will you make sure my house is boarded up or the door is replaced? I'll sort ye out when I can."

"Ok Love. Look after yourself." Ma stood up and we hugged and said Goodbye. She was still sobbing. Da waited for her to let me go and they both walked out of the interview room. Da neither looked at me or said anything as he left.

O'Leary instructed the other Guard to show my parents out. He closed the door after they left.

"How did it go?" O'Leary asked.

"As well as you might expect." I answered.

"Your poor mother is in bits. I'm sure she'll be ok after she has time to digest it all."

"I hope so. Thanks for cutting the interrogation short. Jaysus, I thought Harrison was bad."

"No problem." O'Leary said with a laugh. "I knew it wasn't going to be easy for anyone. There is truth in what I said though. We are working on getting you down to Court asap. You'll be taken back to a holding cell and we'll let you know from there."

"Ok. Thanks again. Oh, and congratulations on the birth of your son."

"Thanks, Michael. Talk to you soon."

The Guard who escorted my parents out of the interview room returned and led me back to the holding cell. On a wafer-thin, tattered mattress, I held my hands over my face desperately trying to forget where I was. Every possible outcome raced through my mind. What if I get fourteen years? That means I'd be touching fifty when I'd be released. Maybe I'd get off lightly because I put paedophile's behind bars? What if Ma took ill and I'm stuck in prison? I could do nothing but lie there and wait for the heavy steel door to be cranked open. I would have given everything I ever possessed for a bottle of whiskey.

12. The System

The jangling of keys and the noise of a bolt sliding from the lock let me know somebody was entering my cell. I didn't bother to look at who came in. The person walked in and stood close enough to me so I could feel their presence. The familiar voice of Harrison said...

"Ok Michael, we'll get you over to the District Court at 2:00 PM. The Court re-opens after lunch at two, your case will be heard between 2:00 and 5:00 PM."

"I can't wait." I replied.

"Neither can I." Harrison said.

Not long after Harrison left my holding cell, I was placed back into the Garda van and driven up the Quays to Park Gate Street. The memories of my first snare came back to me. Standing outside the Court looking for Marty's car. If I could go back to that day, I wonder if I'd still go through with the confrontation. Look where it got me. But on the other hand, look where it got Marty. At 2:45 PM on April 18th, 2011, I was called before Judge Toner in Courtroom two. Judge Toner read the case file and looked at the photographs of the taped up registration on the rented car. He read the chat logs that were found in my house and Harrison updated him on all proceedings up to that point. Harrison then made a suggestion to Judge Toner.

"Judge, if I may, I would like to recommend that the accused is held on remand until we have time to build a case against him. I'm confident that we will find more incriminating evidence on the phones and laptop computer we seized from his home."

"On what grounds would you recommend that the accused be held on remand Detective?"

"The seriousness of the allegations Judge."

Judge Toner sat in silence as if absorbing all the information he had heard. After about a minute, he turned his attention to me.

"Mr.Mills it has already been explained to you why you are standing before the Court today?

"Yes, Your Honour." Having not stood in a Courtroom in over twenty years, all my experience relating to Court came from watching the telly.

"Judge will suffice Mr.Mills. You fully understand the charges against you?"

"Yes, Judge."

"Has your legal representative been contacted Mr.Mills?"

"I would have to apply for Legal Representation Judge."

"On what grounds?"

"I'm currently unemployed Judge, and any financial asset I had were seized by the Gardaí earlier today." Judge Toner turned back to Harrison.

"Detective Harrison, are there any objections to granting the accused request for Legal Representation?"

"No Judge." Harrison replied.

"This is a very complex case. It is obvious that we are not yet in a place where we can bring this case to trial. Detective Harrison and Detective O'Leary will need time to examine the evidence that was seized earlier today. The accused will need time to apply for Legal Representation. In the meantime, the Court will delay the proceedings until a later date. Mr.Mills you will be remanded in custody until your next Court appearance. Your remand date is hereby set on April 26th. You will appear before the Court on this date. Only time will tell where we will be at that point. Should Detective Harrison and Detective O'Leary require more time to investigate this case, they can make such an application on the set remand date. By that time Mr.Mills, you will hopefully have found a Legal Representative who will inform you of your rights as the case continues."

And that was that. No more than twenty minutes were spent in front of Judge Toner before I was packed up and sent off to Cloverhill Prison. Being held on remand until my next Court appearance. Harrison got his wish and had me locked away while he built a case against me.

The first thing that hits you when you enter a prison is the smell. Over four hundred men cooked up in the one place is bound to leave a mark. The next unmissable attribute is the noise. People shouting, security gates slamming, doors being locked, it's never-ending. Hardly a moment passes by without some kind of banging or crashing. It's tough to get used to. Cloverhill Prison is mostly a halfway house for prisoners such as myself. Most men there are held on remand awaiting their court dates. It's a revolving door of prisoners coming and going. I was one more face in the mix, waiting in limbo for my true faith to be sealed. After spending a few hours in a holding cell in what I now know prisoners call 'the check-in desk,' my details and a photograph were taken. It was then time to be escorted into the main prison building. It felt as if all eyes scrutinized my every move as I made the seemingly endless walk to the end of the ground floor or 'Landing One' as it was referred to. I had finally reached the location of my new home. Although it was small, dingy and cramped at least I was the sole occupant. I pretty much kept myself to myself and only spoke to the other inmates when prompted to do so. Most were in on drug charges, and almost all the ones I spoke to had been there before. They knew the system well, and they knew what kind of sentence they faced. When asked about my case I would reply by saying 'fraud'. There was no point of going into exact details, chances were I'd never see any of those men after my remand date.

7:30 PM that night the whole of Cloverhill shut down. All prisoners were sent to their cells and locked in. The slamming of the cell door and the turning of the key compounded the feeling of isolation. The sun still cutting through the window in my cell made me feel like a bold child having been sent to bed early for misbehaving. If only it were that simple. I collapsed, face down on the bed and covered my head with my arms. The prison block descended into a welcome hush as the vast majority of the prison population settled in to watch telly for the night. I had a telly in my cell but didn't bother to switch it on, guessing that every news station would have some kind of report about my arrest.

I knew it was going to be a sleepless night. Every possible scenario and outcome whisked around my head. I tossed, turned and paced around the cell throughout an agonizing first night inside. At home, Ma would be putting herself through the same torment. After what felt like an eternity, morning finally came to put me out of my misery. Straight after breakfast, I was brought to a small interview room near the visiting centre. After a few minutes of wondering what was going on, the door opened and a small ginger man in a blue suit entered.

"Hiya Michael, I'm Derek Fitzgerald, I've been appointed as your solicitor." He switched his briefcase from his right hand to his left and extended his right hand towards me. I analysed him while exchanging greetings.

"How old are you?" I asked. It was a strange first question to ask, but this fella looked like he belonged in primary school. I'm no giant myself, standing at about 5'10, but even I was towering over the slender frame of Fitzgerald.

"Thirty-six," he said with a smile as if he's used to being asked the question.

"But I'm expecting puberty to kick in any day now." With that, he sat at the table, adjusted his glasses, and got down to business.

"Right, Michael, I've read the file on your case, interesting to say the least. It's of the utmost importance that you are completely open and honest with me from the start. Whatever you say is between you and me and nobody else. The more I know the more I will be able to help you. So far you are charged with three counts of blackmail. The Gardaí have seized your belongings and are examining them as we speak. Is it likely they will find more evidence to bring more than three charges against you?"

"Yes." I replied.

"How many more charges?"

"I'm not too sure, to be honest."

"Ok, ballpark figures, are we speaking of less than ten? Or between ten and twenty?"

"It's more than ten, but I can't be sure exactly. I lost count as time went on."

"No problem, and can you talk me through the process of 'snaring' somebody?"

"Yea, some I met on chatrooms, others I met on dating apps..."

"Let me stop you there, chatrooms on your laptop correct? Tell me about the dating apps."

"Chatrooms were on my laptop yea, the dating apps were downloaded onto decoy phones."

"So you bought new phones and downloaded the app onto them?"

"Yes."

"And were these phones seized in your house the morning of your arrest?"

"One of them was, the rest were discarded."

"Ok good."

"Good?" I asked.

"Well, if the phones have no direct link to yourself, the evidence on them can only be circumstantial. It's a lot more difficult for that evidence to be used in Court. Do you know how many people you met via the dating app?"

"Honestly no. My first three snares were in a chat room, then I moved to the app as it was quicker and easier. But I did revert back to the chatrooms so I wouldn't be found out by using the app consistently."

"Ok, no problem, I'm sure we'll find out how many people you met on chat rooms as opposed to the app in due course. What happened after you met these people?"

"I told them they could either go to the Guards or give me €10,000 and it all goes away. After they paid me I sent everything to the Guards anyway."

"Talk me through how you sent everything to the Guards."

"I printed all the chat logs and photographs received by my decoy profile. I sent everything I knew about them to their local Garda Station. Where they lived, where they worked, their car details, anything I had on them went straight to the Guards."

"How did you send this information to the Guards exactly? Post, email, dropped it in yourself?"

"Post mostly. I drove out of Dublin and sent the letters from different areas."

"Different areas every time you sent the information on?"

"Yes."

"Good Michael. This can only help matters. If you sent the letters from the same post office or general area all the time, they would be able to pinpoint your general location by the postmark on the letters. Moving from place to place will cast doubt on who the sender actually was."

"Ok, but the pictures I used on all the decoy profiles were downloaded from a stock photo website. Is this a problem?" I probed.

"Potentially yes. They were downloaded using your own personal credit card details correct?"

"Correct."

"So I assume all the photos are sitting on your laptop. The ones you used on the dating app may be traced back to you, but then again, how can the Gardaí prove exactly what you used them for? Yes, it proves you downloaded the photos. But as long as there is no direct link between you and the profiles on the app, it would be very difficult to use those profiles as evidence."

"Right. I need to ask you about one of the paedophile's I snared. After the initial confrontation, we arranged to meet again in order for him to pay me off. But he killed himself before he came back to Dublin. Do I have his blood on my hands?"

"It depends on what they find on your laptop. If you met him in a chatroom and there are direct conversations between you and him on your laptop. It could be trouble. But proving that you drove him to suicide would be extremely difficult to do. Unless he left some evidence behind saying that you were directly responsible."

"I can't see how he could do that, he didn't even know my name."

"I don't want to promise you anything Michael, it would be very difficult to pin it on you, but it all depends on what they find, and how they can use it as evidence."

"Ok, so I have to wait until then?"

"I suppose so I'm afraid."

Fitzgerald then explained the legalities of the case and what was most likely going to happen.

"You will be held on remand for one week while we wait for a decision from the Director of Public Prosecutions (DPP). Thereafter you can be held on remand for blocks of up to four weeks with your consent or two weeks without consent. At some point, the DPP is likely to direct Trial on Indictment. You will be further remanded for service of a book of evidence. Once you are served with the book of evidence the case will be sent forward to the Circuit Criminal Court."

"What exactly is a book of evidence?" I asked.

"Basically speaking it lists the statement of charges against you. It will also list any witnesses that the DPP proposes to call to Trial. It will outline the statement of evidence expected to be given by each witness. It will also have a list of exhibits, such as photographs or any physical evidence relating to the case."

"And how long does it take to be served with the book of evidence?"

"It depends Michael. Generally speaking, we should have the first contact from the DPP within six weeks of your first Court date. After that, we should be served with the book of evidence anywhere from six to sixteen weeks from that date."

"Jesus. So I'm going to be in Clover Hill for a while?"

"Well, you are entitled to apply to the High Court for bail if you wish."

"I don't know. If they let me out I'll be hounded by every fucker in Crumlin."

"Well, you can give it some thought and let me know."

Fitzgerald turned the conversation back to the paedophile's. We went through every last detail. Setting up the profiles, luring paedo's in, demanding money, collecting money. I told him about renting cars, Q and Dumb-Dumb, the mugging and finding junkie dead. After telling Fitzgerald that at least one paedophile was behind bars because of me and that Europol were involved in another case, he seemed impressed. I answered all the questions Fitzgerald had and began to feel comfortable with him. He was easy to talk to and made me feel he was on my side. Then he asked me the one question that opened the floodgates. I spoke to him about things I haven't spoken about in over a decade. Like he said, the more information he had, the more he could help me. There was no point in holding back anymore.

13. Why?

"The one question that everybody will ask Michael, is why? Why do this? What made you start?" Fitzgerald asked.

"Well, about two years ago the arse fell out of my life. My friend Jumper came to me and told me that he saw my wife in a hotel with one of my best friends. Jumper was on a weekend away with his girlfriend and saw my then-wife, Laura and our mutual friend, Mark staying at the same hotel as he was in Cork. Jumper made sure he wasn't spotted but told me he saw them kissing in the hotel restaurant before getting the lift to their room. Jumper came to me about a week after this and told me everything. I knew he didn't want to do it, but his conscience wouldn't let him be quiet. Laura had told me she was away with her mother, but when I confronted her, she came clean. She said it had been going on for months, she didn't love me anymore, wanted a divorce and was going to stay at Mark's. It hit me hard. I started drinking quite heavily, stopped going to work, lost my job and was in a really bad place. The bank were in touch to say that the mortgage repayments had fallen into arrears. They threatened to start repossession procedures very soon. I needed money and I needed it fast."

"First of all, I'm very sorry to hear this. The breakup of a marriage isn't easy on anyone. But why paedophiles? Why did you see this as your way out?"

"They were easy targets. They rely on power and silence to do what they do. Take that away from them and what are they left with? Nothing. Fill them with fear that you will expose them for what they are, and they have no other choice than to pay you off. And once they think they're all clear to start again. Send their information to the Gardaí and let them take it from there."

"Ok I get it, I do understand the concept. But why Michael? This is a very difficult question to ask, and I'm sure a more difficult one to answer, but...were you ever abused?"

It was time to open up about things I had buried for years.

"Yes. Yes, I was. It started when I was nine and continued until I was thirteen. My Da loves Irish music and arranged for me to have lessons with one of his drinking buddies who played in pubs around Dublin. Flanagan, he lived local and my Ma used to walk me to his house every Wednesday for lessons and pick me up after. It started off ok. I learned a few songs on guitar and tin whistle over the course of a few months, then he started touching me. While I was holding the guitar, he'd wrap himself around me and put his hands on me telling me to hold it 'properly'. He'd make me sit on his knee, then his hands would be everywhere. It was strange and I knew it was wrong, but I was too young to understand what was happening."

"Jesus Michael, I'm sorry to hear this. But it is important that you tell me everything that happened. I know it sounds strange, but it might actually help you."

"The touching and feeling escalated and over time, he had me performing oral sex, and masturbating him. I was eleven when he first raped me. He convinced my Da to let him bring me to a Traditional Music Festival in Wexford. He said I was good enough for an audience. In Wexford, he played a gig in a small pub with some people he knew. He introduced me as his friend's son and bragged that he was teaching me 'everything he knew'. I thought it was strange that he never asked me to play that night. After his gig, he sat drinking pints with his friends until closing time. We were staying in a small house in the middle of nowhere. He drove, full of drink, back to the house. There's many times that I look back and wish he turned the car into a ditch and killed us both there and then. We went into the house where he ordered me to strip and get into bed. I blame myself for so much of it. Why did I do what he told me? I should have ran away or at least said something to someone in the pub. But at eleven years of age you think you're doing the right thing by doing what an adult tells you to. He came into the bedroom, locked the door behind him and got into bed. I was raped that night. I couldn't sleep a wink after it and lay there crying in agony. He snored his head off as if nothing happened. When he woke up in the morning he turned to me and said.

"Tell your Da what happened last night if ye want to, but he'll never believe you. You'll be taken away from your parents and put in a boarding school somewhere. Away from everyone, so you can't cause any more trouble."

As a kid, I believed him. I believed that if I told anybody anything I'd be taken away and never heard of again. The bastard made me feel like it was my fault."

"Michael, this is unbelievable. I'm so sorry that you went through this. Was this an isolated incident? The penetration I mean?"

"No. He raped me whenever he got the chance. If his wife was out when I arrived at his house, I knew it was going to happen. The coast was clear. I lost count of how many times I was raped. He used me as his toy. For four years he had me masturbate him and perform oral sex on him whenever he felt like it. When the opportunity arose, he had full sex with me. He'd teach me new songs every now and then to keep me up to speed, so if anyone asked me to play something for them I could. He loved every minute of it. He was getting paid in pints, supplied by my Da to use me however he pleased. I hated the bastard."

"And when did the abuse stop? How did it stop?"

"The fucker died." The frustration took over and I couldn't speak for a few seconds.

My eyes welled up and my throat tightened. It was obvious to Fitzgerald that this wasn't an easy process for me.

"It's ok Michael. Take your time."

"I point blank refused to go to Flanagan's funeral. My Da was shouting his head off and telling me I had to go. He even wanted me to play Flanagan's favourite song 'Dublin in the rare old times' for him as he was being brought out of the church. That was breaking point for me. I broke down in hysterics in front of Ma, Da and my sister Emily. Ma hurried Emily upstairs and kept her out of earshot. I explained to Da everything that had been going on, and of course, it was my fault.

"Why didn't you fuckin' tell me? I woulda killed the bastard years ago. You fuckin eejit Michael. How could you let him away with it?" Da screamed at me.

Me and Da haven't seen eye to eye from that day to this. It changed everything. I think he feels guilty that he was the one that made me go and get 'lessons' from Flanagan. All the while, he was paying the bastard in drink to abuse me. But Da will never admit it. He pretends it never happened. Then takes out his frustration on everything and anything around him."

"And your mother? How did she take it?"

"She did what any Irish mother would. She marched up to the church that very night. In the middle of the funeral mass, she started screaming and telling people exactly what Flanagan had been up to. She went right up to Flanagan's wife and was screaming in her face. She had to be removed from the church that night, I heard it took three men to carry her out. My mother is probably the only person you're likely to meet that's barred from her local church."

"And what happened in the aftermath?"

"Two more of Flanagan's 'students' came forward and told the Gardaí that they had been abused too. They were older than me, one male and one female. They never spoke up until they felt it was safe to do so, and by then it was too late. The bastard was dead. He got away with it. His family moved out of the area soon after he died and that was that. There was nothing more anyone could do."

"And how did this affect you in the coming years?"

"I started drinking at a young age, dabbling with drugs and hanging out with the wrong people. I got into a lot of trouble. It started off small, like shoplifting, vandalizing, breaking into cars. When I was fifteen it finally caught up with me. I was caught joyriding for the third time in quick succession. That time I wasn't going to get away with a slap on the wrist. I was sentenced to spend sixteen months in St.Patricks Institution in 1995."

"And how was that?"

"As amazing as you might imagine. A couple hundred juvenile offenders locked up in an old Victorian style prison. It was hell."

"And after your release, you didn't re-offend until now. Am I right?"

"Yea."

"So do you think your time served in St.Patricks put you off reoffending?"

"Well, not exactly. My Uncle George, well my Great Uncle George, really put his neck out for me when I was released."

"In what way Michael?"

"I had mentioned to him when he visited me in St.Patricks that I enjoyed the woodworking class. I liked the fact that I could take a piece of wood and make something useful out of it. When I got out, George had a carpentry apprenticeship already lined up for me. A good friend of Georges's from the Liberties had a son who ran his own carpentry company. George pulled some strings and arranged for me to start about two weeks after my release. The only problem was, I lived in Crumlin and would have to travel from site to site to work as a carpenters apprentice. George's solution, he bought me a car. Everybody thought he was crazy, 'buying a joyrider a car, it's a one way trip to prison'. But I knew I wouldn't let him down. He took out a substantial loan to pay for the car and the insurance. As you can imagine, the insurance was astronomical for a convicted joyrider. But I promised him that I wouldn't fuck it up. And I'm proud to say I didn't."

"So you spent the best part of twenty years staying out of trouble as far as the Law is concerned?"

"Yea. I was never arrested as an adult, until yesterday."

"Did you know you were going to get caught one day Michael?"

"I didn't really think about it, to be honest. I was making money, keeping the bank off my back and exposing paedophile's. It felt good. It was great knowing that the shoe was on the other foot once I confronted the perverts. The power changed hands and they were the ones with nowhere to run, nobody to tell. They now know what it feels like to be a victim, and I hope that feeling stays with them for the rest of their lives."

A knock came to the door and a voice called out. "Times up. Wrap it up please gents."

It was about a ninety-minute meeting. And in those ninety minutes, I told a complete stranger more than I have ever told anyone in the last decade. The last person I opened up to was Laura, and look how that turned out.

"Ok Michael. This was a good meeting. Very productive. I appreciate your honesty and believe me I'll do everything I can to fight your corner. I will need to meet you again and go into more detail about the amount of paedophile's you snared. How it happened, where and when, etc. But we'll play it by ear. If you think of anything else that I need to know, just jot it down and we can discuss it at our next meeting."

"Ok, Derek. Thanks for your help."

"No problem. Your remand date is set for April 26th. Personally speaking, I think Detectives Harrison and O'Leary are going to request more time to investigate this case before going to trial."

"So, I'll be here for a while?"

"The maximum time that they will be able to get is thirty days, so you could be here for another three weeks or so."

"Lovely." I replied.

"We'll get to your remand date and take it from there." Fitzgerald said as he closed his briefcase and stood up from his chair.

"By the way Michael, have you seen the news lately?"

"No." I replied.

"You might want to take a look. The story broke that you were the one responsible for throwing money all over Grafton Street. Details of what happened are trickling out."

"How? Who reported it?"

"The Media are everywhere. But it can only be a good thing. If people realise what you were doing they might get on your side. It could be a positive."

We shook hands and Fitzgerald left. I think he purposely left me on a positive note. When you're leaving a prison to go back to society, why not leave an incarcerated man with a hint of optimism. That night I made sure I tuned in to the six o'clock news. One of the main headlines read.

'Man arrested for Christmas Cash incident on Grafton Street.'

It wasn't the top story that day. When it came time to give more detail, the report started by showing footage recorded outside my house.

'It was here early yesterday morning that Gardaí arrested a man suspected of blackmail. The man reported to be in his early thirty's who has yet to be identified was removed from this address on Kildare Road for questioning. It is understood that the man was posing as a minor on internet chatrooms. Once he lured individuals into meeting who they believed to be a minor, the accused demanded money from them in order for him to stay away from the Gardaí. One such transaction went sour on Grafton Street at Christmas last year. An estimated €50,000 rained down on one of Dublin's busiest shopping streets. More details on the case are said to be forthcoming as the accused awaits trial.'

On a positive note, the door to my house was boarded up. On a negative, everyone in Crumlin would know exactly who I was. News like that travels fast in a small community.

Wednesday, April 20th, 2011, it was time for Ma and Da to pay a visit. The visiting room was a large hall with about thirty prisoners allowed to visit with their loved ones at the same time. I was able to tell Ma and Da a little more information about what was happening without a Guard being too close. But still, I didn't want them knowing too much. Reporters, neighbours, friends, and family would be hounding them for information. If Ma or Da accidentally blurted something out it could have ended up being used against me at trial. Ma's eyes were as red as they were in Pearse Street, she looked like she hadn't slept. Da, as usual, had a face like thunder. It was obvious they weren't speaking to each other as they approached the table. Ma walked at least five paces ahead of Da, he followed with both hands inserted in his pockets.

"Michael love, are you ok?" Ma asked as she sat at the table.

"I'm grand Ma, seriously."

Da arrived at the table, pulled his seat out, sat down and cleared his throat. I thought he was getting ready to say something, but no. He placed his right elbow on the table, rested his head in his hand and just sat there.

"Cameras were up outside your house. It was all over the news." Ma informed me.

"I know, I saw it."

"People were ringing our house and knocking on the door all night."

"Tell them nothing. The less they know the better."

"Everybody's sayin' you were responsible for throwin' money all over Grafton Street at Christmas." I smiled and looked Ma directly in the eye.

"Oh, Jaysus it was you! What happened?" Still not a word from Da. I looked around and made sure none of the patrolling prison officers were anywhere near.

"I was meeting a paedophile, he was to pay me €30,000 to stay away from the Guards."

"€30,000?" Ma gasped.

"Yea, he arranged to meet a minor and share her with two of his buddies. I was chargin' them €10,000 each to keep quiet."

"And what happened."

"They went and told the Guards, and they were waitin' for me on Harry Street. They grabbed me before I got onto Grafton Street."

"And how did the money end up in the air?"

"How else was I gonna get away? I knocked the money out of the Guards' hands and legged it."

"Jesus Michael. And you sat and had Christmas dinner with me and HIM a few days later?" The fact that Ma referred to Da as 'HIM' confirmed my suspicion that they weren't speaking.

"Well, what else could I do Ma?" I replied. "If I skipped dinner you would have known there was something up. That's why I even went to yours the year before when my face was black and blue."

"That was something to do with paedophile's as well? It's going on that long?"

"Yea, I was mugged. But I was mugged for €10,000 I collected from a paedo."

"Oh, Jesus. And what's going to happen now?"

"I met with a solicitor yesterday. I told him everything. And I mean everything. Flanagan and all." With the mention of the name 'Flanagan' Da's eyes darted towards mine. I could feel him holding a stare for an uncomfortably long time. Still not a whisper.

"What did the solicitor say?" Ma asked.

"He said the more he knows the more he can help. He can use what happened to me in my defence. Everything from Flanagan, Laura and Mark, my job, everything. He's going to do what he can to help me."

"And did he say if you're going to stay in prison or not?"

"I'm in Court again on April 26th and we'll go from there. His name is Derek Fitzgerald, expect him to be in touch."

I filled Ma in on all she wanted to know but warned her not to say a thing to anyone who asked for detail. She told me that Emily rang and could tell Ma was upset over something. Ma had to tell her that I was arrested and sitting in Clover Hill. Emily was shocked and told Ma that she thought I was 'over all that'. Visiting time came to an end and everybody started to say their goodbye's. Ma was wiping away tears and told me she'd be back the following day. I told her there was no point in coming down again until my next Court date. But I knew she wouldn't listen and visit religiously. Just as we were about to part company, Da finally broke his vow of silence.

"Are ye alright son?" I looked at him in complete shock. Dumbfounded by his question. It took me a few seconds to answer.

"Do you realise that's the first time you asked me that in nearly twenty years?" He didn't know where to look. At first, he stared at the ground, then he looked to Ma, and back to me. It was uncomfortable, nobody knew where to look or what to say. I almost felt sorry for him.

"I'll be grand," I said right before they left. Why did he ask me that? And why leave it until visiting time was over to say it?

As expected, Ma took no notice of me when I said there would be no point in visiting again before my remand date. She visited every day. By that Friday she seemed to be herself again. She wasn't crying and was able to hold a conversation. It all started to sink in and she came to terms with what was going on around her. My solicitor, Fitzgerald, had been in touch with Ma and Da and talked them through the case. He explained what was likely to happen at each stage of the procedure. He also broke it to them that I was likely to spend some time in prison. He had no idea how long my sentence would be, it would all depend on what evidence Harrison and O'Leary could find. Although Ma's visits were comforting and I was delighted to see her, she must have been so disappointed in me. After doing so well for so long, I had basically turned the clock back by twenty years.

14. Back to Court

My remand date was mentioned in almost every media report relating to my case. It had also become a hot topic of debate within the walls of Cloverhill. Some prisoners were even betting 'ash' on what would happen next in my case. Ash is loose tobacco that smokers on the inside roll into the form of a cigarette. It's one of the many methods of currency in prison, plus it's cheaper than tailor-made name brands.

'Five rollies says he gets bail'. 'A pouch says he'll be back here the day after his remand', were some of the bets I overheard being placed. It was next to impossible to ignore the looming Court date. The days leading up to it were unbearable. I tried to keep my mind off it as much as possible by reading or drifting into a semi-conscious existence in front of a telly. But even when I allowed myself to relax and began to switch off, a sudden bout of reality would pounce without warning, reminding me of where I was. The whole saga had barely begun, and I already wished it was over.

April 26th, 2011, the morning of my remand date. After another sleepless night, I was due to arrive in Court on Parkgate Street by 10:00 AM. Four other prisoners were due in court that day too. We were loaded into a prison van and began our journey at 9:15 AM. A sombre mood engulfed the interior of the van. Not a single word was exchanged between the confession box sized transport cells. I can only imagine that every occupant sat there doing exactly the same thing. Quietly pondering the outcome of our respective cases. A small rectangular perspex window sat above my head. Leaning my right shoulder on the wall of my cell I could just about see some clouds. I couldn't help but be brought back to my childhood. I'd sit in the back of Da's car looking out the window trying to get a hint of where he was taking Ma, Emily and me. On a good summer's day, we'd go to

Brittas Bay, Howth or Portmarnock. Emily and I would run and play on the beach while Ma and Da looked on. We'd sit and munch on a special blend of jam and sand sandwiches as the seagulls circled, crying out for the crusts. After washing down our lunch with fizzy orange, that had been sitting in the sun for hours, we were free to play again. My reminiscence of a far happier time was brought to an abrupt end. The first burst of violent blows came crashing against the exterior of the van.

It's an unnerving experience sitting in a confined area while the van was attacked from all directions. Slowing to a crawl, I could only guess that we were in close proximity to the Courthouse. Sirens blared while agitated voices shouted in unison. It was impossible to hear what the mob were chanting. The thunderous blows continued to rain down on the exterior, sending deafening echoes throughout the tiny cell. After what felt like an age, which was probably no longer than thirty seconds, the pandemonium outside came to a sudden halt. The van stopped and the ignition was switched off, indicating that we had made it into the grounds of the Courthouse. My cell door swung open and I looked up to the prison officer. "What the fuck was all that?" I asked.

"There's supporters here Michael." He replied. "The media are all over the place, TV, radio, newspapers everything!"

"For who?" I naively asked.

"You Michael. Former victims of sexual abuse have gathered outside the Court to show their support for you. It's mad stuff altogether."

My gut instinct told me he was joking. He had to be. Surely one of the other prisoners must have been a serial killer or notorious drug kingpin that people wanted to get their hands on. There was no way they would support a paedophile hunter. We were escorted into the Courthouse and placed in separate holding cells.

"Your solicitor will be with you shortly." A pot-bellied Guard said before he slammed the door shut.

A short time later the door was opened and Fitzgerald came in.

"Good Morning Michael. How are you feeling?"

"Grand, yea. What was all the banging on the van?"

"Nothing to worry about. They're here to support you."

"Who are?"

"The news broke that you were exposing paedophile's by setting up false profiles online. Most of the people outside are victims, or should I say, survivors of sexual abuse. They came here to back you up. You're a cult hero out there Michael."

"That's crazy."

"That it is, but anyway, let's focus on the case. I have found that there are nine letters containing information on paedophile's that were sent to various Garda Stations throughout the Country. Does that sound about right?"

"Yea, about that."

"And the one found in your house the day you were arrested, brings us to ten. I'm certain they are going to ask about the number of calls and texts made to 'Q' on your personal phone. I know you already told me he was a hired hand, but are you willing to work with them by revealing Q's identity?"

"Even if I wanted to I couldn't. Once he backed out, he changed his number, I haven't seen or heard from him since."

"But you do know where he either lives, works or socialises. So he can be tracked down. I'll ask again, are you willing to assist the Gardaí locating him?"

"No. He had nothing to do with this. He thought I was dealing drugs."

"Fine Michael. Moving on, are you any clearer about how many snares you had on chatrooms or app?"

"No. Sorry, I can't remember."

"Grand, we'll cross that bridge when we come to it, I suppose. Anything else you want to ask or tell me before we head in?"

"No, nothing."

"Ok. Your case is to be heard at 10:30. I'll see you in there." Fitzgerald said as he exited our brief encounter.

Thankfully the agonizing wait in my holding cell was a short-lived one. Had my case been in the afternoon I would have driven myself demented. The overthinking, anticipation and insecurity is enough to break anyone. I was soon removed from my cell and brought into Court number one to face Judge Toner. The Courtroom was packed yet eerily silent. I had one quick scan around the room, and every eye was on me. It was a ghastly feeling. I lowered my head and focused my gaze to the floor. Conscious that my body language already made me look guilty, I jolted my head upright and tried to assume a look of confidence. Through the sea of scrutinising glares, Ma's bleary, tear-filled eyes stood out, almost demanding attention. She flashed me a conspicuous but comforting smile right before I sat beside Fitzgerald. Harrison and O'Leary sat on the opposite side of the room, facing the Judge's bench. Judge Toner emerged, settled himself into his seat, and we were ready to begin.

"Mr.Mills, since our last meeting I believe you have found Legal representation with a Mr.Fitzgerald, am I correct?" Asked Judge Toner.

"Yes, Judge." I replied.

"Detective Harrison, Detective O'Leary," Judge Toner began. "You've had sufficient time to carry out your investigation into this case. Can you please inform the Court of your findings since our last hearing?"

"Certainly Judge." Harrison replied. "Within the last week, Detective O'Leary and I have been able to link the accused to twelve cases of blackmail. As you will see, each case is strikingly similar to its predecessor. We have nine near-identical letters containing information and chat history between the accused's decoy profiles and the people he blackmailed. We will be able to prove that these letters all came from the accused. On top of that, we seized cash amounting to €41,670 in the accused's dwelling. We have photographs of a car that the accused rented to collect a payment. And also a letter addressed to the Gardaí, containing information of his most recent case, which we also found in his home,"

"Mr. Fitzgerald?" Judge Toner asked for a prompt response.

"Judge, If I could ask the Detectives where the nine letters were sent from?"

"Detective?" Judge Toner directed to Harrison.

"Judge, I don't see the importance of that question..." Harrison replied.

"Judge, if I may..." Fitzgerald interrupted. "My client lives in Dublin. Were all the nine letters sent from Dublin?"

"No, Judge" Harrison replied. "Eight of the letters have a different postmark. One was handed into Pearse Street Garda Station by a member of the public. However, we are confident that they all came from the accused."

"Judge, if the eight letters all came from different postcodes, they could have been sent by anyone." Fitzgerald claimed.

"Detective..." Judge Toner awaited Harrison's response.

"That may be true Judge. But we have proof that all the photographs used on each of the decoy profiles were downloaded by the accused."

"May I ask where exactly the photographs were downloaded from Judge?" Fitzgerald quizzed.

"The photographs were downloaded from a stock photo website." Harrison replied.

"A stock photo website Judge." Fitzgerald quipped. "These photographs are mainly used in the media for advertising purposes etc. If I want a picture of a sunset, I type it into this website, find the picture I want, pay to download it and use it how I please. The photographs downloaded from this website could have been used for anything. There is no direct link between these downloaded photographs and my client's involvement in this case."

"Judge," Harrison began his reply "To date, we have proof that the accused has used five of these photographs as profile pictures on a dating chatroom."

"So you can link only five of the twelve cases to the accused Detective?" Judge Toner asked.

"No Judge. We can link the accused to more than that. The five profiles on the chatrooms, the one profile that led to that ugly incident on Grafton Street," Harrison was interrupted by gentle giggling and soft whispers by members of the public gallery, at the back of the courtroom. Judge Toner cast a frowning look of disapproval towards the small pocket of people disrupting proceedings.

"The five chatroom profiles," Harrison repeated. "The well-publicised incident, and another meeting where the accused didn't show up."

"So seven of the twelve Detective? And what of the remaining five?" Asked Judge Toner.

"Judge, with the information that was sent to various Garda Stations throughout the Country, we can see that the remaining five profiles were created using a dating app. The chat logs have striking similarities to the ones directly relatable to the accused. There is no doubt in my mind they were sent by the same person." Harrison replied.

"And the origin of the remaining five profiles Judge?" Fitzgerald asked. "There is nothing to indicate that my client had anything to do with these five profiles. Can they be linked to my client's address, his phone number?"

"Judge, we have information from the phone carrier service that each of the five phone numbers used on the decoy profiles were mainly used in the Crumlin/Dublin 12 area."

"The Dublin 12 area Judge. A small area which includes Crumlin, Walkinstown, Bluebell, and Drimnagh. How could you possibly pin the five profiles to one person?" Fitzgerald questioned.

"Judge, taking into account the information we have on the chatroom profiles and the well-publicised incident, we can clearly see that the photographs used on each of those decoy profiles were all downloaded onto the accused's laptop computer. All the letters that were sent after he had been paid off by the people he blackmailed in chatrooms are identical to the letters sent after the cases on the dating app. I'm confident that after we have been given adequate time to investigate these matters, we will be able to prove they have come from the same person."Harrison finished.

"Ok, so my client had some pictures downloaded onto his computer," Fitzgerald started. "But you have no proof of exactly what he did with them. You say that the pictures were used for profiles on a dating app. Great. But these app's were on a mobile device not purchased or owned by my client. You have nothing to tie my client to these phones, apps or chat logs. You say the phones were primarily used in Dublin 12. But as I already explained, Dublin 12 is a big area with, at a guess, some twenty thousand people living there. Any information you have on these five dating app profiles are purely circumstantial. I would suggest that Detective Harrison and Detective O'Leary have thrown a rock in the air to hit someone guilty."

"Given time Judge I'm 100% positive that I can prove the accused was involved in the remaining five decoy profiles." Harrison hit back.

"On that note Judge, I have my doubts about my client's involvement in one of the other cases. Detective Harrison said my client was a no-show for one of the payoffs. Can Detective Harrison elaborate on that particular case?"

"Detective Harrison," Judge Toner directed at Harrison.

"I'm glad Mr.Fitzgerald brought this case into question Judge. This is a particularly sad incident. The person in question was contacted by a decoy profile," Harrison began.

"Judge If I may?" Fitzgerald interrupted.

"Go on Mr. Fitzgerald." Judge Toner replied.

"When this person was contacted. May I ask how? Was it a chatroom or app?" Fitzgerald asked. It was obvious to everyone why he asked that question. Everybody, including Harrison, knew where the conversation was going.

"Detective?" Asked Judge Toner.

"I believe it was an app Judge." Harrison replied. "But that doesn't take away from the severity of this case. The person in question never made it back to Dublin to payoff the accused. He committed suicide after a text was sent to him ordering him to pay up. The Gardaí in Drogheda discovered a text message on his phone ordering him back to Dublin and got us involved. It was a carbon copy of what had happened that Christmas, so we knew it had the accused written all over it. We waited for the accused to contact the deceased's phone again to arrange a meeting point. We waited there ready to arrest him."

"But he never showed up?" Fitzgerald asked.

"After the deceased phone rang I had no choice but to answer. I confirmed I was in the meeting spot and asked the person to describe what they were wearing."

"And? Detective?" Judge Toner impatiently asked.

"The person on the end of the phone gave me a description of himself and that person was promptly arrested. But it wasn't the accused. The person we apprehended was an innocent bystander," A quiet eruption of giggles and whispers filled the courtroom once more.

"I will not have such childishness in my Court." An irritated Judge Toner directed to the public gallery. "Continue please Detective."

"In my first interview with the accused, he stated that it was him at the other end of the phone. He said he didn't show up because he knew my voice was different from that of the deceased's. This clearly shows that he interacted with the deceased before that day."

"Mr. Fitzgerald?" Judge Toner asked Fitzgerald to respond.

"This profile was on a dating app Judge, which I have already shown casts doubt on the identity of the person behind it. No phone number linking my client to the profile. No evidence linking my client's computer to the profile. Any information sent to the Gardaí would, I assume, have been sent from outside Dublin."

"The accused has already confessed to having been at the scene Judge." Harrison stated.

"Judge, before we came to Court today my client couldn't confirm how many cases he was accused of being involved in. Let alone any specific details of any particular one. Might I remind the Court that my client was arrested very early in the morning on the day that he 'confessed' to being involved in this particular incident. My client was out of work for almost two years before his arrest and had no reason in recent times to be awake that early in the morning. I suggest he was confused and disorientated and had no idea of what exactly he was 'confessing' to."

"Judge, a man committed suicide because of the pressure he was under to pay €10,000 to the accused." Harrison was the first to mention a specific cash figure per case.

"€10,000?" Judge Toner repeated.

"Yes Judge, that is the figure that the alleged paedophile had to pay the accused. Believing their money would buy the accused's silence." Harrison informed Judge Toner.

"In the five cases that you can directly trace back to the accused, you have evidence that €10,000 was paid to him in each case Detective?" Judge Toner asked.

"Yes, Judge. And in the well-publicised case at Christmas, that fee was €30,000. The accused believed that he had snared three individuals at once, so he tripled the figure."

"And did he Detective? Did the accused snare three people at once?"

"Yes, Judge." Was Harrison's only reply.

"Can you elaborate Detective?"

"The investigation is ongoing and involves Europol. We apprehended the three individuals and have since found links to a paedophile ring in the U.K and mainland Europe." Harrison reluctantly confessed. Fitzgerald was content to allow the Court to fall silent. It seemed as if everybody in the Courtroom was taking a few moments to process what Harrison had just said.

"This is a very difficult and complex case," Judge Toner stated. "Detective Harrison, Detective O'Leary I thank you for your hard work in gathering your evidence in such a short space of time. I can only assume that upon completion of your investigation, a file will be sent to the DPP. Mr.Fitzgerald, your client will continue to be held on remand until he is served with a book of evidence from the DPP. The court is adjourned." With that Judge Toner began to leave the Judge's bench.

"What's happening?" I asked Fitzgerald.

"We can't go any further until we hear from the DPP," he replied.

"Is that a good thing?"

"It depends. If they find that there is enough evidence to get a conviction on all twelve counts, it's trouble. If they find that there's only enough evidence to convict you on five or six counts, its decision time?"

"Decision Time?" I asked.

"Guilty or Not Guilty. If you plead Not Guilty to the charges brought against you there will be a trial with a Judge and Jury. If you plead Guilty to the charges, there will be no trial, just a sentencing hearing".

"And what do you think will happen?"

"Nobody knows Michael. It all depends on the findings of the DPP."

"But how do you feel it went?"

"It went ok Michael. It could have been better, but it could have been a lot worse. I said everything I wanted to say and made every point I wanted to make. We have to play the waiting game now." I couldn't help but feel that Fitzgerald was somewhat dejected. He gave me the impression he didn't want to answer my questions. I felt he was disappointed with how it went.

There was no time for me to question Fitzgerald any further. The Guards approached me ready to escort me back to the holding cell.

"I'll be in touch as soon as I hear anything from the DPP. Best of luck Michael," were Fitzgerald's departing words.

Sitting in the cell waiting to go 'home' to Cloverhill, I couldn't help but think about the case. Fitzgerald made some encouraging points. 'Circumstantial evidence' was a new concept to me, but I liked the sound of it. Even though I committed the crimes, legally speaking they couldn't pin them on me. The photographs were on my laptop, but still had no link to the profiles on the app. Honestly, I believed that anyone would be able to see that the letters I sent to the Guards were near identical. I snared everyone in the same way, charged them the same amount and double-crossed the ones who paid me off. But once there is an ounce of doubt about who was behind the decoy profile, there was no Jury who could say it was definitely me.

Shortly before lunchtime, the door to the holding cell opened and the two Guards who escorted me into the Courthouse were waiting to load me back into the van and make the trip to Cloverhill. I shared the journey with three of the original prisoners who were in the van that morning. The van was started up and we began to make our way out of the Court grounds. The banging and crashing on the exterior erupted again. Whistles blowing, sirens blaring and a mob chanting echoed throughout the tiny cell. After about a minute of mayhem, we picked up speed which ended the furore. I gazed at the clouds rolling past the perspex window along the journey. Freedom felt so close but unattainable. Knowing full well the final destination, I wished that van journey would never end. There was something therapeutic about watching the sky flash past. It was nature in motion, something I had barely caught a glimpse of since my arrest. Arriving back at Cloverhill, I was content to retire to my cell and try to unwind after such a hectic day. One prisoner interrupted my solitude by coming into my cell and inquiring about my case...
"How'd ye get on Mick?"
"They're waiting to hear from the DPP." I answered.

"Ah right, pain in the bollix isn't it?" Before I had a chance to reply, my lacklustre interrogator vanished. "He's waiting on the DPP." I heard him cry on the landing. What followed next was a mixture of shouts and screams about who owed rollies to who, which included...

"Shane, you owe me 10 rollies. Pay up Sunshine!" "Fuck your rollies I won a pouch!" "Shut up sulkin' and put your money where your mouth is!"

My case was featured on the news that night, which resulted in another uproar.

"Gwan Mick ya mad whore" "Yer fuckin' famous man!" I watched the programme intensively, wanting to see what it looked like from the outside in. I was astonished to see about forty people outside the Courthouse. Some held banners reading 'Free Mick Mills'. Others were interviewed by reporters and posed for photographs. Footage of the prison van arriving was played. As soon as it was in sight, the supporters rushed the van and start pounding the exterior. It was incredible to think that people would actually support someone who was arrested for blackmail.

I couldn't sleep a wink that night. I fretted about what the DPP would find. Was there enough evidence to charge me with all twelve counts? Would they only charge me with five or six? And if so, what are my options? Guilty or Not Guilty. A Guilty plea to all twelve charges was out of the question. With the points Fitzgerald made in Court I wasn't going down without a fight. A Guilty plea to five or six charges? I wasn't sure. Accepting my fate could go in my favour in terms of how long I'd serve in prison. The negative side, I still faced a maximum sentence of fourteen years. I could do nothing until the DPP made a decision.

Much of the next few weeks were spent agonizing over every last detail of my case. The only thing that broke that train of thought was the visits. Ma came to see me every day she was allowed to and Da tagged along the odd time. They kept me up to speed with everything that was going on outside the four walls. Aido and Jumper came up to see me a few times too. It was great to have contact with people who cared for you. It really made me feel like I was never alone. The days and weeks rolled on while I waited to hear from Fitzgerald. It was only a matter of time before my faith would be sealed.

15. Guilty or Not Guilty

Tuesday 7th June 2011. First thing in the morning, I
received word that I would be meeting with Fitzgerald that
afternoon at 2:00 PM. If I thought the weeks leading up to
that meeting were excruciating, that day was worse by far.
I paced the landings while constantly checking the time. It
took me back to pacing around my house before I was
about to confront a paedophile. Reading or getting lost in
front of a telly were some of the ways of trying to occupy
myself. But nothing worked. My mind was fixated on the
meeting and wouldn't allow me to concentrate on anything
else. Finally, after what felt like a life sentence of its own,
a prison officer appeared at my cell.

"Mills, follow me." Was his way of escorting me to a
meeting room near the visitor's area. He opened the door
and upon entering the small room, I was greeted by
Fitzgerald who was already waiting for me.

"Jesus Michael, you look terrible." Were the first word's
out of his mouth.

"Thanks. Haven't been sleeping, everything's running
through my mind, ya know?" I answered him.

"Yea, yea. I can understand. well sit down and we'll get
straight to it."

I settled myself into a flimsy white plastic chair and
trembled in anticipation.

"The DPP has served you with a book of evidence. The
Investigation indicates that there is sufficient evidence to
get a conviction on six charges against you. Five of the six
charges are connected to the chatroom logs which were
recovered from your laptop computer. The sixth charge is
the one on Grafton Street where Detective Harrison and
Detective O'Leary can positively identify you at the scene.
All other charges against you were deemed to have
'insufficient evidence to prove beyond reasonable doubt'
that you were the person who set up the profiles. Basically,
Michael, the DPP is confident that a Jury will find you

Guilty on the six charges where you snared people via the chatrooms. All other charges via the dating app are off the table. It's as if they never happened. This includes 'Joe' who we both know committed suicide. It can only be a good thing that they can't trace that particular case back to you. As for 'Q', they found that he was a bit-part player in all the cases and will seek no further information on him or his whereabouts."

"Jesus Christ." I exhaled while lowering my head towards the table. Tears were streaming down my face. It was a lot of information to absorb. Twelve counts were reduced to six. They couldn't come near me for Joe or Q. I dared to allow myself to feel a hint of optimism.

"There is more Michael. 'Marty' from your first case, 'J.J' from your third, and 'Alan' from the case on Grafton Street, have all given a statement to Gardaí and are willing to testify against you at trial if needs be. Their version of events are near identical. All three say that they began conversing with a minor online. Arranged a meeting where they were instead confronted by yourself, and you demanded cash for your silence."

"Fuck," I muttered as the trace of optimism faded to a distant memory. "Even though they faced, or will face, prosecution for their own actions, they can still come to my trial and hang me? How is that possible? Did they make a deal with the Gardaí?"

"I don't know Michael, and to be quite honest with you, it's irrelevant. The fact is that there are three people who can positively identify you as the person who lured them into a meeting and demanded €10,000 from them. They have already given statements and are willing to stand as a witness for the prosecution."

"Bastards. So what happens next?"

"Typically speaking Michael, the case will be heard at the Circuit Criminal Court about three weeks from today. As I said to you the last time we met, it's decision time. If you indicate a Guilty plea you will be held on remand until your Court date is set. This Court date will be a sentencing hearing where a Judge will determine how long you spend in prison. Indicate a plea of 'Not Guilty' and the trial will begin with a Judge and Jury."

"What do you think is best?"

"Well Michael, they have all the evidence they need to get a conviction on the six charges brought against you. They have the chat logs and a large amount of cash. They have proof that you rented a car and altered the registration plate to pick up cash. And both Detectives were at the scene on Grafton Street. On top of this, they also have three of your victims who are willing to give evidence. The only thing going in your favour in relation to the six charges is the fact that you got convictions against the men you snared. But that doesn't take away from the fact that you blackmailed these men. You still committed a crime, and these crimes are punishable by up to fourteen years imprisonment. As your legal representative, I would advise that you plead Guilty to the six charges. At least that way you are admitting what you did was wrong, and it will be seen that you are co-operating with the Gardaí and the DPP."

"How long do you think I'd get if I plead Guilty?"

"It's hard to say, Michael. With a Guilty plea, it's up to the Judge on the day. All that you will have in your defence is your final mitigation. This means that we can put your story forward and hope that the Judge will sympathise with your situation. The fact that you were abused as a child, you went 'off the rails' and spent some time in St.Patricks. But after that, you were doing well until the break up of your marriage. That's when you began to drink heavily and everything fell to pieces. You were angry and needed someone to blame. Our only hope would be that the Judge would take some pity on you and hand down a more lenient sentence. But there's still no guarantee this will work. In my personal opinion, I can't see any Judge giving you less than five years. Ten would be harsh, but that's only my opinion, it's completely up to the Judge on the day."

"At least five years? Fuck me!" The severity of the whole situation finally dawned on me.

"That's only my opinion, Michael. But there are other aspects of your sentence to think about. Whatever sentence you receive, you can reduce it while serving it. They look favourably on prisoners who use their time inside wisely. There are a number of courses you can do to prove that you will be ready to re-join society in a productive manner once you are released. You can further reduce your sentence with good behaviour. No matter what sentence you get, you can always proactively work towards reducing it."

We discussed the whole situation in some finer detail, but the outcome was always the same. In Fitzgerald's opinion, a Guilty plea was the best way to go. He explained that in Circuit Criminal Court he would no longer be speaking directly to the Judge. This would be done by a Barrister. I had no idea how the whole procedure worked so I had to take Fitzgerald's word for it. He recommended a Barrister and gave me his contact details. The state does not cover Barrister fees, so my family would have to make their own arrangements to pay him. I'm sure that would delight Da. My 'legal team' would then prepare my final mitigation and deliver it to the Judge. That was of course if I pleaded Guilty. Plead Not Guilty and I'd face a complete trial. A Judge and jury would examine all evidence, listen to statements from both the prosecution and defence and make a final ruling. My head was all over the place. Fitzgerald left me with a copy of the book of evidence to read over and told me to contact him with my final decision as soon as possible. I was escorted back to my cell and lay on the bed trying to figure out my next move. The ceiling seemed to be lowering towards me in an uncomfortable, claustrophobic way. Covering my eyes with the palm of my hands did nothing to escape the reality that I had at least five years of this ahead of me, according to Fitzgerald.

Harrison and O'Leary crossed my mind. I wondered how they were feeling. They must have been disappointed that I only faced six of the twelve charges. Harrison knew I was at the scene to meet Joe at the G.P.O. But he didn't physically see me there and couldn't prove it was me on the phone. I'm sure that drove him crazy. After another sleepless night mulling over every possible outcome, my decision was made.

The hush of the early morning was interrupted by Cloverhill slowly erupting to life.

Footsteps pounding the landings. Cell doors being unlocked. Shouting and whaling echoing the cellblock as breakfast was served. It was an all too familiar sound that I may as well get accustomed to. Ma was due to visit that morning, I'd have to break the news to her.

She arrived alone. I was glad she was alone.

"Fitzgerald was up with me yesterday Ma." I told her.

"Yea? And what did he say?"

"I face six counts out of twelve. The DPP has decided that there's not enough evidence to convict me on all twelve charges." Her eyes lit up.

"That's great news. So only half of the cases?"

"Yea Ma. But I'm still facing at least five years according to Fitzgerald." Her wide excited eyes almost suddenly welled up. She turned her head away and tried to hide her face from me.

"It's all right Ma. Even if I get five years I could be out in two with good behaviour." I lied. She looked back towards me and gave me a faint smile.

"Did you do the twelve of them, Michael?"

"Yea Ma".

"€120,000 you conned people out of? If you needed money you should have come to us!" She said as if my Ma and Da had the kind of money to keep the bank off my back.

"I know Ma, but there's no point in talking about that now. What's done is done and we have to move on from here. I want you to do me a favour Ma. Ring Fitzgerald when you go home and tell him I'm pleading Guilty to the six charges."

"Jesus are you sure love?"

"Yea. It's the only way out. They have all they need to convict me, there's no point in dragging everyone through a trial. It could be worse, I could have faced all twelve counts."

"But what if...."

"MA". I interrupted her. "I've been awake all night going over everything. Guilty is the only way forward. Ring Fitzgerald and tell him I'm pleading Guilty. It's my final decision."

"Ok love, if you're sure."

It broke my heart to tell her that, and I'm sure it broke hers to hear it. Her only son was facing a good stretch in prison no matter what happened.

16. My fate in his hands

Ma followed through with my instructions and told Fitzgerald I was pleading Guilty to the six charges against me. A few days later, he came back to Cloverhill to have me sign the Guilty pleas. There he explained that the Barrister he recommended was named Turlough McAdam S.C (Senior Counsel). I accepted Fitzgerald's recommendation on the basis that I didn't fully understand how the whole Court process transpired. Fitzgerald tried to clear the confusion.

"The prosecution evidence will be given by Detective Harrison and Detective O'Leary as they are now witnesses for the prosecution." He started. "They will be lead through the evidence by counsel for the DPP. McAdam will be given the opportunity to cross-examine both Harrison and O'Leary to elicit any information that may assist your defence. McAdam will then address the Court in mitigation. Here he will explain your actions and why you committed the crimes you did. He will explore your background, including your history of sexual abuse. I will warn you, Michael, it won't be easy to listen to. But anything we can present to the Court to try and make your crimes appear less serious is an attempt to obtain a more lenient sentence."

After the papers were signed and I was given a crash-course in Court proceedings, Fitzgerald said that he would 'get the ball rolling' from there. He called me two days after the meeting to inform me the Court date had been set for June 30th, 2011.

I had one sit down meeting with both Fitzgerald and McAdam, about two weeks before the trial. McAdam was a tall but heavyset man in his fifties. He towered over Fitzgerald as they both entered the meeting room I was already waiting in. He was bald on top and had grey hair covering the back of his head from ear to ear. His well-spoken, almost over pronounced words seemed to echo inside his puffy cheeks before exiting his mouth. He spoke with 'marbles in his mouth' as Ma would always say. My first impression of him was that he was quite a likable person. He never spoke down to me or tried to make me feel inferior. The meeting lasted about an hour. When McAdam and Fitzgerald felt they had everything they needed, they left. I wouldn't see them again until my final Court date.

June 30th, 2011, the morning of my sentencing hearing finally arrived. As strange as it might sound, I sat on my bed early that morning feeling a huge sense of relief. In one way, the waiting, sleepless nights, worry and heartache was coming to an end. But in another, it was only beginning. My Trial was to be heard at 11:00 AM. Shortly after 9:00 AM I was escorted to the check-in desk and placed in a holding cell waiting to be transported to Court. I was given breakfast but couldn't manage a bite. My stomach was in knots. I managed to drink half a cup of orange juice and that would have to suffice until after my hearing. The door to the holding cell eventually swung open and Prison Officer Sullivan entered. Sullivan had a straight-laced, 'do it by the book' mentality. He removed his hat, something I never saw him do before and tucked it under his arm. He leaned one shoulder against the cell wall, appearing awkward and out of place.

"Michael." He started in a dull Dublin tone. "We've got word from the Courthouse that there are a number of people outside who've shown up to support you. Some forty or fifty people strong we hear. The Media are present too. TV, papers, radio the works. The Gardaí have roadblocks in place near the Courthouse to ensure we get to Court without incident. I'm letting you know this in case you hear extra sirens or people banging on the side of the van. Is that ok Michael?"

"Grand. Yea."

"Ok so. We'll be on our way any minute now. Best of luck son."

"Thanks."

Sullivan placed his hat back on, turned and exited the cell. He nodded to his colleagues waiting outside, that was the signal to handcuff me and bring me to the van. I was escorted into one of the lockable confession boxes once more. For this trip, I was the only prisoner in the back of the van. My only travelling companion was a clear plastic bag containing everything from my cell in Cloverhill. It was packed up in the driver's compartment, ready to escort me to my new dwelling after the sentencing hearing. We crawled and manoeuvered our way out of Cloverhill on our way to Court. Along the approximate twenty-minute journey, I listened to the gentle hum of the engine increase or decrease as our speed followed suit. I allowed my body to lazily sway with every turn and bump along the road. My mind was in a daze. At times it felt as if I were on the outside looking at a prison van bashfully sitting among civilized vehicles in traffic. The droning of distant sirens grew louder as we were inevitably lured in by their call. I was snapped out of my daze by the now familiar sound of people attacking the van. The screaming, shouting, and pounding seemed to last longer than before. Indicating that more people than ever showed up to the Courthouse. Eventually, the van came to a halt inside the court grounds. I was ushered from my transport cell into a holding cell, in the basement of the Courthouse. Fitzgerald came to see me shortly before my hearing started.
"Morning Michael, still having trouble sleeping I see."
The bearer of compliments as always.
"Yea. A lot going through my mind."
"Completely understandable." He said with a sympathetic smile. "I'm here to give you a general briefing on what will happen in there. The Judge over the case is his Honour Judge Simon Flynn. I'll be honest with you Michael and say that I'm not one hundred percent happy with this. Judge Flynn is close to retirement and very old school. I would be a lot more comfortable with a slightly younger Judge. One who is more 'in tune' with modern technology such as chat rooms and the like. But in saying

that he is known to be a very fair Judge. Nine times out of ten the punishment matches the crime."

"Wonderful." I sarcastically replied.

"Chin up Michael! The support outside cannot be ignored. The media coverage is mostly favourable, the people are on your side. They see you as someone who set out to protect children, let's hope Judge Flynn sees it that way too."

"Are my Ma and Da out there?"

"They are. And they're holding up well. Your friends Adrian and 'Jumper' are outside also. I was introduced to a ton of your aunts, uncles, and cousins too. Everyone has your back, we're all rooting for you."

"And McAdam?"

"Turlough is all set and ready to go. You'll be brought in to Court soon Michael. As usual, stand when prompted to do so and speak only if spoken to. I doubt you'll need to say a word, so sit and let myself and Turlough take care of things. I'll see you in there Michael." Fitzgerald outstretched his right hand to shake mine. He almost pulled my arm out of my socket while shaking my hand.

Shortly after our brief encounter, it was finally time to face the music. I was escorted from my basement holding cell up to the entrance to Court Number three. The door to the Court opened slowly and I could feel every eye boring a hole through my body. 'Look down, look guilty. Look up, look overconfident'. I said to myself as I walked towards Fitzgerald and McAdam. I picked a spot on the wall in front of me and stared at it intensely, desperately trying not to make eye contact with anyone. I settled in beside McAdam and he gave me a jovial "Good Morning Michael." His bald head was covered by a comical grey wig and he wore an intimidating black grown. Fitzgerald sat facing McAdam and me, he gave me a wink as our eyes met. I glanced past McAdam to see the prosecution side. Harrison and O'Leary sat beside a wigged and caped barrister like I did. A solicitor sat facing them also.

"All Rise." Was the order that broke the deafening silence. The sound of a packed Courtroom shuffling to get to their feet filled the air.

"Case Number 433 on June 30th, 2011. His Honour Judge Simon Flynn presiding." Judge Flynn made his appearance. He was a small man to begin with. With age, his body was beginning to bend forward, as if his spine was giving up long before the rest of him. At a guess, I'd say he was mid-seventies. His grey wig was longer on the sides than McAdam's but looked as ridiculous. A neatly framed pair of glasses sat perched at the end of Judge Flynn's nose. He used them to examine the documents in front of him. When he spoke, his head didn't move an inch, only his eyes would re-adjust and focus on the person he was addressing. He gave you that look that a schoolteacher would give you if you misbehaved in class. A sharp stare over the glasses was enough to stop any child in their tracks. I guess that's why his body was bent forward. Decades of leaning forward to read documents and not readjusting his body afterwards had taken its toll.

"You may be seated." Was our next instruction. The sound of the packed Courtroom all sitting in unison was as if somebody played a recording of us all standing in reverse. The prosecution started by calling Detective Harrison to the stand. He was asked to point me out in the Courtroom and from there he was lead through all the evidence they had on me. Chat logs, photographs of the registration plate on the rented car. The letters I sent to the Guards, everything. He positively identified me at the scene on Harry Street on December 23rd, 2010. Detective O'Leary was next to the stand and he pretty much repeated Harrison's testimony word for word.

McAdam was then given a chance to cross-examine both Harrison and O'Leary respectively. But there wasn't much he could do. They had all the evidence found on my laptop. The taped up registration was linked to my address and my driving license. A large amount of cash was found in my house and both Harrison and O'Leary could positively identify me from the incident on Harry Street. The cross-examination was a very short exercise. One which didn't seem to change the course of events one way or another.

"Mr.McAdam you now have the opportunity to deliver your final mitigation in defence of Mr.Mills. Please proceed." Judge Flynn ordered McAdam, from his statuesque pose at his Judges bench. Judge Flynn didn't waste any time.

"Thank you, Judge." McAdam started. "As I'm sure you are aware, this is a very complicated, delicate and unique case brought before this Court. My client has pleaded Guilty to the six charges brought against him. He knows what he has done is wrong, immoral and illegal. He is here to face the consequences of his actions. But let me assure you that Mr.Mills is not a man of malice or hatred. He is simply a product of his own personal history. Mr.Mills grew up in the suburb of Crumlin in Dublin twelve, he has spent all of his life there. He had a normal childhood of going to school, playing football with his friends, and getting into mischief as any boy that age would. But at nine years of age life as he knew it changed for good. On his father's persuasion, Mr.Mills began taking music lessons from a social acquaintance of his fathers. My client's mother would walk him to the house of his music mentor every Wednesday evening and pick him up one hour later. Everything was fine at first and Mr.Mills quite enjoyed learning different songs on guitar and tin whistle. But a few months in, his teacher began to molest him. The touching and kissing advanced until the terrified young boy was groomed or shown how to masturbate and perform oral sex on his attacker. My client was sworn to secrecy. Threatened that if he told anybody what was going on between him and his music teacher, nobody would believe him. He'd be taken away from his family, so his lies couldn't hurt them anymore. Mr.Mills was a boy of eleven years old the first time he was sodomised."

McAdam stopped speaking briefly as if to let the Court digest what they had heard. It wasn't easy to sit there and listen to McAdam tell a room full of strangers what happened to me. But if it was all to help me get a more lenient sentence I was prepared to let him say all he could. "My Client was raped a countless amount of times in the space of five years." McAdam stated, interrupting the silence he had cast upon the Courtroom.

"The abuse continued on a weekly basis for the same period of time. Every Wednesday at 7:00 PM my client's mother would walk her son to the house of his attacker. Sometimes my client would learn how to play new songs, other times he'd be molested. The abuse only stopped when my client's attacker died suddenly and unexpectedly. Mr.Mills refused to attend his attackers funeral. He did not want to show any respect to the man that had been abusing him for years. Mr.Mills's father insisted that he attend the funeral and play his abuser's favourite song as he was being carried out of the church. This was the final straw for my client. He broke down and told his parents exactly what had been going on for the previous five years. The news was met with shock and disbelief. How could they be so foolish to allow their son to be abused for so long? Why couldn't they see the signs? And worse still was the fact that my clients years of abuse would go unpunished. His abuser died before anybody found out exactly the kind of person he was. And there was nothing anyone could do about it."

The burden of the guilt and the shame of what had happened to my client certainly took its toll. At the age of fourteen, my client began drinking and experimenting with drugs. He mixed with the 'wrong crowd' and was involved in minor criminality such as shoplifting and vandalism. His criminal activities advanced to stealing cars and joyriding. At the age of fifteen, my client was sentenced to sixteen months in St.Patricks Institute. It was there that my client focused his attention to woodwork. He excelled at it and found peace of mind by constructing items such as birdhouses and various types of cabinets. Upon his release from St.Patricks, my client's Great Uncle George secured him a carpentry apprenticeship. George put a lot of trust in my client. He went as far as getting a loan to buy a car so that my client would have transportation to complete his apprenticeship. Of course, everybody thought George was throwing his money away. Buying a convicted joyrider a car was obviously a recipe for disaster. But George would reply "I know Michael won't let me down." And Michael never did. He worked hard and completed his apprenticeship with distinction. Proving George right, and everybody else wrong. My client well and truly put his criminal past behind him. In the coming years, he would marry a local girl, buy a house on Kildare Road, Crumlin and prepare to start a family. But his dream of living a quiet, simple life, was about to take another drastic turn."

It was a strange experience listening to a virtual stranger narrate your life in front of a Judge. I knew what he was saying was true and I knew what he was about to say next, but it seemed as if he was talking about someone else. "In the space of eighteen months, my client's life fell to pieces. A close friend of his rang my client one day and requested to meet him at a local bar. This wasn't uncommon for the two friends to do this so my client thought nothing of it. But when Mr.Mills met his friend he knew that something was wrong. His friend confessed to Mr.Mills that he had seen his wife in a hotel with another man. But not just any man. A childhood friend of them both. The man in question even stood as a groomsman at my client's wedding. Mr.Mills waited for the punchline to this elaborate joke, but it never came. Upon confronting his wife with this information, she confessed that it was all true. She had been having an affair for a number of months with his close friend. She told my client that after six years of marriage she didn't love him anymore. She wanted to end the marriage and continue her relationship with her new lover. She left the house she had purchased with Mr.Mills and took his trust, confidence, and hope along with her. Mr.Mills was alone and his future looked bleak. He began to drink heavily to try and cope with the situation he found himself in. Over time he lost his job as a result of his drinking. His mortgage lender was in contact. With no income, Mr.Mills had fallen into arrears. He was alone, angry and desperate, and needed someone to blame. His decision at that point in his life led us all to be in this Courtroom today. Although my client accepts that he is Guilty of the charges brought against him. I would like to present to the Court the reasons behind Mr.Mills's actions and the positive impact he has had on many peoples lives in recent times. I know it sounds preposterous that a person's crimes can have positive elements. But I hope to show the Court there is a method to my madness as we delve deeper into the six cases brought against my client."

McAdam closed a folder on the desk in front of him and opened another. It was as if he had finished his starter at a meal and he was about to begin his main course. "Paedophiles require two main elements to fulfill their sexual desires. Power and secrecy. Take away one or both of these elements and where does it leave them? Without power, there is no control. Without secrecy, they face the full wrath of the law. Mr.Mills decided to use a paedophile's core strengths against them, and they had no option but to play by his rules. The first decoy profile my client set up was 'Erica-Iz-New'. Although it stated she was eighteen on her profile, my client made it absolutely clear that Erica was fourteen to any person who contacted her. A fifty-six-year-old married man from North Dublin with the screen name 'Marty216', took a very keen interest in Erica. He knew from the beginning that she was fourteen, and felt there was no issue in conversing with her. The conversation turned sexual, and within a few days of messaging and texting Erica, a meeting was arranged. Marty216 sent Erica explicit pictures of his penis before they met. He booked a hotel room near the city centre. He purchased two bottles of wine and a bunch of flowers for Erica. On the day he was supposed to meet a fourteen-year-old girl and take her virginity, he was instead confronted by my client.

Mr.Mills made it clear to Marty216 that he was, in fact, the person behind 'Erica's' profile and that there was no fourteen-year-old girl. Mr.Mills showed all of the chat logs, text messages and pictures that Marty216 sent to Erica. He realised he was in trouble. It was then that my client offered Marty216 a way out. Option one, Marty216 could go to the Gardaí himself and face the legal consequences of his actions. Option two, Marty216 could pay my client €10,000 and nobody would ever find out about the whole situation. The power was now in my client's hands, he had turned the tables on this alleged paedophile and he had nowhere to hide. Go to the Gardaí and ruin his marriage, career, and reputation. Or pay €10,000 and nobody ever finds out. Marty216 chose to pay. About one week on from their first meeting, a second meeting was set up in order for the money to exchange hands. My client drove away from the meeting with €10,000 in his pocket. His idea had gone exactly according to plan. My client could have accepted his profit and give no more thought to Marty216. But his conscience wouldn't allow it. Mr.Mills sent every piece of information he had gathered on Marty to the Gardaí. From there, an investigation would be launched.

All six of the charges against my client worked exactly the same way. Set up a decoy profile, engage in conversation with an adult. Arrange to meet with that adult with the intent of sexual relations. Confront the person with all the evidence against them, and give them the option of going to the Gardaí or paying for anonymity. In total my client collected more than €45,000 from the six individuals he interacted with using fake profiles. It could have been more. But at one of the meetings where Mr.Mills was to be paid off, Detective Harrison and Detective O'Leary were waiting at the scene. My client's only way out? Create a distraction big enough to allow him the opportunity to escape. Mr.Mills knocked the cash from Detective Harrison's hands. An incident which was well publicised around Christmas time 2010.

And there we have it. This is why we are all here today. My client lured six paedophiles into a trap, blackmailed them and then double-crossed them. But what if Mr.Mills never made a decoy profile? These individuals would have still been on the internet seeking out the attention of minors. How many children did my client stop from being physically and psychologically abused? We may never have an answer to that question. But one thing is for certain. If Mr.Mills never demanded money from the people he met online, we would not be standing here. Instead, I believe Mr.Mills would receive some form of award for the work he did. He single-handedly has removed very dangerous people from society. If they did not receive a custodial sentence, at least now, they are on the radar of the Gardaí. In the first case brought against my client, Marty216 is now serving an eight-year prison sentence for the charges that were brought against him. Eight years. He was also placed on the Sex Offenders Register indefinitely. My client's findings also gave a former victim of Marty's the courage to come forward and express the abuse, her uncle, Marty216 subjected her to when she was a child. The second case whose screen name was 'Dr. Octave' received a prison sentence of eighteen months with the last six months suspended. He was already on the Sex Offenders Register when arrested. Profile number three, screen name 'J.J_38'. He received a six month suspended sentence and was placed on the Sex Offenders Register for three years. Profile four, screen name 'Denis.Mac'. Denis received a twelve month suspended sentence and was placed on the Sex Offenders Register for a duration of two years.

Profile five, screen name 'AllThatYouWant'. Unfortunately, I am limited to what I can say about this case as the investigation is ongoing. All that I am permitted to say is that the investigation involves a paedophile ring that stretches as far as the U.K and into mainland Europe. Europol is currently leading the investigation. This is all a direct result of my client's decoy account." McAdam rotated his body and outstretched his left arm proudly towards me, to emphasize his latest point.

"Profile number six, the final case brought against Mr.Mills. Screen name 'Cathal_Canz' received an eighteen month suspended sentence and was placed on the Sex Offenders Register for five years. All six individuals were arrested due to the findings of Mr.Mills. In each case, these six men were fully aware that they had arranged to meet a minor for sexual interaction. Had Mr.Mills not set up a single decoy profile, these individuals would be online trying to make contact with children. Mr.Mills dragged them from the shadows of the darkest corners of society and cast them into the spotlight. In doing so he exposed these individuals for who they truly are. Gone was their power. Gone was their secrecy. Once their main attributes were taken away from them, they could do nothing but face the consequences of their actions.

Judge, my client sits before you not only as a man who has pleaded Guilty to the charges brought against him. But he is also a victim of abuse. When his life began to unravel before his eyes he became angry and needed someone to blame. His past will never leave him. The abuse he suffered as a child can never be forgotten. My client decided to vent his frustrations on the very people who were the cause of so much suffering in his own life. Paedophiles. He lured them in, blackmailed them and then double-crossed them. But as I have already said, he could have accepted their payments and thought no more of it. But instead, he sent everything he found to the Gardaí. With this information, six people stood before a Judge. Two of them received prison sentences. Three received suspended sentences and one will learn his faith in the coming months. These six individuals will find it increasingly difficult to re-offend without the intervention of the Gardaí.

My client is a good man, and he has already proved that he has the ability to 'bounce back' from making bad decisions. Upon leaving St.Patricks Institute as a young man of seventeen, he proved to himself and others that he had the ability to reform and become a respectable member of society. I conclude my mitigation by stating that I have no doubt whatsoever that Mr.Mills will reform once again and become the well-respected person he once was. Thank you, Judge."

McAdam took his seat. He looked relaxed and seemed content with the speech he delivered. He didn't look or speak to Fitzgerald, he just sat there looking up at Judge Flynn. My body was pulsating in unison with every beat of my heart. I knew what was coming next.

"Thank you Mr.McAdam." Said, Judge Flynn. "Mr.Mills, firstly I want to say that I sympathise with your situation. No child should ever endure the abuse you suffered in your formative years. It was harrowing to hear. But my sympathy does not take away from the fact that you committed a crime. As Mr.McAdam stated in his mitigation, you had the opportunity not to demand money from your victims. If you forwarded the information you gathered to the Gardaí, you would not be standing here today. It was your greed and personal vengeance that was the driving force behind your criminal activities. You demanded €10,000 to stay away from the Gardaí collecting at least €45,000 in the process. And what about the money you didn't collect? The incident on Grafton Street for instance. It is my understanding that the sum of money you demanded in that particular case was €30,000. You were almost apprehended at that point Mr.Mills. But in order to evade arrest, you struck the cash from the hands of Detective Harrison. €30,000 was sent raining down on Dublin's busiest shopping street at the busiest time of year. Your actions that night were reckless and careless. People were hurt and you made a mockery of the Gardaí and the Detectives at the scene.

No man is above the law Mr.Mills. Nobody has the right to act in the manner you have. Although the men you targeted have faced the consequences of their actions, the ways and means you went about achieving their convictions are totally wrong. We as a nation cannot have our citizens making up laws and rules as they deem fit. With your sentencing Mr.Mills, I must also keep in mind that I want to deter any other person from following in your footsteps and building upon the foundations you have laid. Mr.Mills, I hereby sentence you to six years imprisonment for the crimes you have committed. Twelve months for each case to run consecutively. I have taken your Guilty plea into account and the fact that you cooperated with the Gardaí once you were arrested. Detective Harrison, Detective O'Leary thank you for your inexhaustible efforts in bringing Mr.Mills to Justice. Mr.McAdam, Mr.Fitzgerald thank you for the service you have provided for the Court."

Six years. I wasn't quite sure what to think about it. In hindsight, I suppose it wasn't too bad. It could have been fourteen, so in that sense, I got off lightly. What if they charged me on all twelve counts? Would that mean I would have got twelve years? Thank God for circumstantial evidence. Being led out of the Courtroom, I glanced over my shoulder. Ma was crying hysterically. Da had his arm around her, I couldn't remember the last time I saw them make physical contact. The door to my holding cell slammed shut behind me and sent a swirling echo throughout the confined room. I may as well get used to it. Mayfield Prison was to be my new home. I didn't know very much about it at the time, but we had six years to get acquainted. Sitting on the bed in the holding cell, I heard the door being opened. Detective O'Leary was first to enter, followed shortly by Harrison.

"Ye alright Mick?" O'Leary said as he presented his right hand to me.

"I think so." I answered as I stood up to shake his hand.

"It was a good chase son, but I always get my man."
Harrison piped in. He delivered that line with such an air
of complacency. The right corner of his mouth was
smiling, the left corner didn't budge. It was a strange
forced half smile that he wanted me to see.
"Six years isn't so bad Michael, with good behaviour, you
could be out in three or four. Chin up and best of luck!"
O'Leary said. Harrison nodded but didn't make another
sound.

They were gone as quickly as they entered. It was a
strange and awkward meeting. O'Leary was genuine when
he wished me luck. I guess Harrison came to see me to rub
my nose in it. He 'got his man' and wanted to gloat. Soon
after, I was transferred from the holding cell into the
prison van. Unlike any of my other trips to or from Court,
this time two Guards on Motorbikes escorted the van out
of the Court grounds with sirens blaring. I suppose they
were trying to act as a deterrent to the people waiting
outside. But it didn't work. The thundering blows on the
exterior were worse than ever. The van rocked from side to
side as it inched onto the road and tried to find space. It
was terrifying. Although the people responsible were there
to support me, it felt like I had been convicted of murder
and everybody was trying to get at me to deliver their own
form of Justice. Eventually, we picked up speed until the
sirens grew louder than the chants of the agitated mob.
Before long, I was well on my way to Mayfield Prison.

17. A L2 6

I've been inside for almost ten months now. Mayfield
Prison is Ireland's newest 'State of the Art' prison. It sits
on a two hundred and ten acre-site on the Dublin/Wicklow
border. Mayfield consists of three identical Prison Blocks,
A, B, and C. They sit parallel to one another and each
contains three floors with eleven cells either side. At max
capacity, each floor can house forty-four prisoners and
each Block can house one hundred and thirty-two
prisoners. Mayfield has a total maximum capacity of four
hundred and twenty but for the most part, the actual figure
is under four hundred.

On my first day here, at the check-in desk, located in
the Admin Block, I was asked if I knew anyone already
detained in the prison who might help 'get me settled'.
After telling the prison officer no, his next question was if
I was a tradesman. Hearing I was a carpenter, he suggested
putting me to work in the maintenance division or helping
out in the woodwork class. But having worked at the one
profession all my adult life I suggested learning something
new. He nodded in agreement and said,
"As soon as you get adjusted I'm sure you'll find
something that sparks your interest. Let us know, and we'll
see if there's an opening in that field."
I have since learned that the Admin Block also houses the
main security room, the camera Room, the isolation units,
the medical units, all the holding cells and the visitation
hall. After spending about an hour going through the
administration routine of paperwork and getting my photo
taken, it was finally time to be escorted to my cell. 'A L2
6' was the order of a supervisor in the Admin Block. Two
prison officers led me out of the Admin Building, down a
seemingly endless corridor. The smell of fresh paint told
me that the lime walls were recently coated. The blue
Industrial type floor reflected the fluorescent lights
hanging above. Our footsteps echoed throughout the

empty hallway as a door to my left read 'Kitchen/Bakery'. A door to my right read 'Education/Recreation'. We continued straight ahead and entered the security area of Cell Block B. To the left, behind a metal security gate, is the corridor leading to Cell Block C, and to the right is the corridor leading to Cell Block A. 'A L2 6' was repeated to the prison officers in Cell Block B and they opened the electronic gates leading to Cell Block A.

The first time stepping into Cell Block A was daunting. Prisoners on the ground floor stared as I was led into the block. On the two landings above, bodies leaned over the guardrails desperately trying to get a glimpse at their new resident. I kept my head down and tried my best not to lock eyes with anyone. I was escorted up a metal staircase in the middle of the ground floor and we made our way to the second landing. 'A L2 6' finally made sense. Cell Block A, landing number 2, cell number 6. I don't have the luxury of having my own cell in Mayfield, this one I have to share. A bulky man of about 6'2 was waiting in the cell to greet me. I guessed he was in his mid-fifties. He looked like a stereotypical biker, his grey hair was pulled back and tied in a ponytail. A grey, unkept, wispy beard grew from his face. I've since told him that he looks like Santa Clause's evil twin, although I didn't dare say that to him the first time we met. He stood up to greet me and welcome me to my new abode.

"Are you Mills?" He asked.

"I am." I replied.

"Put her there son." He threw out his right hand to shake mine. When I shook his hand he grabbed me in closer and patted me hard on the back with his left hand.

"They call me 'Barreller'. Welcome to hell." The prison officers left and instructed Barreller to help me find my feet. I quizzed my new cellmate on his peculiar nickname.

"It's my weapon of choice, a double-barreled shotgun. I'm in for armed robbery. In my trade, most people choose a smaller shooter, something that they can hide. But I've always used a double barreller. The end of each of the barrels is roughly the same circumference as the human eyeball. Stick that in someone's face and they're bound to do whatever you tell them. It's more threatening than a little cowboy gun."

I suppose you can't argue with that logic. Me and Barreller get along well, we stay out of each other's way and help one and other when we can. I've since heard why Barreller is really in Mayfield, although I've never heard it from the horse's mouth. Yes, he's an armed robber, but what he tried to rob was a cash in transit van. He acted alone but never did his homework. The van he tried to rob was on its way back to the depot having made all it's deliveries that morning. Barreller is doing time for trying to rob an empty van. Some of the other lads give him stick about it, but I keep my mouth shut. He's alright with me, so why rock the boat.

"You're a fuckin' genius," Barreller said to me.

"I am?"

"Yea, what you did son is nothing short of a stroke of genius. Made money but at the same time taking pervs off the street. Six years is harsh in my book. They shoulda let you go."

"I wish, but as the Judge said, it was my 'personal greed' that I got punished for."

"Fuckin' Judges. What do they know about the real world?"

That first-night Barreller filled me in on the day to day routines of prison life in Mayfield. We would be 'banged out' at 7:30 PM every night. Banged out means being locked into your cell for the night. You would be awakened at 8:00 AM the following morning and breakfast would be served between 8:00 AM and 9:00 AM. Contrary to what most people believe, there is no dining hall or cafeteria in prison. There's no way that any prison would want over four hundred prisoners congregated in one place at the same time. It doesn't make sense. Instead, every meal is served in your Cell Block. It's wheeled in from the kitchen in stainless steel transport carts. Landing number three is always the first to get served. They make their way down the staircases, queue to be served, and then return to their cells where they are locked in. This procedure is then repeated for landing two and then landing one. Every prisoner is locked in their cells for every meal time. After you're given thirty minutes to consume your food, the same sequence repeats. Landing three return their trays, dishes, etc to the canteen staff and head back to their cells. The same thing happens for landing two then landing one. Lunch at 12:30 PM and Dinner at 3:30 PM work exactly the same way. At 9:00 AM every prisoner is released from their cell. Those who have jobs around the prison head off to work, those who don't are left to their own devices, hanging around the landings.

In my early days as a prisoner, I would seek permission to gain access to the library, located in the Education/Recreation (Ed/Rec) building where I could lose myself in fiction. As the library is located in a different area of the prison, your access to it is at the discretion of the Acting Chief Officer (A.C.O). The A.C.O is the highest ranking Officer in each Cell Block. If you stepped out of line in any way the A.C.O has the right to revoke your access to the Ed/Rec building. If you commit a serious offence, the A.C.O can recommend further punishments to the Governor. These include loss of visitations rights and phone privileges. For more serious offences he can request that you spend some time in solitary confinement. The A.C.O of Block A is Mr.Martin, a straight-talking, no-nonsense skinny man in his fifties. 'What Martin says goes' is a much-repeated phrase within Block A. Some prison officers use it to deflect decision making away from themselves and put it back on Mr.Martin. I can't blame them really, there are not a lot of prisoners who will choose to go toe to toe with our authoritative A.C.O.

To this day I have a good relationship with Mr.Martin. I never give him any unnecessary headaches, and he returns the favour. After breakfast, he would always see to it that I was escorted to the library. I first had to leave Cell Block A and gain access to the security area in Cellblock B. From there I entered the corridor that connects the Admin building to the Cellblocks. The Ed/Rec building is about halfway up this corridor on the left. The building itself looks a lot similar to a Cellblock, although slightly shorter in length. Behind a continuous lime wall to the left-hand side is the library and study area. Above the library on the second landing are the classrooms. There a prisoner can partake in any one of the courses on offer. From basic education to Junior and Leaving Certificate all the way through to College qualifications. The music school is on the third landing. Lessons here are held later in the afternoon so they don't clash with the classes going on below them. On the right-hand side of the Ed/Rec building is the gym. Every Cellblock has an allocated time that they are permitted to use the Gym. Block A is from 9 AM to 11 AM, Block B, 1:30 PM-3:30 PM and Block C, 4:30 PM to 6:30 PM. Above the Gym, there are four workshops where a prisoner can learn new skills such as woodwork, woodcarving, metalwork, computer-aided design and information technology. The third landing is basically used as a storage area, raw materials for the workshop are stored there along with any old or broken equipment that has no use anywhere else in Mayfield.

My daily visits to the library didn't go unnoticed and before long it was suggested by Mr.Martin that I apply for a job there. I've been working here for nearly seven months and honestly quite enjoy it. I was introduced to the 'Dewey decimal system'. A complicated classification system that allows books to be added to the library in their appropriate location based on their subject. It's difficult to get used to, but thankfully we have limited stock, so it's easy to get to grips with. The library is run by a thick black-bearded Westmeath man named Brendan. Housed in Cell Block C, Brendan is serving time for theft. Like myself, he wants to keep his head down, take each day as it comes and get the hell out of here. We work well together, and my time spent in the library keeps me from getting wrapped up in any unnecessary bullshit on the landings.

After about a month in Mayfield, I got a surprise visit from someone I thought I'd never see again. It was Q. At first, I was surprised that he would actually come up to see me, pretty stupid I thought. He was lucky the Guards didn't think he was important enough to find.

"Howya Frankie." Q greeted me. We both laughed off his joke.

"I came by to say thanks for not gettin' me involved." He said.

"No worries. Sure you didn't even know what you were involved in."

"True, but you still coulda ratted me out, thanks anyway. And by the way, I knew Dom used to like them young, but I didn't think he was like that." So the penny finally dropped.

"Yea, I wanted to tell you but wasn't sure how you'd react." I told him.

"I woulda bounced his head off the fuckin' ground. You're lucky you didn't tell me or I'd be in here with you!" I laughed off his bravado.

"Listen, I'm here with a message." Q told me in a semi-whisper.

"Yea, go on..."

"Henry got word of what you were up to. At first, he wondered why you didn't tell us, we could have helped you out. But after all that he wants to do you a favour."

"Henry wants to do me a favour?"

"Yea. His brothers in here. His name is Graham McNair. Make yourself known to him, and he'll look after ya." I'd heard the name 'McNair' been mentioned around the prison. But couldn't put a face to the name. I never knew Henry's surname so I had no idea that his brother was in Mayfield.

"What's he in for?" I asked Q.

"Drug possession." He answered. Those two words gave more information than Q intended. It finally answered the question I had when Henry first invited me into the drug business. Why did Henry, a man that had been in business for many years, all of a sudden need a new supplier? The answer was sitting in Mayfield. Graham was obviously Henry's right-hand man but got caught handling the drugs himself. After he was tossed in here Henry needed a new supplier fast. He tried to lure me in but thankfully I backed away.

"Tell Henry thanks for that, it's much appreciated." I told Q.

"No worries Fra...Mick. And another thing. He told me to tell ya when you get out of here go and find him. He'll give you a job whenever you want it."

"Nice one Q. Tell him thanks very much for the offer."

The unexpected reunion with Q came to an end and I returned to my cell and asked Barreller what he knew about McNair.

"Stay the fuck away from him." Was his only advice. "That fella is nothing but trouble. He runs this kip. Any debt that's owed in here is owed to him and his cronies."

I decided to introduce myself to Graham in any way. What had I got to lose? Henry had probably already told him about me and he might think it very strange if I didn't make myself known to him. Barreller pointed out McNair's cell to me. It was the last cell on the third landing. The furthest from the staircase, a very coveted cell away from prying eyes. I walked up to McNair's cell and saw four prisoners sitting inside. I obviously startled them. Upon seeing me in the doorway three of the prisoners sprang to their feet.

"I'm Michael Mills. I know Henry. He told me to introduce myself to Graham." I nervously explained.

"Ah Michael," The remaining sitting inmate said as he slowly rose to his feet. "Nice to meet ye, have a seat." Graham said as he invited me in. He is by no means a large man. About 5'8 but stocky for his height. Short, black, well-gelled hair sits on top of his head almost in spikes. I doubt he's forty but his weather-beaten face would suggest otherwise.

"Henry told me all about ye, a smart lad so ye are," Graham said in his thick Northern Ireland accent.

"Yea, well Henry didn't know what I was at until I got arrested."

"Aye, that's what I mean, not everyone gets one past our Henry." Graham informed me. I nervously laughed and smiled back at him.

"If you run into any trouble in here Michael, you come to me. Henry told me to sort ye out with whatever ya need, so if there's anything I can do for ye, anything at all, you let me know, ok?"

"Thanks a million Graham."

"Aye no bother. Now tell me all about your snaring business."

We spent about half an hour talking about how I ended up here. Setting up the profiles, luring paedophiles and how exactly that led me to Henry. Graham seemed impressed by what I had done. He never spoke about how he ended up in here, so I never asked. I had made a well-known comrade in here so why fuck it up by asking stupid questions.

From that day to this Graham and I get along very well. He comes into the library quite regularly and always makes a point to ask me how I'm getting on. I always politely decline his assistance, but it's good to know that if I need anything sorted out, Graham is there to help. I've never seen Graham go anywhere unaccompanied. The three prisoners I originally saw in his cell are always close by. 'Sexy' acquired his nickname through irony. He is by far the ugliest man I have ever laid eyes on. He has a constant mess of 'bed-head' sitting on top of his head. His eyes are crossed so badly that you can never tell if he is looking at you. He has one prominent buck tooth, God knows what happened the other one. And to top it all off he has bad acne scars all over his face. I once heard another prisoner referring to Sexy as having 'a face like a stepped in dog shite'. Harsh to say the least, but truthful. 'Daryl' can be summed up in one word 'Big'. Everything about him is big, his head, arms, chest, feet and especially his ego. Daryl will lift anything not nailed down in Mayfield and brag about it for weeks. It's a brave or stupid prisoner that would ever dare to challenge Daryl to a 'Lift-Off'. Mostly it's the younger, immature, new to Mayfield prisoner that think they are tough enough to beat Daryl. But every time without fail, Daryl destroys his competition, exerting his dominance in the process.

'Whisper' is the oldest of the quartet. A Bald, broad-shouldered, hefty man in his fifties. A natural observer, Whisper will never engage in any conversation going on around him. Instead, he studies or even examines his surroundings at all times. His eyes constantly look past you, and his head turns from side to side and looks behind him so often that I'm surprised he never gave himself whiplash. It's uneasy being around him, I constantly feel that an attack is coming at any time due to his overwhelming sense of awareness. If Whisper ever needs to talk to a prisoner, he leans his bald, sweaty head uncomfortably close to his victim, covers their ear with his hand and 'whispers' whatever he needs to tell them directly into their ear. I've witnessed him doing this a handful of times and on occasion, the person who received the message would mysteriously show up with visible cuts and bruises on their face a day or two later. I have no idea what they're up to, and I have no intention of finding out.

Around November 2011 I had another surprise visit. This time it was none other than Harrison and O'Leary. As usual, O'Leary greeted me with a smile and asked how I was getting on. Harrison reluctantly shook my hand sat down and opened his briefcase.

"Alan's trial is over, we thought you might like to hear the outcome," Harrison said. "The investigation into an individual who used the screen name 'AllThatYouWant', who we later discovered to be called Alan led to a total of nine arrests. As you know Alan had arranged to meet a minor for sexual intercourse. He wasn't going to meet her alone and had two others waiting in a hotel room. We arrested Alan on the 23rd of December 2010. We later arrested his two accomplices. Through our investigation, we found that all three men were involved in a paedophile ring. With the help of Europol, a further six men were arrested. Two in Glasgow, one in Bristol, and three in Amsterdam. These men made and distributed photographs and videos of themselves and others engaging in sexual activity with children, both male and female. Some of the victims are estimated to be as young as two years old. The oldest victim is estimated to be fourteen. Alan received a custodial sentence of fifteen years for his involvement in this paedophile ring."

"Jesus," I said. I was delighted with the news.

"There's more Michael," O'Leary said. It was a polite way of telling me to shut up so Harrison could continue.

"As for the other eight men involved in this paedophile ring, their combined prison sentences equate to seventy-four years." Harrison finished.

"Eighty-nine years? You're telling me I'm responsible for a total of nine people serving a combined eighty-nine years?" I asked them to confirm.

"That's correct Michael." O'Leary delivered with a smile. "In case you're interested Michael, the other cases which you were not charged with have all been tried also. I presume you were too occupied with your own case to pay any attention to them." O'Leary reached across Harrison and began to list the cases.

"Screen Name: Vinnie.KK. Two year suspended sentence. Two years on the Sex Offenders Register. Screen Name: Charlie4fun. Eighteen month suspended sentence twelve months on the Sex Offenders Register. Screen Name: TomIsHere. Six month prison sentence relating to indecent images found on his personal computer. Five years on the Sex Offenders Register.

Screen Name: True_Rumer. Twelve month suspended sentence, two years on the Sex Offenders Register.
Screen Name: TheDominator. (Dumb-Dumb) Twelve month prison sentence for breaching the terms of a bail bond. Two years on the Sex Offenders Register.
Screen Name: Joe -D. Deceased. Over three thousand indecent photographs were found on his computer along with two videos involving child rape. He would more than likely have faced prison time had he lived to be arrested.

In total Michael. All your decoy profiles, be it on chatroom or app, are responsible for thirteen men serving a combined sentence of one hundred and one years. That figure certainly dwarfs your six years doesn't it?"

I was speechless. I leaned back in my chair, threw my arms behind my head and couldn't hide the huge smile that was etched on my face. Tears began streaming down my cheeks. I didn't know what way to feel. I lost interest in researching what happened to the perverts after confronting them. Even in the cases where I didn't get any money, they were still brought to justice. One hundred and one years. Thirteen men were jailed because of what I did, another six received suspended sentences. But how many minors did I save from being abused? To think all this happened because of me was overwhelming. I never thought it would come to this. If Marty never paid me, maybe I wouldn't have continued trying. Or if I didn't see the article about his niece coming forward I might have simply lost interest and tried to get my life back on track.

Harrison hasn't come back since that meeting, but O'Leary has been up to see me twice since then. We are around the same age, he has two small children and tells me all about them. I'm not quite sure why O'Leary comes to see me. Maybe I was his first big case? Maybe he has some kind of a guilt complex? Whatever it is, it's nice to get a visit from someone outside my immediate family.

My First Christmas here was tough. Inside it's a day like any other. The same old routine. But you can't help but think about your family on the outside. I'm not ashamed to admit that I cried thinking about Ma sitting at home with Da and a turkey. Emily stayed in New Zealand and I was locked up here. It broke my heart knowing that I let Ma down so much. She'll never admit it, and always tells me how proud she is of me, but I know deep down, she must be so disappointed in me. Ma still keeps up her regular visits. She comes to see me twice or three times a week. It's encouraging to see that she's back to her old self and finally got over the initial shock of me being in prison. She could do nothing but accept things the way they are. Da comes up about once or twice a month. We still don't exactly see eye to eye, but things are getting better. We chat more and more every time he's here. We don't take sly digs at each other and the ice between us is beginning to thaw.

On Ma's most recent visit she told me some fantastic news. Emily is expecting her first child in October. She wants to come home and have the baby in the Coombe Hospital. Nearly every member of our family was born there so she may as well carry on the tradition, especially if the baby's going to grow up in New Zealand. She has written to me quite a bit and told me she'll visit me the next time she's over. I told her not to, I don't want the animals in here lusting over my little sister. A grandchild will be just what Ma and Da need too. It will take their minds completely off me. They could even go to New Zealand in the future, give them a much-needed break.

Laura's solicitor sent me plenty of letters too. She wanted, and succeeded, in getting her name off the mortgage on the house we bought together on Kildare Road. The only way out was to sell it. I had no means to cover the repayments and with me sitting in here, it wasn't likely I was ever going to be able to keep the house. I loved that house and worked my arse off to buy it. But sometimes these things are beyond your control and you simply have to let them go. The sale of the house barely covered the amount we borrowed and the legal fees. My share of it all was a grand total of €427.16. That amount will barely put a dent in the money I owe my parents for the barrister fees.

Aido and Jumper come up to me quite a bit too. Sometimes they're together, other times they're alone. They keep me informed of everything going on in the outside world. They say that strangers in the pubs around Crumlin are still buying them pints when they discover they're friends of 'The Paedo Hunter'. The media coverage has made me something of a celebrity in my own community. Aido and Jumper are reaping the rewards of my good work. It's a pity I can't enjoy the free drinks with them. It's one of the things I miss the most, heading out with friends without a care in the world. I'd give anything to turn back the clock to our 'Underground' days. Friday, Saturday and Sunday drinking away like there was no tomorrow.

On Jumpers most recent visit he seemed uneasy. He wouldn't look me in the eye and was fidgeting relentlessly. I knew he had something to tell me.

"What is it Jumper?"

"Watcha mean?"

"Don't give me that. I know somethings up."

"There's not Mick. I swear."

"The last time you acted like this was when you told me Laura was cheating on me. Somethings up. C'mon Jumper, out with it."

"Alright. It's Laura... she's pregnant." It was a right kick in the gut. Although I knew our marriage was over and there's no way of us ever getting back together, it still hurt. The woman I loved, who is still legally my wife, is having a baby with one of my closest friends. He even stood as a groomsman at our wedding. Beautiful.

"She was in a hair salon in the village and Beth (Jumper's sister) was there too. She overheard her telling one of the hairdressers. I'm sorry Mick."

"It's not your fault Jump. Listen, I'm gonna go, but thanks for telling me." I cut the visit short and just wanted to get back to my cell. There was nothing more to talk about.

Jumper said what was on his mind, I hope he got the burden off his chest.

The most common question I'm asked by people in here or from visitors is "Are you proud of what you've done?" I still don't know how to answer that. I'm neither proud or ashamed of what I've done. I had an idea and tested it to see if it would work. It did, and I made over €60,000 in the process. But when you look at it another way, €60,000 over the course of nearly two years really isn't that impressive. Granted it would have been more if Alan didn't run to the Guards, but that decision got him locked up for fifteen years. On the other hand, I have to allow myself to feel some kind of pride in the fact that I took thirteen paedophile's off the streets. Even if I stopped one person from being molested, sexually assaulted or raped I think what I did was completely worth it. Through it all, I can't shake the tormenting feeling of how it all could have worked out so differently. If Laura didn't cheat on me, maybe she'd be pregnant with our kid? We could have had a good life, a roof over our heads, both of us in steady jobs, and that kid would have never wanted for anything. I would have gone to the end of the earth to make sure Laura and our child were safe and protected. If I was never abused as a child, everything could have worked out fine. I would have never gone 'off the rails' as a teenager and wound up in St.Patricks Institute. But then again, if that never happened, George would have never bought me a car. Maybe I wouldn't be a carpenter, I may not have met Laura. God only knows where I'd be right now. But life dealt me a major detour. I lost it all. My wife, my job, my house, my freedom. With nothing better to do all day, I can't help but think about how it might have been. What I could have done to change this or that. But that's what happens to you in here. Prison gives you a lot of time to think, and a lot of time to write.

Snared.

Thanks for reading! If you enjoyed Snared and have a moment to spare, I would really appreciate a short review on Amazon as this helps new readers find my book.

Thanks again for your support.

Paul Cunningham.

Printed in Poland
by Amazon Fulfillment
Poland Sp. z o.o., Wrocław